A Crooked Tree

Una Mannion
A Crooked Tree

faber

First published in 2021
by Faber & Faber Limited
Bloomsbury House
74–77 Great Russell Street
London WC1B 3DA

Typeset by Faber & Faber Limited
Printed in the UK by CPI Group (UK) Ltd, Croydon, CR0 4YY

*This is a work of fiction. All of the characters, organisations and
events portrayed in this novel are either products of the author's
imagination or are used fictitiously*

A CIP record for this book
is available from the British Library

ISBN 978-0-571-35795-6

10 9 8 7 6 5 4 3 2 1

for my mother

1

The night we left Ellen on the road we were driving north up 252 near where it meets 202 and then crosses the Pennsylvania Turnpike. To the west were open fields, stretches of golden prairie grass and butterfly weed, the final line of sun splintering light through them. To the east, King of Prussia – grey industrial sites cast in dusk, cement trucks, cranes and a maze of highways and expressways. The Blue Route was somewhere over there too, like an amputated limb, started in 1967 but fourteen years later still unfinished, the asphalt ending at a line of overgrown grass and trees where the money had run out. Teenagers learned to drive on it or partied there late at night. The road to nowhere, we called it. We drove. Cars switched on headlights and straight ahead the hills of Valley Forge had become shadows, the trees already dark silhouettes.

The six of us were in the car, Marie up front in the passenger seat, Ellen between me and Thomas in the back, and Beatrice lying in 'the way back' with all our school bags and work folders from the year spread around her. It was the last day of school and we were officially on summer vacation. My mother was driving. Erratically. She hit the brakes, accelerated, revving high in first gear before shifting. She was angry. I could feel it in the car's sickening motion and from the seat behind I could see it in glimpses of her jawline, how it moved and twitched under the skin, even when she wasn't speaking. She and Ellen had been arguing, Ellen pestering her about going to an art camp that summer.

'I told you no.' She called it promotional blackmail, sending home brochures in school bags, and it infuriated her. 'I have enough to handle as it is.'

I was dreading the coming summer.

I pressed my forehead against the window and looked toward that final thread of light. Sage would be working at the mall, waitressing in J. C. Penney's diner. For the summer they'd offered her full-time. I'd spent almost all my summers with her. I thought about forging my mom's signature to get working papers. At fifteen, I could officially work, but I knew I wouldn't be allowed, that she needed me to look after the younger ones when she was at the hospital. Her job was admissions receptionist in the ER at Paoli Memorial. Sage said I was lucky. She complained about the other waitresses in their support hose and orthopaedic shoes, splashing coffees on the counter for other geriatrics who sprayed tester perfumes in the morning over their eggs and toast. But I envied her real job with regulars and tips and people who stiffed her and the stories she told. One customer in her nineties drank half-and-half from the white porcelain creamer left on the counter every morning, leaving behind a sloppy lip-print in bright orange. It wasn't about money or work – I had my Friday-night babysitting job for the Bouchers. I was afraid of all the days ahead of me alone.

Thomas was reciting the periodic table in a low whisper on the other side of Ellen. 'There's holmium, hafnium, erbium—'

'Stop,' she said.

'—phosphorus, francium, fluorine, terbium.'

'Shut up. Just shut up!' Ellen put her head down on her knees and crossed her arms over her shins. She was crying. A throbbing pain that started in my neck had moved across my skull into my forehead. I wanted them both to shut up.

'You're annoying everyone, Thomas. Just stop,' I said.

'Did you know tears contain glucose, sodium and potassium?'

'Shut up, you weird science freak.' Ellen kicked his shins twice with her heel, shoving the driver's seat which she had gripped for support.

'Stop it this instant. Do you want us to crash?' My mother was furious.

'Tears contain a natural chemical painkiller, enkephalin,' Thomas whispered. 'You'll feel better afterward.'

'Make him stop.' Ellen's voice was muffled.

Her whine and his murmurs made me want to hit him or someone. Ellen's head was back on her knees. I reached across her and pushed him hard on the shoulder with my knuckles.

'Shut up, Thomas. What do you know about tears?'

I said it and wished I hadn't because there was something wrong with him, the way he didn't cry after all that had happened to us, how he just disappeared into himself and his room. Right then, teasing Ellen, he was more like the old Thomas.

3

He turned toward the window and didn't say anything back. It would have been better if he got angry. I tried to undo it, remembering a joke. 'Hey, Thomas, if you're boring and a moron, guess what that makes you?'

He turned to look at me, waiting. 'Well?'

'A boron.'

'Very funny, Libby, but you don't even know what boron is. You've just admitted that I'm supernova material, not even of this earth.'

'All of you stop,' Marie said from the front, and she looked back at us over the seat. Her hair on one side was dyed black and spiked out like Siouxsie Sioux's. She'd pierced her cheek and shaved the other side of her head before the graduation mass at school, and it was growing back in blonde stubble. Both Thomas and I went quiet. Marie was almost eighteen, only a year older than Thomas but we listened to her, especially since she was giving away the rock albums she didn't want any more. She'd left *Who's Next* on my pillow after I stayed home with Beatrice while she snuck out to a party, and Thomas got *Quadrophenia* for winning the highest GPA in his class. We both wanted *Tommy*. Thomas said he should get it, given his name and all. I didn't want to point out further similarities, like a dead father, a mother with a secret boyfriend and not being allowed to say anything. Neither of us even had a record player. Marie had a portable turntable, and we all used that.

Outside, dogwoods lined the understorey where the woods met the fields, and even in the falling light I could see they were stripped of their bloom. *Cornus florida*. Oval leaves with primary veins that curve upward along

4

smooth wavy margins. Clustered flowers surrounded by bracts that people mistake as the petals. My father had bought me *The Field Guide to the Trees of North America* the last Christmas before he died. I'd read and reread the book, committing to memory every tree fact I could. I'd started a tree notebook, identifying all the trees I saw with descriptions of them in different seasons; I sketched them, took bark rubbings, pressed their flowers.

His gift had arrived in a package with a postmark from New York City, where he'd gone to live, working with a cousin, an Irish immigrant like himself. He'd gotten us each a card. For me, a forest of spruce, one tree separated out in front with a star on top. His handwriting was small and uneven, as if he weren't used to signing cards, which I guess he probably wasn't.

For Libby, always in a tree. Merry Christmas.
Love, Dad.

I don't know if I spent so much time with trees because I loved them or because of how much he loved me loving them, and I cannot separate these things. When I was maybe six, and he still sometimes lived with us, I'd come home at the end of a day in the woods, barefoot and filthy. Once, he sat me on the washing machine, turning on the tub next to it, and washed my feet. He lathered up the soap and gave them a vigorous scrub, even using a nail brush on my heels, where dirt was embedded deep in the calluses.

'There's copperheads in those woods, Libby – you have to wear sneakers. You can't keep going around barefoot.'

Jagged scabs scored my shins from climbing trees and crawling under laurel and rhododendron thickets.

He took my hand and pulled my finger across the ridge of a particularly bumpy scab.

'See that? You're already turning into a tree. Your legs are becoming bark.'

The furrowed scab was raised and dark. I traced it with my fingers and ran my hand up both my shins, feeling the crusts.

'I think I am,' I said. I looked up at him, happy, and he laughed and towel-dried my feet and shins, even between the toes, and then slipped socks over my clean feet.

'Now you can go up to Her Ladyship and not be in trouble. And keep your feet clean.' But I knew he loved my black feet.

He had picked a book for each of us that last Christmas. Even now I think of him in that bookstore in New York City, selecting the books we would like, choosing our cards, deciding on the paper, then wrapping the gifts: folding, tearing tape and tying ribbons with his thick fingers, more conditioned to working machines or hauling cinder blocks. For Marie, he had bought *Rock On: The Illustrated Encyclopedia of Rock N' Roll, The Modern Years*. I'd lost hours looking through pictures. It covered 1964–1978 and pretty much all my favourite bands. Thomas got *The Illustrated Encyclopedia of Astronomy and Space*, which he kept in its original wrapping paper and wouldn't let us touch. Ellen's book was on art history and came with a watercolour set and brushes; for Beatrice he'd bought a book on breeds of dogs, with stickers. I wondered now if he'd told the person at the cash register they were for his children. I imagined him with his bag of presents on the subway back to the Bronx, sitting among the other Christmas shoppers, and there in the car I suddenly felt like I couldn't breathe. I wished I could tell him how each book had become a cipher for us, how we couldn't lose the picture he had of us or stop trying to fill it.

Next to me, Ellen was still bent over, the bumpy bones of her spine visible beneath her school pinafore. 'A little sprite,' my aunt Rosie had said when she came from Ireland for my dad's funeral. She'd sent us food packages and at Christmas a bottle of sherry to improve Ellen's appetite; she said she wasn't 'thriving', a turn of phrase that had made us all laugh, as if she were talking about a farm animal. But she was right, Ellen was small. At twelve years old, she was just over four feet and only sixty-some pounds. Looking at her now, she seemed so tiny and unhappy, and I tried to pat her back.

'Get off,' she mumbled, and shoving me she banged into the back of the driver's seat.

My mom swerved the car toward the verge and back on to the road again, exaggerating the power of Ellen's knock against her seat. 'You could kill us doing that. Do you understand? That's enough. You can vacuum the downstairs when you get home, and fold the laundry.'

'No. I won't,' Ellen said. 'You should make Beatrice do something for once.'

'Leave Beatrice out of this.' I could see my mother's large hair bun and just one eye in the rear-view mirror as she looked back at Ellen.

'It's okay. I don't mind doing it.' Beatrice leaned forward from the way back, fretting that she was somehow the cause of what was happening.

'Thank you, Beatrice. If only Ellen could be sweet to others.'

'You hate all of us and you just love her. And your fat boyfriend.' Ellen was going too far. I elbowed her to make her stop.

'One more word and you'll walk.'

'It's true. You hate us.' Ellen was shouting. 'You hated Dad, and I hate you.'

His name in the car punched the air out of us. We didn't talk about him in front of my mother. The car skidded into the shoulder, right where 252 crossed the turnpike.

'Out. Get out.' My mom said it with her voice low, which let us know she meant it. Ellen reached across Thomas, opened the back door and started to climb out.

'You can't leave her here,' Marie said. 'It's getting dark. I'm going with her.' She started to gather her school bag from the floor of the front.

'You'll do no such thing.'

'Wait,' said Thomas. He looked stricken, blaming himself for the teasing. Ellen was standing on the gravel verge of the overpass in her school pinafore, tennis shirt and knee socks. Marie was opening her door when my mother threw the car into gear and accelerated forward.

I looked back. Ellen was facing away from us, looking down over the bridge, where columns of cars funnelled along the turnpike.

'Mom, don't. Please,' Thomas said, but she didn't answer. We sped up 252 into the national park and then
turned west toward Valley Forge Mountain, where we
lived. Ahead of us, the sun had fallen below the fields.

'You can't leave her. It's dark,' Marie said.

We were still five or six miles from home. I hadn't said
anything to make my mother stop. We careened down the
road, went through the covered bridge, past farmland and
fences. Beside us, the shadows of dogwoods blurred in the
dark as my mother kept driving, each tree hemmed in a
halo of white where the bracts had fallen.

2

Valley Forge was best known for the winter that George Washington spent there with twelve thousand soldiers of the Continental Army camped in makeshift log cabins, trying to survive. They were malnourished, half-naked and barefoot. Over two thousand died from exposure, disease and injuries, and another three thousand were unfit for service. Miss Esposito, our ninth-grade history teacher, had said that Valley Forge was the turning point in the war, that it symbolized the revolutionary spirit and America's sense of itself. I was the only one in my class who actually was from there. When I walked through the woods on the mountain, I thought about those freezing men who came up here to drag timber and fallen branches down to the encampment, who ran through the trees, deserting the army, or who may have crawled here to lie down and die. Some weren't even men, only boys, Thomas's age.

The army hospital was set up at Yellow Springs, the other side of the mountain, so the sick and dying men must have come through our woods, along the trails, to get there from the encampment. Men with no shoes trudging through snow, sick, walking the same woods as me or being carried. What would they have seen from a stretcher in the winter, looking up, no canopy of leaves? Just bare black branches against a grey sky, thinking it might be the last time they were witnessing the earth and the sun wouldn't even show itself. Maybe they didn't even see trees at all; I'd read somewhere that to keep warm and build their cabins, the soldiers had felled nearly all the trees.

Valley Forge Mountain was not so much a mountain as a hill. Washington's headquarters was less than two miles from my house if I cut through the woods. In the 1950s, the mountain was zoned for housing, but the woods were preserved as part of the park. Behind my house was the Horseshoe Trail, a hiking and bridle path that started in the park and went 140 miles until it met the Appalachian Trail in Harrisburg.

The trail divided the mountain into two townships: Tredyffrin, where Sage lived, and Schuylkill, our side. Sage's side of the mountain seemed more affluent – houses were bigger and better kept. Schuylkill's main town was Phoenixville, an old ironworks and steel-mill town at the bottom of the mountain. While we were growing up, steel mills were downsizing, laying people off, closing. Phoenixville suffered. Marie said the town was caught in a time warp: the 1980s had started but Phoenixville was stuck in the '60s and there weren't many prospects there for young people. On the mountain, Schuylkill kids went to Phoenixville High School and those on the Tredyffrin side to Conestoga, one of the best public schools in the state. We didn't go to either. We went to Catholic schools closer to Philadelphia.

I spent most of my time on the mountain in the woods or walking down to Washington's Headquarters. Thomas and I had tried fishing in the Schuylkill River which ran alongside it. He said we could try for catfish or perch. We never caught anything and the riverbank smelled like sludge, with hubcaps, old toasters and other garbage visible in the shallows. On the mountain, off-trail, there were traces of old quarries in the woods, and at the bottom of my road, about a quarter of a mile in, was a deep ravine that used to be a quartzite quarry. They would mine the quartzite ore and bring it away to be crushed into sand. Quartz was everywhere on the mountain – giant glimmering rocks sitting on the surface of the earth and flashing edges jutting up from the ground, as if it were growing there. Dad had told me that in prehistoric Ireland quartz was sacred and was buried with the bones of the dead.

After we left Ellen on the road, we drove up the mountain in silence. I watched the car's headlights hit the trees as we turned the corners. Each time the car downshifted and slowed, I hoped my mother might be changing her mind, that she would turn around, drive back and take Ellen off the road, that none of us would be angry any more because we would be so thankful to have her safe in the car again. But we drove on. Lying in the way back, Beatrice was the only one to speak.

'There's no streetlights. How will she see the way home?' Nobody said anything.

We pulled into our driveway and Marie got out to open the garage door. The Walkers had switched on their lamp posts across the road; under their light, I could see our yard's overgrown grass, knee-high and gone to seed. Things felt wrong. The house, the uncut grass, Ellen on the road, Dad gone. A few months earlier, Mr Walker had written a note, a barely disguised complaint about how the house looked. The card read *Thinking of You* on the front and inside he'd sympathized with all we had been through in the past year, how we'd been on his mind. He said he and his wife Minnie had been praying for us and then he ended the note: 'We were thinking that it might help alleviate your burden if you had someone to cut your lawn this summer and do odd jobs for you. I know one of the De Martino boys is looking for that line of summer work. Let us know if we can be of any help.' He signed it 'Your neighbour and friend, Harry Walker.'

Marie had threatened to march over there. 'I am going to ask him, if he's such a big Christian and so worried about the length of our grass, why doesn't he drive over here in his Cadillac sit-down lawnmower and sit his fat Elmer Fudd butt down on its real leather seat and cut it for us?'

We'd all laughed, even my mother. Mr Walker did look a bit like Elmer Fudd with bright plaid pressed shirts and khakis pulled up too far. Marie performed *Stepford Wives* imitations of Minnie Walker. She'd put her hair in curlers like an old-fashioned set, stuff her bosom with soccer balls so that she nearly fell over, wear a full-length apron and apply bright-red lipstick all over her mouth, smearing outside the lines. She'd carry an imaginary tray across our living room with a glass of lemonade: 'I'm so busy with my Christianity and charity, dearest Harry Walker, I nearly forgot your refreshment. You must be so tired sitting on your ass cutting these grass blades. And it must be so exhausting for you, poor Harry, to look across at that disgraceful house and those disgraceful people.' She made us all laugh with abandonment. Thomas laughed so hard no sound came out of his mouth. I knew the grass bothered him the most, that he felt it should be him cutting it. But we didn't have a lawnmower and we'd never gotten my father's machines back from his cousin in the Bronx. We'd never asked, and he never offered. We didn't get anything of my father's back except his truck, which my mother sold, and his body. I wondered what had happened to all the cards and gifts we'd sent him. All the things we'd made him at school. I knew he kept them. I felt sick imagining his cousin just throwing out his stuff.

I watched Marie rolling up the garage door in the headlights of the car. Now, with her head shaved on one side, she couldn't do Minnie Walker's curlers any more. Marie stepped to the side of the garage and my mother drove in, pulled up the handbrake, switched off the engine, grabbed her pocketbook from the floor of the front seat, and went straight into the house and up to her bedroom.

I hauled out my own school bag and folders, as well as Ellen's, and carried them in. Ellen had brought a large art folder with her work from the school year. She had drawn *Ellen* in large cursive and then outlined it over and over in different colours, extending outward in a psychedelic flourish with flowers and patterns, like a Cream album cover. I opened her folder and spread the pictures out on the lower trundle bed where she slept. There were colour wheels and pencil drawings, still lifes of fruit and flowers. There was a family portrait with just five figures; she hadn't included Dad or Mom, just us. She made Marie the largest even though Thomas and I both towered over her. In the middle of the pile was a self-portrait, done with wax and oil pastels. She'd used all blues, purples and black. It wasn't meant to be realistic, but it captured something about Ellen, her large blue eyes, the dark lashes and brows, how her eyes always looked hollowed-out with slight streaks of purple beneath them, the parting on the side of her head. Her face didn't have a clear outline; it seemed to float out of the dusky shapes. There was a note on the back of the folder done in green felt-tip.

A beautiful and expressionistic portfolio, Ellen. Great work all year and so artistic. I've left a set of oil pastels inside the folder with information about the art camp and a reference. I've put a green circle on the back of work I think you should submit with the application. While you are young, I have no doubt that you would be accepted. Miss LeBlanc.

I reached back in and pulled out the large envelope. Inside was a brochure for Chestnut Grove Art Academy Summer Camp and a smaller sealed envelope with *Recommendation for Ellen Gallagher* typed across the front. Ellen hadn't mentioned the gift, the note or the recommendation earlier in the car. I put all the pictures back inside the folder and left the envelope on my bed. I had to get ready for babysitting.

Every Friday night, I sat for Mrs Boucher's two small boys. She was the only divorced person I knew other than my mother, except she made it look glamorous. Marie said that was the difference social class made. If you had money and social status it was acceptable to break the rules. Mrs Boucher wore fitted black dresses, turquoise necklaces and large hoop earrings. She had raven-black hair that she wore down when she went out. She told me that she was part American Indian and that her hair was Shawnee, from her grandmother's people. She was a lawyer and lived in what my mom would call a contemporary house, deep in the woods, with walls of glass that reflected the trees all around them. She called it her tree house.

I took off my uniform and pulled on jeans, a T-shirt and sneakers. My big toes were pushing through the canvas. I'd already saved up enough babysitting money to get a new pair. Mrs Boucher paid me $10 a night basically to watch television, which for me was a treat because we didn't have one at home. I didn't want to leave with Ellen still out on the road, but I couldn't call Mrs Boucher this late to cancel. I looked out the window into the darkness, holding my hands on either side of my face to block out the light from the room. Someone had turned on the outdoor lamps, probably Marie. I could see the large quartz rocks at the end of our driveway, the long grass and the empty street.

Marie came into the room and flopped on her own bed across from the trundle beds where Ellen and I slept. 'Don't leave your stuff on mine.' She threw my kilt back at me. 'You can stop looking; she won't be back for hours. It could be ten or eleven before she gets here.'

'She shouldn't have mentioned Dad.'

'Why not?' Marie asked. 'Why should we go around walking on eggshells all the time? We're not allowed to talk about anything, so when someone does it's a catastrophe.' Marie had taken off her kilt and school blouse. She tugged a black T-shirt with a picture of burning cars across the front over her head. 'And once again, she just shuts herself in her room.' She shoved her heel down into a black boot. She was right, Mom would stay in there for the night. 'Anyway, it wasn't mentioning Dad that upset her so much.' Marie sat back down on the bed and started putting on thick black eyeliner. 'It was the fat-boyfriend comment.'

After Dad died we had gone to family counselling twice. On our first visit we each met individually with the counsellor, Gwen. I told Gwen about my mother's boyfriend, Bill, how she kept him a secret from all of us except Beatrice, that the rest of us had never met him even though he'd been around for years. That it was obvious he was Beatrice's father and how I was angry with my mom all the time. I never asked any of the others what they talked about.

In our second session, Gwen brought us into the room together and we sat in comfortable chairs arranged in a circle. I looked at Gwen and at my mother and I knew this wouldn't work. Gwen's dangling earrings and sky-blue eyeshadow, her gold ankle bracelet against her tan leg. My mom's clear, pale skin, her hair pulled back in a bun, her lack of frivolity. She'd never worn make-up and hardly ever spent a penny on herself. Gwen wanted her to talk about Dad, how things were before they split up, things that had happened. One of us had said something. Was it just me? I felt pain in my chest. Mom wasn't going to budge and her face was set. She wouldn't say anything bad about Dad. She didn't tell things. There was a poster on the wall of Holly Hobbie in her rag dress and her ridiculous gigantic bonnet, smelling a flower. We couldn't see her face. We looked at the walls, at the green industrial carpet on the floor, the tweed weave of the chairs we were sitting on, anywhere but at each other. My mom's loyalty to my father hurt me. I had betrayed her over and over, most recently to Gwen, a stranger, who was writing her notes on the clipboard with a pencil that had troll hair sticking out at the end with googly eyes glued on. Marie's eyebrow raised as she watched her write. Gwen wasn't going to get anywhere with us.

Afterward, my mother decided that counselling was useless, that she couldn't bear Gwen's patronizing sweet voice. 'We just need time,' she said. We never went back.

Now Marie took out white powder and started blotting it across her cheeks and forehead. I watched her for a minute. Our features were different. At school, people didn't believe we were sisters. Marie, like Ellen, was small-boned, her face petite. Mine was wider and flatter. While Marie was alert and pretty, Sage said I was more 'ethereal', as if I was always preoccupied. My eyes were a lighter blue than Marie's, more like my mother's than any of my siblings, and while they all had light-brown or blonde hair, my hair, eyebrows and lashes were all dark. Hippy hair, Marie called it. It just fell straight down either side of my face, all the way to my waist. It was shapeless compared to her punk cut or Sage's layers, but I'd never really had any good ideas about how to get it cut. A lot of the girls in my class had gotten Dorothy Hamill haircuts, but I didn't think that would suit me. I had a gap between my two front teeth, so I smiled with my mouth closed. Marie was applying purple lipstick now, so dark it was almost black.

'I have to go babysit. Will you call me at the Bouchers' when she gets here?'

'Yeah.' She looked at me in the mirror. I didn't understand her putting on her punk face when she wasn't going anywhere.

I went down to the kitchen and opened the refrigerator. There was hardly anything in it. My mother always kept the bread in the crisper drawer, so it wouldn't go stale. I took out a slice and a stick of butter to spread on it. The bread was cold and I could barely chew. I thought for a moment I might be sick. 'The Worrier', Gwen had called me. It was true. I worried about everything. When everyone else climbed the fence of the swimming club to go skinny-dipping, I stayed outside keeping watch on the road, in case they set off the alarm or a neighbour reported them to the police. When Marie snuck out the window at night, I couldn't sleep until she was back, imagining all the bad things that could happen to her, listening for my mother in the hallway. Even before Dad died, I was already like this. My mother had once bought us each a poster. Mine was a picture of a lion cub wailing with a wide-open mouth. *Stop worrying*, it read. *The world is sad enough without your woe.*

For Marie she'd bought a poster of cartoon animals playing musical instruments with the line *Music hath charms to soothe the savage beast.*

Ellen had gotten *Don't take the fun out of dysfunctional*. I threw the bread in the trash. I couldn't swallow it.

In the rec room, Beatrice was folding the laundry on the couch and Thomas was vacuuming. They had started the chores Ellen had been told to do. Beatrice was seven, five years younger than Ellen and seven years younger than me. Ellen was right, she was coddled by our mom, by all of us actually, but she wasn't a brat, and she didn't like being separated out. I sat next to her on the couch and started folding a school shirt.

'I don't know why Ellen was so mad at me.' Beatrice looked up. There was a gaping space in her mouth where she had lost two teeth. Her wavy hair was pulled into fat bunches just behind her ears.

'She wasn't mad at you. It's not your fault, Bea.'

'What if she can't find her way or gets hit by a car?'

'She'll be fine. We're used to going around the mountain in the dark. She knows the roads. Help Marie look out for her, okay?' Beatrice nodded.

Thomas shouted over the vacuum cleaner: 'Stop slacking on the job! Get folding. Hup, two, three, four.' Bea brightened and rolled matching socks together.

'I have to go. Make sure someone calls me at the Bouchers' when she gets home.' I went back up the stairs to tell my mom I was leaving. The door was shut. I knocked. 'I'm going now, Mom.' She didn't answer.

Marie came out into the hallway on her way downstairs. 'It's better to leave her alone.'

'I'm only telling her I'm going.' I wanted to kick and stamp the door. I went back into our empty room and picked up Ellen's folder, sifting through the sheets to find the green circles from Miss LeBlanc: the floating self-portrait, the family minus parents, a series of studies of a stag, just the face and antlers, all done in different gradients of black pencil shading. They weren't childish, sweet drawings; they were stark, detached and sad. I knew Ellen must be completely exceptional in her class. I took the note, brochure, reference and drawings. Mom needed to know. I walked back to her room and knelt on the rug, sliding each of them under her door before leaving.

Our house on the mountain was a split-level. There were four floors with small staircases of five steps between each of them. We had four bedrooms. My mother's room, Bea's box room and the one I shared with Ellen and Marie were on the same floor. Bea's was very small and right next to my mother's. Thomas had a large room on the very top floor. I loved the house and the woods all round it. We'd moved to the mountain after Ellen was born. Before that we rented a house in Ardmore. I don't think my father ever felt at home on the mountain. He was different from the other dads up there. It wasn't just his job; he had never been to school after fifth class, the same as our fifth grade. He said in Ireland this was common for children reared on farms. They were expected to work. And my dad worked harder than anyone I knew. But he never seemed to be able to save.

Before Beatrice, my parents went through a some-times-together, sometimes-apart phase, but by the time she was born, he wasn't living with us any more. We saw

Dad less after that, but I still worked with him cutting lawns and raking leaves. He stayed in the Philadelphia area and lived in different places but never anywhere for long. Then a distant cousin offered him the job and place in the Bronx; he had a contracting and landscaping business. We went there just once – Marie, Thomas, Ellen and me. We took the Amtrak train from 30th Street Station in Philadelphia and he met us at Penn Station in Manhattan. He was standing at the top of the escalator as we came up from our platform. He had showered after work and put on a shirt and tie, something old-fashioned that he'd done when he lived with us if we were going anywhere. He never wore casual clothes like my friends' fathers. He'd never owned a pair of jeans or khakis or shorts. Not even sneakers, which would have looked wrong on him. He wore white short-sleeved undershirts, but never a T-shirt with writing on it, work trousers when cutting grass, and he always had his wavy hair parted on the side and combed back.

'Dad's 1950s,' Marie would say with pride. She said it was weird how grown men in America had started to dress like little boys and had no sophistication.

We took the subway out to Woodlawn in the Bronx, where he had moved. The houses were close together with chain-link fences between them. The streets and yards seemed naked. There were no trees, a few scattered thin shrubs, and it seemed strange for my father to be in a place without leaves. At some of the houses where we'd worked with him, the leaf fall would be so thick I could wade through it up to my waist. Dad would turn on the blower and the leaves would swirl up all around us and fall again. In the Bronx he'd rented what he called an efficiency apartment, a room attached to another house with its own separate entrance. It had a little kitchenette by the window. He made us a steak dinner and mashed potatoes on a two-ringed electric stove. There was a tiny bathroom with a shower and he had a couch that doubled as his bed. He pulled out foam that he kept behind the seat of his pickup truck and rolled it out on the floor, and we all spent the night, the four of us and him, in that one room together in the Bronx. He had bought new plates and forks and knives for our visit, so that he'd have enough to feed five. I sometimes still fall asleep remembering that night. All of us together, lying in the dark, talking, breathing in the one room.

3

I stepped out into the dark. Lightning bugs blinked around the edges of lawns where they met the woods. The night air was warm, and it felt like summer. The Bouchers lived on the other side of the mountain; it would take me twenty minutes to walk there. I had to pass the Addisons', or 'the Manson House', on the way. The Addisons had moved to the mountain from California and were a street up from us. Shortly after they moved in, people had started talking. They said that in California Mr Addison's company had cut down redwoods that were never used and later dumped in the Pacific Ocean, that he was at the top of the 'Death List' Charles Manson had written in prison. A few years earlier, one of the Manson Family had tried to kill President Ford in order to save California redwoods. No one knew for certain if the stories about Mr Addison were true. Marie had a copy of *Helter Skelter* and I'd read it. There was a section in the middle of the book with photographs. I studied them intently, trying to read the faces of the young women who became part of Manson's group, memorizing them in case I ever saw them here. I still walked away fast whenever I saw a Volkswagen bus.

The Addisons' house was set deep in the woods. I slowed as I got closer, preparing to run. They had lights on some sort of a sensor, so that at night when anyone passed they clicked on and lit up the house and the woods around it. I crossed the road to avoid setting them off and about five yards from the start of their property I sprinted, running as fast as I could for a hundred yards, imagining the women assassins in the woods, waiting. I looked over my shoulder to see if there was anything coming behind me. At the top of High Point Lane there was a shortcut straight ahead through the woods that went past the water tower and was part of the Horseshoe Trail. It was dark, but I knew the path. I'd run it often. The trail was marked by painted yellow rectangles on the trees that caught splinters of moonlight, lighting up briefly in the dark. I always felt reassured by the markers; as if in a fairy tale, I was still on the right path. But tonight a wave of panic washed through me. How far had Ellen walked?

Ahead of me, the trail broke into a gravelled clearing with two towers. One was a colossal metal water tower, a hulking grey presence in the surrounding stands of oak and maple. Some days, in the late afternoon when the sun started to fall below the canopy, the trees cast perfect shadows across its flat surface so that it almost seemed to be part of the woods. The other tower was taller, a framework of criss-crossing metal parts. It seemed like it might start moving, extending its limbs to crush human intrusion. We thought this tower had something to do with electricity. Both towers were surrounded by a high fence with angled strips of barbed wire along the top. It didn't work; kids still climbed over and jumped to the lowest rung of the water tower's service ladder, then pulled themselves up to scale its side. Everyone was afraid of the other one, the one that might be electric.

I could hear voices and laughter on the far side of the lot, most likely some of the Phoenixville kids who hung around getting stoned and drinking beer. Red lights blinked from the top of both towers, a warning to aircraft or a beacon to other alien beings.

The winter before, Thomas and I had come up here with Jack Griffith, Thomas's oldest friend on the mountain. We hadn't seen him much since Dad's funeral. Thomas had stopped going out or returning phone calls. It was dusk, a day or two after New Year's; we were still off school for Christmas, and it was snowing. Marie, Thomas and I had been outside trying to shovel the driveway when Jack rumbled up in a little Datsun. He was driving now, he said, and thought he and Thomas could look around, that the snowploughs hadn't been out yet. Marie told Thomas to go. As they were getting in the car, Jack turned to me and asked if I wanted to come and, without thinking, I said yes and climbed into the back.

We drove through thick snow. The roads were empty and there were no car tracks; only the trees defined the path of the road. It was dark and we drove around the mountain cocooned in Jack's Datsun as it snowed all around us. Supertramp's 'The Logical Song' came on the radio as we were trying to get up Horseshoe Trail Road, the car spinning wheels and sliding back. Jack couldn't get the car up any further, so he stopped and we got out and walked up to the water tower lot to see what it would look like up there at the top of the mountain, all white. The three of us stood in that quiet of snow at night, our faces cold, the thick flakes falling and lights blinking, and I felt happy. I remember looking over at Jack and he had become beautiful, his dark hair and red cheeks. I could see he was happy too, just being there with us. Ever since, I'd had a kind of crush on him, something I didn't even admit to Sage. I hardly ever saw him anyway. Neither did Thomas.

Cutting past the tower, there was more laughter and the shattering of glass, and I broke into a run before any of them saw me. But I hadn't yet reached the woods on the other side of the clearing when shadows moved ahead of me in the dark. I slowed to a walk. Five or six teenagers were standing in a haphazard circle, the smell of pot hovering around them. Abbey Quinn stepped out on to the trail.

'Hey, Gallagher. That you? Where you headed?'

I stopped. I liked Abbey but the others she was with made me uncomfortable. 'Hi, Abbey. Babysitting.'

'The beautiful Mrs Boucher?' Abbey giggled. She was stoned.

I looked over at the others, trying to make out their faces. 'Yeah.'

'I heard there's someone who thinks Mrs Boucher is beautiful,' she said, and started laughing again.

I didn't know what she meant and shrugged. Abbey put her arm around my shoulders. She'd been drinking too.

'You should come out more often. It'd be good for you. With Sage.'

'I'll try,' I said. 'Better get going. See ya.' I kept walking down the trail.

The path ended on the road where the Bouchers lived, and I turned left to head down the hill. Beyond their house was a Nike Site, owned by the US government. Because

Philadelphia was a major American city, it was surrounded by these sites which were supposed to detect incoming missiles and launch anti-missile missiles that would hit them and bring them down. Some sites had radar and some sites had missiles. I didn't know which one we were. Either way, it meant that nuclear war was close to us, that we could be a target and that missiles were buried in our ground. I worried about nuclear arms and radiation. A couple years earlier, when the Three Mile Island meltdown happened, people had needed to evacuate. We'd listened to the radio in Dad's truck on the way to school. Harrisburg was only an hour and a half away, even less as the crow flies. I'd imagined the people fleeing on foot, looking behind them in terror at something invisible carried on the air, how everything could be obliterated by a contamination you couldn't even see. People said the sites hadn't even been used since the 1960s. Did that mean they took out the surface-to-air missiles or were they still here in the ground? No one knew.

Mrs Boucher's house sat several hundred yards from the road, at a steep drop and barely visible from the top of the driveway. As I walked down I could see the lights of the house in slices through the trees. I decided then that I would tell her what had happened with Ellen. Maybe she would take me and the boys in the car and go down the mountain to look for her along the road. Or I could stay in the house with the boys and she could go. I knew she would help us. But when I got to the front door, Mrs Boucher opened it before I'd even knocked. She had a light scarf wrapped around her shoulders and was holding her pocketbook and keys. She moved back to let me in, keeping her hand on the open door.

'Hi, Libby. Sorry, I'm rushing tonight. The boys are in their pyjamas. There's ice cream in the freezer. I got mint chocolate chip for you.' I hesitated before stepping inside. Mrs Boucher looked at me. 'Is everything okay?'

'Oh, yeah, fine. Thank you. And for the ice cream. I finished school for the summer today,' I added, as if this explained something. I stepped past her into the hallway.

'Ah, the paradox of freedom,' said Mrs Boucher, like she understood. 'I'll see you when I get back', and she shut the front door.

Why hadn't I told her? I put my hand on the door to open it and call her back, to say we needed help. But I hated asking people for things. Maybe she would pass Ellen on her way down the mountain. I began to think of all the people that might pass Ellen on their way home. Surely one of them would stop. In her uniform she would be easily recognized.

I played games with the boys and put them into bed. I read *Goodnight Moon* to Bruce, who was two, and *Peter Rabbit* to Peter, who was five. Bruce sucked his thumb and snuggled into me. He had a moon lamp in his room and was asleep by the time I'd gotten to the 'Goodnight, room' part. Peter liked to take his book after I'd read it and look at all the pictures in detail. I pretended that he was a rabbit, so we rubbed noses goodnight and I reminded him to clean his fur and to put down his ears to sleep.

I left him and went upstairs to the living room. The whole time I listened in case the phone rang. At ten I picked it up and made sure the dial tone was working, then placed it carefully back on the cradle. I wanted to call home but my mother would answer the extension in her bedroom. I called Sage, who was the one person in the world other than Marie or Thomas who would instantly understand.

'Hi, it's me.'

'Why are you whispering?'

'I don't know. I'm at the Bouchers'. My mom kicked Ellen out of the car tonight when it was dark. On the bridge over the turnpike. She's walking home, but I don't think she got there yet.'

'By the turnpike? Poor Ellen. That road's so lonely.'

'Yeah. I don't know what to do.'

'I'll get Charlotte to go out in the car,' Sage said. 'You know she would.'

'No. Please don't. It would make things worse. My mom could get in trouble.'

'So what if she does?'

'Don't say anything to your mom. I'll call you when I hear that she's home.' I went back to the couch and tried to watch television but couldn't concentrate. If I had just told Mrs Boucher, maybe we would have found Ellen and all this would be over. At ten thirty the phone rang.

It was Marie. 'She hasn't come home yet.'

'Oh God. I feel sick.'

'She's not on the road. She must have tried to go through the woods.'

'How do you know?'

'Wilson McVay went out and drove the whole route on his motorcycle, and he didn't see her.'

'You called Wilson McVay?'

'Yeah. Who else could I call?'

'Anybody but him. He's crazy, Marie.'

'People who say that don't know him.'

'People say it for a reason. It's because he's done stuff that's crazy.'

'He helped us, Libby. Grow up.'

I could think of plenty of things wrong with Wilson McVay. Our dead cat, Mr Franklin, for one. (Thomas had named him after Benjamin Franklin who, according to legend, had once spent a night lost on the mountain. We'd found Mr Franklin as a kitten in the woods.) We believed Wilson had killed him. People said he killed neighbours' pets with his BB gun, and when we found Mr Franklin dead he had circular wounds in his side. I had seen first-hand how crazy Wilson was and so had Marie. Years earlier, when I was eleven or twelve, we were sitting on the swings at the Sun Bowl and Wilson was circling around on a dirt bike, making attempts to go up the rock hill at the far end. He'd try a few times and then come up toward the swings and rev the bike, kicking up the dust on the ground in front of us. A group of older guys had shown up and were hanging around on the basketball court. I didn't like the look of them either. When Wilson passed them on the bike one of them, a guy with no shirt, called something after him, like 'Psycho'. Wilson circled back around. When he passed, the same guy commented, 'Even the lunatics came out to play', and the others laughed. Wilson turned again and drove straight at him. He never hesitated or veered, only missing the shirtless guy because he jumped out of the way. The guy picked himself up and shouted, 'Who let you out of the asylum, asshole?' Wilson dropped the bike, ran straight at him and jumped, smashing his own head against the guy's forehead. He stood stunned for a second, and then just folded to the ground at Wilson's feet. 'He's knocked him out,' someone shouted. Wilson walked past where we were on the swings, and I saw how he looked.

I knew why the guy had called him crazy – everyone did. Maybe six months before that, the police had been called after Wilson punched out his neighbours' windows. Three houses in a row. He smashed panes of glass over and over with his bare fists, shouting in the middle of the night. When it stopped, Mr Pascall who lived next door went outside. He found Wilson stark naked on the road, crying, his hands and arms bleeding. Wilson had looked up and said, 'You should call the cops now.' Not long after the Sun Bowl, we heard he'd been involved in a hold-up that went wrong, where a gas station attendant was tied up. Some people said Wilson had been the get-away driver. He must have done something because after that he was gone for a few years, no one was sure where. When he came back, he started showing up at parties, hanging around teenagers not much older than me, just there on the edge of things.

'Maybe Ellen hid when she heard the motorcycle because she was scared it was Wilson.'

'You don't even know him. I'll call you when she gets here.'

I watched the television with the sound turned down low. *Fantasy Island* came on. It all looked so ridiculous, the little man shouting 'De plane! De plane!' and the guy in the tuxedo who was supposed to have godlike powers telling all the staff to smile for the rich clients; I switched to *The Rockford Files*. I couldn't sit still. It was almost eleven, over three hours since Ellen got out of the car.

Mrs Boucher had subscriptions to magazines and newspapers and walls lined with books. The *Philadelphia Inquirer* and *New York Times* were on the coffee table. The main story on both covers was still the Atlanta Child Murders. I tried reading the story but couldn't concentrate on the words. I had heard it on KYW News that morning when we drove to school. The police had been keeping all of Atlanta's bridges under surveillance, and the week before had observed a car stop on one of the Chattahoochee River crossings, and then heard a splash below in the water. They pulled the driver over and two days later, downriver, a body washed up. They thought they finally had the murderer. I prayed it was him. Over twenty black children were missing or dead. I felt scared in the Bouchers' house alone. It was all glass and at the back the ground sloped so that in the living room I felt as if I were floating in the trees. I could see why Mrs Boucher called it her tree house. There were no curtains, and windows everywhere.

I decided to call Sage back and get her to ask her parents for help, even if it meant they had to call the police. As I walked toward the kitchen phone, a shadow flickered at one of the windows to the front of the house. For a split second, I saw something white. I stopped, held my breath. I heard rustling. Then tapping against the glass. I looked down at my white T-shirt and wondered if I had seen my own reflection. More tapping. There was definitely someone at the window. I walked to the door, casually, as if I weren't scared, and hid behind it and waited. I reached to flick on the porch light, turned to look out, then screamed. I opened the door, and Ellen stumbled in across the threshold.

'Oh God, Ellen.'

There was dirt and blood smeared across her face. Below her right eye was a cut, still bleeding. There were cuts down her right arm and leg and her whole side seemed to be studded with parts of the road. Her white polo shirt was spattered with blood and mud.

'I jumped out of a car.'

'What? What do you mean?' I shut the front door. I could feel the blood rushing into my head, making a sound like the ocean in my ears. 'Are you okay? Are you hurt somewhere?' My voice seemed too loud.

'I don't think so. I don't know. I walked here. I couldn't go home.'

I have to clean her cuts. That's what has to be done. 'Come on.' I brought her down to the bathroom Mrs Boucher used for herself and visitors. Ellen's pinafore and knee socks were caked in dried mud. I tried to ease her down on the white porcelain tiles, her back against the cabinets under the sink. She was shaking. Everything in Mrs Boucher's bathroom was white and monogrammed.

'Hold on a minute.'

I ran to the linen closet, grabbed a set of brown towels and came back. In Mrs Boucher's bathroom Ellen looked like a ghost, her face blue-white, paler than the sink and cabinets behind her. The veins on her temples and fore-head stood out, and the threads of darker veins beneath her eyes and at the sides of her cheeks looked black, as if her skin were see-through. I put the white floor mat into the bath and spread the towel across the tiles.

'Scooch up.'

Ellen raised herself and I slid the towel under her, then wrapped another around her shoulders. I turned on the water, adjusted it to warm and ran the brown washcloth under it.

'I'll be careful, I promise,' I said. I squeezed the excess water from the cloth and touched it to Ellen's face, just under her eye where the cut was still oozing. Ellen winced and pulled back, banging her head on the cabinet.

'Ow.'

'Just let me clean it.' I dabbed at the scratches on her face and wiped the dirt from her chin. My hand was shaking. *She jumped out of a car.* I pulled back the towel and looked again at Ellen's right arm and leg. They were both torn raw. The cuts weren't deep but they stretched across the skin and were dotted black with dirt and grit. I opened Mrs Boucher's medicine cabinet above the sink and found a bottle of hydrogen peroxide.

'Don't look.' Ellen turned her face away, and I poured a capful and tipped it down her right arm, flushing the cuts. 'We have to take off your shirt.'

I undid the shoulder buttons on the pinafore and folded it down to her waist. Ellen pulled her shirt over her head and winced as she raised her right arm. She tugged the towel toward her chest, caving in on herself. She looked so small in her white training bra, the one she didn't need that we teased her about. There was grit all the way up her forearm and elbow, to her shoulder. I kept thinking she might have hit her head and didn't know it, or there could be internal injuries. Her face was sickly white. She began talking.

'After you guys drove off, I started walking toward home, but I knew I was going to end up in the pitch-black because it was so dark already. I know it was stupid, but I decided I'd hitchhike.'

'Oh shit. Ellen, no.'

'I walked a few yards and just turned to face the traffic and put out my thumb. I was scared, but I just thought it would be better to hitch than try to walk in the dark. And my thumb wasn't out even thirty seconds when a car pulled up.'

I sat back from her and kneeled up to rinse the washcloth in Mrs Boucher's sink. Bits of cinder washed out along with swirls of blood.

'A car stopped. Then what?'

'It came up right beside me. It was black, low to the ground. I didn't even look to see who the driver was. I just opened the door and sat down inside, thinking I was lucky to get a ride so fast.' She began fiddling with the ends of her hair. 'I didn't see the driver until we started moving. I turned to say thank you, and I saw him then. I knew I'd made a mistake.' Her right leg started to shake. 'He was so creepy-looking. He had long white-blonde hair, so long he was sitting on it.'

'Oh my God.'

'His hair was like a Barbie doll's, except on a man, and whiter.'

'How old?'

'I don't know. Maybe thirty? Older? He looked like Gregg Allman, except ugly. Even his eyebrows were white.'

'Like albino?'

'No.' Ellen shook her head. 'Not like that boy in Bea's class. His hair was shiny, almost fake, like a doll's. He asked, "Where you headed?" and I told him that I needed to get to Valley Forge Mountain so could he drop me off near the covered bridge. He said, "Yeah." But we had hardly driven at all when he put his hand on my leg, sort of on my knee, and was, you know, rubbing it.'

She paused.

'I didn't know what to do. I didn't say anything. He kept driving with his hand on my leg and then he moved his hand up. All the way up my leg. I couldn't move my hands to push his hand away even though his hand was as far as it could go.'

Ellen took a deep breath. Her voice was steady; she wasn't making any crying noises but tears fell from her eyes.

'When the car was getting closer to the covered bridge, I said, "You can just pull over and I'll get out here", but he didn't say anything back. He kept going. And I knew then he wasn't going to let me out. So when we started into the bad corner just before the bridge, when he had to really slow down, I jumped. I already had my hand on the door handle, and I just pushed it open and jumped, and I stumbled a bit and then fell and rolled on the road.'

I thought I might pass out; black specks and silver flashed on the edge of my vision. When I spoke, my own voice sounded very far away.

'Were there other cars coming?'

'No, but his car stopped just ahead of me. I could see the red from his brake lights on the road. He got out. I thought he was coming for me, but I think it was to shut the car door. I got up and ran across the road toward the creek. I went down the bank and straight into the water near the bridge. It was only waist-deep, and I tried to run through it, but it was like I was going in slow motion, and I kept falling. The rocks were covered in slime.' She looked down at the skirt of her pinafore. I could see the track of the creek water and the mud on her socks. 'When I got to the other bank, I ran as fast as I could through the woods, even though I knew then he wasn't behind me.'

'Why didn't you go back down to Yellow Springs to one of the houses for help?'

Ellen shook her head. 'I don't know. I just kept running in the woods. I was going up the side of the mountain, and I knew that he would never find me in there. I tried to just keep going. And finally, I saw lights. Someone's house at the back of Hamilton Drive.'

'You were almost home. Why didn't you go home?'

Ellen shrugged. 'I remembered you're here on Fridays. Mom would kill me if she found out I hitchhiked.' Ellen wiped her nose with the back of her wrist on her good hand. 'And plus I still hate her.'

39

4

It was early morning and in the shadow of the trees the air was still cool. I paused and breathed in the smell of loam and damp earth. In the distance a chainsaw hummed a discordant scale, pitching high and low, and somewhere a lawnmower started. It was Saturday, the first day of summer break from school, and the familiar woods and the routine of work in the world seemed reassuring, even if just for a moment. I hadn't slept. Shafts of light fell diagonally through the trees and dust glittered and floated in front of me. I walked through them, deeper into the woods.

I'd told Sage to meet me in the Kingdom as soon as she could and told her what Marie said we needed: antibiotics and Valium. Sage would need time to sneak it from her dad's clinic without being seen. Grady Adams was a physician and ran a practice next to the house. Sage's mother, Charlotte, worked as his secretary. They were both Southern. Sage referred to them by their first names when she spoke about them. 'Grady and Charlotte had a dinner party last night and Mrs Nelson was drunk and trying to play footsie with Grady while Charlotte and I were right there in plain view.' Sage spoke like this, recounting little dramas that always made her family seem interesting. She spoke about them like they were characters that she was friends with. I envied it. When I thought about them,

Grady, Charlotte, Sage and her brothers, it was always through a haze of happiness, their bright lives, even when Sage said differently.

Spots of early-morning sun broke through in patches on the forest floor, lighting clumps of resurrection fern and dense tufts of moss. I tried to slow down and think. *Mom won't find out. She's taken Thomas to swim practice. Beatrice went with them. Marie's with Ellen. She'll be okay.* But I was scared. Ellen wasn't right. She hadn't slept at all. This morning she was weak and dizzy and Marie said her heart rate and breathing were both too fast. Marie said it was probably shock and that we needed Valium to help her body calm down and antibiotics to prevent the cuts from getting infected. I still worried about the injuries inside her that we couldn't see.

I walked down the Horseshoe Trail toward the Kingdom, a secret fort Sage and I had made several summers before. Ahead of me was the crooked tree, our marker for leaving the path to circle into the Kingdom from the back, a routine we had so that there would never be a trace of track or footfall for anyone else to find. We imagined that the crooked tree was one of the ones Indians had used as signposts along trails to signal where there was good hunting or soft ground for shelter. It was an oak that had started to grow upright but suddenly the trunk made a complete right angle for two or three feet and then grew up straight again. Before the Kingdom even existed, Dad had shown me the tree. He said it might have been a marker, but it could also have been caused by a bigger tree falling on the oak when it was young, and then over time the bigger tree rotted away or fell apart. The young tree survived but was left with this strange shape.

The Kingdom was an enclosure about four feet above the trail and set back in a natural ring formed by a stand of red oak and thick mountain laurel. Inside, deep green moss provided a natural carpet. Sage and I had dug a deep trench to bury a large suitcase filled with supplies: flashlights, batteries, canned food, sleeping bags and pillows – our own nuclear bunker. The hole had taken us a month, slicing through and around the network of roots. We'd told no one but Ellen and even then only because I was in charge of her the day we hauled the suitcase. I had one of Dad's tarps that he used for raking leaves, which had a waterproof side and punched holes. We'd hammered hooks in the oaks around us so we could give ourselves a roof should we ever need it. We'd covered the suitcase bunker with a board, leaves and moss. It hadn't been opened for several summers and roots had started to track across it. We had other stashes, shallow holes for cigarettes and matches or beer. In the Kingdom we talked, smoked Charlotte's Kent menthol cigarettes and on a few occasions drank lukewarm bottles of Yuengling or Rolling Rock, stolen from Grady's refrigerator in his downstairs den. This far down the trail, neighbours didn't pass, just hikers, and from within the Kingdom we could see them coming first and duck to stay hidden. If we ever had to run, no one would catch us – we knew every root and ridge. I could run the trail barefoot at night.

Inside the Kingdom, I sat down against the trunk of a large red oak and pulled my knees into my chest and waited, peeling thick moss off the earth in sections and re-arranging it in patterns. It was strange how it could grow without roots. I brushed my hand across its gentle purple spores on their thread-like stalks.

It was Sage who had brought Ellen home. I'd called her and asked her to come up and bring a change of clothes. When she arrived at the Bouchers' it was nearly midnight. She was wearing her cut-offs and a faded Rolling Stones T-shirt with the tongue on the front – her favourite band. Sage had long wavy gold-blonde hair cut in layers and a spatter of freckles across her nose. Her two front teeth turned in slightly, an imperfection somebody else would have fixed with braces. She liked her teeth. 'It's charac-ter,' she said. With Sage there, I felt safe. We told her what had happened and Sage listened, the whole time holding Ellen's hand. She knew what to do. She had Ellen move all her limbs to make sure they weren't broken. Then she asked her questions I would never have asked.

'Ellen, I know this is hard, but did the man touch you inside your underwear?'

Ellen shook her head no.

'Are you certain? Did the man make you touch him at all?'

Again Ellen shook her head.

'Is there anything you haven't said that you're scared about?'

'No. I'm sure.'

Then Sage told her everything was going to be fine, and I felt for a moment like it was. Ellen put her head on Sage's shoulder.

'There's no way she can walk home, Libby,' Sage said. 'Either you tell Mrs Boucher when she gets home, or I'll get Charlotte to come.'

'No. No parents. It will just make everything worse. Give me a minute.' I called home and Marie answered right away.

'It's me.'

'Mom just left,' Marie said. 'She must've gone out to look for her.'

'Ellen's here.'

'What? Oh, thank God.'

'Yeah. But listen: something's happened. She's okay but won't be able to walk home.'

'I'll get someone. Have her ready.'

We'd been waiting less than twenty minutes when headlights started down the driveway toward the house. I panicked. What if it was Mrs Boucher? How would I explain Sage and Ellen in the house? A car door slammed, the headlights stayed on and a dark bulk moved toward the outside light. A man. He tapped lightly on the door. I looked out. He was broad. I recognized the dark hair and suede leather-fringe jacket. It was Wilson McVay with his dad's Buick. Ellen was ready in Sage's clothes, and Sage was carrying Ellen's uniform. I opened the door and Wilson stood at the threshold looking at us.

'Well, you must be the Florence Nightingales,' he said.

'Hey, Wilson,' said Sage. She started walking with Ellen to the door.

'Yeah, hi,' I said.

'This is Ellen,' said Sage.

45

'Hey there, Miss Ellen,' Wilson said, slightly bowing. 'Your taxi's ready.' Ellen broke a smile. Wilson smelled of leather, cologne and a hint of alcohol. Ellen and Sage followed him out to the car while I fanned the door in and out to make sure the smell of him was gone before Mrs Boucher came home.

I watched the tail lights disappear through the trees. How had Marie managed to get Wilson and how had I just let Ellen into his car after everything that had happened? In the bathroom I cleaned the sink and floor, put the bath mat back and threw the towels we'd used into the washing machine.

It was close to two, later than usual, when Mrs Boucher came home. She drove me to the top of my road without saying anything. She seemed tired and preoccupied, driving with the window down while she smoked.

'Are you okay for next Friday?' she asked when I was getting out.

'Yeah. That'd be great. Thanks.'

The back door was unlocked. I tiptoed up the steps. In our room, Marie and Ellen were still awake. Sage and Ellen had gotten out of Wilson's car at the top of our road and walked down to the house together. Marie had met them at the back door and taken Ellen inside, and Sage had gone back up to where Wilson was waiting. Marie had brought Ellen upstairs and put her into bed. I crawled on to my half of the trundle, and we all lay there in the dark.

'Does Mom know Ellen's home?' I asked.

'She must have heard us because after we'd turned off the light, like twenty minutes ago, she came in. She stood over Ellen's bed, but she didn't say anything.'

'She pulled my blanket further up,' said Ellen.

I looked down at Ellen's trundle. In the dark I could see the glow of her forehead, the shape of her face, but I couldn't see that she was hurt. None of us spoke for a few minutes.

'What a fucking creep,' Marie said. 'He should be castrated. Did you see any of the licence plate, Ellen? Was it Pennsylvania?'

We never slept. I could sense us all awake in the dark and every hour or so Marie or I would ask, 'El, you still awake?' or 'Does anything else hurt?' I thought about the art camp and the letter Miss LeBlanc had written.

'Ellen, why didn't you tell Mom about Miss LeBlanc's note? I don't think she understands how good you are.'

'It wouldn't have made a difference. She wouldn't have let me go anyway.'

In the Kingdom, all around me, the laurel was in bloom, the flowers like wide-open cups, and I pulled one from its cluster on a branch. The white petals were pink-tinged and speckled with deep burgundy dots. The flowers and pollen of laurel are poisonous, but the leaves can be medicinal. The Cherokee used the leaves on cuts for pain relief and rubbed them against skin for arthritis.

I heard a low whistle. Sage. Her silver bracelets jangled as she walked, and I watched her coming down the trail through a small gap at the top of the embankment. She turned at the crooked tree and came around the back and into the ring. Before she sat down, she pulled a ziplock bag with two cigarettes in it from her knapsack. She put a Kent in her mouth and lit it, then handed me the bag. I shook my head. Sage pulled the smoke into her mouth first, then breathed it in deeply, the way she always smoked. Charlotte smoked the same way.

'How is she?'

'Marie thinks she's in shock but that she'll be okay.'

Sage exhaled. I breathed it in; the smoke was cool and fresh. Jack Griffith had told me and Sage that menthol cigarettes had fibreglass in them and were the worst ones to smoke. He and Thomas had caught us smoking behind the house two summers ago. 'What a nerd,' Sage had said when they'd walked away. Sage was the same age as Thomas and Jack and she and Jack were in the same class. Sage thought he was annoying. 'Smugly virtuous,' she said.

'Does your mom know yet? I hope she feels like shit.'

'Oh my God. No. She can't find out. She'd kill Ellen for hitchhiking in the first place. We've all agreed not to breathe a word.'

Sage recited lines from 'Jumpin' Jack Flash' and I made a sound that wasn't a laugh.

There were times when I did think my mother was some kind of hell-hag, but I didn't like other people saying it.

Sage was obsessed with Mick Jagger and we had an on-going joke using Rolling Stones lyrics when they fit our situation. They were coming to Philadelphia in September. Sage was going.

She pulled out a tube of ointment. 'Neosporin's for her cuts and scratches. It's the same stuff we used last night.' She handed me a small brown pill bottle. 'These antibiotics

48

are the ones I got for the burn. It's the second dose I didn't end up taking, but I know they're good for skin and infection.' Last October, up at the water tower, Sage and some others had tried to start a small campfire. Sage helped pour gasoline on the woodpile and some of it splashed on her down jacket. When she went to strike the match, a small explosion erupted in her hands. There were flames and someone put them out right away, but nobody went for help. Sage walked home with her hands and arms burnt and her dad took her to the hospital. Her hands healed perfectly but she had puckered scars on the soft underside of her forearms, where her jacket had melted on to the soft skin. For Sage, it was like her crooked teeth: she didn't see the scars as a blemish but as experience written on her body, marks that added to her story about herself. She didn't want braces, and she liked her scars.

'I couldn't find Valium. I looked everywhere. I don't know if you should give it to Ellen anyway. I still think we should tell Grady. He could look at her.'

'No, Sage. Please. You can't tell anyone. Ever.'

'Jesus, Libby – Ellen looks like she's nine. That guy who picked her up. We should tell someone.'

I didn't want Grady Adams to know. He already didn't like things about my mom and I didn't want him to know any more. I loved Sage's dad. He played classical music and collected jazz records. He had a downstairs den with a bar in it and sometimes I'd seen him through the door, levered back in a leather swivel chair, his eyes closed, listening to music. He had a soft Southern drawl and always spoke to me like he was interested in what I had to say. He never seemed quite part of everything. Charlotte was the opposite, nervous and elegant. She was blunt in her opinions and loved a good story and wasn't afraid to exaggerate to make it more colourful. Sage called her dramatic. My mother said Charlotte Adams could land airplanes the way she talked, swinging her arms and moving her hands.

'No. We're not telling anyone. Please, Sage. Promise.'

Sage stood and reached out her hand and pulled me to my feet. 'Let's go see Ellen.'

We walked back down the trail, sunlight falling through the canopy all around us. Fallen trees lay collapsed across one another, the bole completely broken on some, leaving upright jagged stumps like open wounds. I held the ointment and pill bottle in my closed fist. I thought about my mom driving the empty roads looking for Ellen. I wondered if she had waited at her own window, looking, whether she had seen Sage bring her home, how she had tried to tuck Ellen in. Even though I was angry with her, it hurt to think of her like that.

5

Wilson McVay was in my bedroom. He was leaning against our clothes drawers by the window, as relaxed as though he were a regular visitor. He was wearing heavy black boots, black jeans with a black Harley-Davidson belt and a black T-shirt. Sage and I sat on the lower trundle. Ellen was behind us, propped upright against the wall with pillows all around her. She was still very pale and the area around her lips was shadowed dusky-blue. Marie sat cross-legged on her own bed, in a black skirt and T-shirt; a long strand of rhinestones dangled from one ear.

Aside from Marie and the Siouxsie and the Banshees poster on the wall behind her, our room was mostly pink. Wilson was totally out of place in it. Maybe he was nineteen or twenty, but he already looked like a fully grown man, someone who would have to shave every day. His presence in our room changed it, as if something dark and looming had cast its shadow straight into the heart of us. I wanted him gone.

They were listening to a tape Wilson had brought for Marie, and I realized that they had punk in common. They must have met at a show. Or maybe they had gone to one together. Did Wilson take her to those places? He didn't look anything like a punk rocker but I could see how the music might appeal to him, the angry parts. On the mountain, everyone listened to rock or heavy metal, and where you stood between Creedence Clearwater and Black Sabbath said something about who you were and who you hung out with. My sister was the only person I knew who was into punk. Girls at school thought she was a freak. Now, Marie and Wilson were talking about bands they knew or had seen that Sage and I had never even heard of: Flipper, Killing Joke, The Stickmen. She told Wilson she had gone to watch some band in a DJ's basement in West Philly and that she had had to stand on a washing machine to see them. They talked about being at The Hot Club.

'Don't you have to be twenty-one to go there?' I asked. Marie ignored me. Since Christmas, she'd been going into the city to clubs and to see bands. She told Mom that she was staying with her friend Nancy. As far as I knew, they hadn't been friends since the tenth grade. In the school cafeteria, Marie sat alone with a book at the far end by the window. Nancy sat with other girls with long greasy hair like hers, who tended to look down at the ground or at SAT flash cards. The only friend Marie had from school that I knew of was Rae. She had graduated the previous year and was a freshman at Moore College of Art and lived in her own apartment downtown.

This year Marie had thrown out her tie-dye Grateful Dead T-shirts and bleached jeans in favour of black vintage clothes, fishnets, Doc Martens and rhinestone jewellery. She'd go into Philadelphia to meet Rae and hang around South Street, Zipperhead and the basement of Rage Records on Third, which had the best collection of punk music in the city. Over the past weeks, she'd started skipping school, taking the bus into Philly after my mom dropped us off at the gates. The nuns didn't really do anything about it. Sister Benedict brought her in one day to talk to her, but I think they were afraid of adding to my mother's difficulties and they didn't get along with her. Plus, Marie had the best SAT scores in her class and had been accepted into Penn on a full scholarship.

Marie was telling Wilson about an English band, X-Ray Spex, and the lead singer, Poly Styrene. Wilson said he knew 'Oh Bondage Up Yours!' Sage nudged me. Marie said that Poly Styrene had been singing against consumerism but now she'd left the band. Wilson said it was inevitable that she'd eventually be disillusioned, even by punk.

'Wow. You're both a barrel of laughs,' Sage said. I knew she found conversations like this pretentious, and even though she loved Marie she wasn't awed by her punk-self the way I was. When Marie dyed her hair black and shaved the side of her head, I thought she was cool, that she was brave to reject what people said was beautiful. Sage said it was just another uniform.

Wilson took out a clear plastic baggie of drugs he'd brought with him. There were tablets of different sizes and colours, pastel pinks and blues and white ones. There were small red pills.

'My mom's basically got a pharmacy in her medicine cabinet. She won't miss any of this.' He stuck his hand in the bag and pulled out a very small tablet, which he put on top of our pink chest of drawers and split in half with the tip of his pocketknife. He gave Ellen half. 'It's diazepam, same as Valium.'

'Are you sure you're giving her the right one? They're all mixed up in there.' I wondered if powder from other drugs like hallucinogens or something dangerous could have rubbed off on what he gave Ellen.

'It's diazepam, trust me,' he said. 'Diazepam's the actual drug. Valium's a trademark.'

'Oh, right. You're, like, a narcotics specialist?' Sage asked.

'Something like that,' he said.

While Ellen swallowed her half-pill with a glass of water, Wilson popped the other half into his mouth. I wanted to scream at Marie to get him out, to get him the hell out of our bedroom and our lives. She was looking at the cassette tape cover he had made.

Sage leaned over toward me, humming the tune to 'Mother's Little Helper'. I wondered what it was like to have a mother taking drugs. Was it because of this that Wilson was so messed up or did she take drugs because her son was so messed up? Either way, I wanted him to get out.

Marie started telling Wilson about a job offer she had from Rage Records. He went there too.

'It's only minimum-wage. My friend Rae has an apartment in West Philly, and she could use help with the rent. My room will basically be the living room couch, but it's only until the dorms open in August.'

'What?' I asked. 'You're leaving?'

'Yeah. I'm not going to stay out here in the middle of nowhere. I need a job.'

'You can get a job at the mall.'

'I'd rather die than work at the King of Prussia mall.'

Marie looked over at Sage. 'Sorry, Sage, but I couldn't do Chick-fil-A again. It's like I would have lost my will to live.'

'Believe me, it's probably worse than you remember.'

'What about us?' I felt as if I'd been slapped.

'I'm not your mother, Libby. I was never planning to stay here for the summer.' Marie's eighteenth birthday was in three weeks and I realized then that no one was going to try to stop her from going.

'How will we see you?' Ellen asked.

'By train, dummy,' Marie said, throwing a pillow at her. Ellen flinched. 'Oh shit. Sorry. You okay?' Ellen nodded.

'Does Mom know?' I couldn't believe Marie was telling us in front of Wilson, like it was nothing, and I resented him even more for seeing me exposed and hurt like this.

'Yeah. She knows.' She was being so casual about leaving. She went across the room and sat next to Ellen on the upper trundle. 'You're going to have to sleep, Ellen. But before you do, Wilson wants to ask you just a few things.'

'I don't want to talk about it. Please.'

'You don't have to talk about what happened. It's just to identify the guy.'

'It's what I said already. He had long almost-white hair, so long he was sitting on it. Blue eyes. Oh, I forgot. He had really long fingernails for a man.' Her picture gave me an involuntary chill.

'Was it both? Did he have long fingernails on both hands?' Wilson asked.

Ellen thought for a moment. 'No. It was his right hand. The hand on my leg. Not the one on the steering wheel. And he had to sort of bend over the way he drove, like his body was too big for the car.' She paused. 'I can't think of anything else.'

'What about the car?' Wilson asked.

'I don't know. It was black. It looked like the car Chicken De Martino drives except a different colour.'

'Chicken drives a Camaro,' Wilson said. 'Was it a Camaro?'

'I don't know,' Ellen said. 'It was black on the inside.'

'What were the seats like?'

'They were low, like we were sitting on the ground.'

'Bucket seats?' Wilson asked.

Ellen shrugged. She yawned and her hand moved to the cut under her eye. 'They had furry covers, like the lid of the toilet seat in Meredith Hunter's house.'

'That's shag,' I said.

'And disgusting,' said Sage.

'Shag,' said Ellen. 'But fluffier and dark, like purple-black.'

'You told Libby he played a tape.' Wilson picked up the ziplock and stuffed it back in his pocket. 'Do you remember what?'

Ellen stared straight ahead for a moment. 'He put in the cassette and when he leaned over his head knocked a rabbit's foot hanging from the mirror. It was yellow. The song was something about being a child.' She started to hum, her hand moving to a beat. 'They had a fever?'

'"Comfortably Numb",' said Marie. 'Pink Floyd. You've heard me play it too?'

Ellen nodded. 'I can't remember anything else.' She was groggy. 'I feel like I could sleep now.'

'That girl is worn out,' Sage said, 'and I have to get home.' She stood up, straightened her cut-offs and leaned over to give Ellen a kiss on the top of her head. 'See you later, munchkin. Get some sleep.'

Ellen settled down into the pillows around her. The rest of us walked downstairs together and out to the driveway.

'I'll call you later, Libby,' Sage said. She walked to the back of our house to cut through the woods. Wilson, Marie and I stood facing the street. Mr Walker was sitting on his drive-around mower with his glass of lemonade, watching us. Everyone knew who Wilson McVay was and now Mr Walker had seen him come out of our house when our mom wasn't home. He didn't talk to our mother ever, but what if he decided to call her? I stared back at Mr Walker until he looked away.

'Why are you guys asking her all those questions?' I asked. 'Are you going to report it to the police?'

'No,' Marie said. 'But someone's got to get him. Wilson knows people and if he's from around here it won't be hard to find a giant blonde man with hair down to his ass who drives a black Camaro. Someone'll know him.'

'And who plays the guitar,' said Wilson.

'What?'

'The fingernails on the right hand. He must keep them long for plucking.'

I looked at the two of them. Marie was acting as if all of this was perfectly normal.

'Do you think you're detectives or something? What will you do if you find out who he is?'

'Skin him alive,' Wilson said in a deadpan voice. It gave me a jolt in my stomach. I looked at him and remembered that day in the Sun Bowl when he'd passed us on the swings. He saw my face and started to laugh. 'Calm down. I just want to find out who the shithead is.'

He walked back up our driveway and into the woods toward the trail where Sage had gone. A few seconds later we heard a motorcycle start. Wilson must have come to our house through the woods and left his bike up there. Why hadn't Sage and I heard him when we were up in the Kingdom? He made me uncomfortable. People instinctively moved away from him. There are trees – allelopathic trees – like black walnuts that are poison to whatever is nearby. They release chemicals from their roots, their decaying leaves, their bark, that start to destroy the life around them. I thought of Wilson like that, bringing toxins and danger just by coming near us. We didn't know anything about where he'd been. Juvenile prison, a mental institute, reform school? I blamed him for Mr Franklin. Was a BB gun even strong enough to kill a cat? I'd been shot loads of times by a BB gun. The De Martino boys used to wait for us to pass on our way up to the Sun Bowl and shoot us. I'd been hit in the behind and got bruises, but the metal balls had never broken my skin. Maybe Wilson had done it with some other kind of airgun, or a real gun. Marie had an airgun that shot darts, a Marksman, and it could definitely hurt or even kill an animal. No one else knew about it but me. She had begged Dad for it. We took it out into the woods sometimes and kept it hidden in our bedroom closet.

'Marie, what if Wilson killed Mr Franklin? Why are you hanging around him?'

'That's just people talking. He's not bad if you get to know him. He's had a shit childhood.'

'So?'

'He's helping us, Libby.'

We could hear the revving of the gears on Wilson's bike as it hit Forge Mountain Drive from the trail. He was a blur when he passed the top of our street at full throttle, the front wheel elevated in the air.

'God, what an asshole,' I said. 'Please tell me you don't go around with him on that.'

Marie didn't say anything, and we stood there together for a few minutes watching Mr Walker cut perfect circles on his lawn.

6

A door clicked shut. I sat up. The room was dark. Ellen was below me, sleeping. She'd slept almost all day, and I could see Marie's shape across the room in her bed, the soft rise and fall of her breath. Another sound came from the hallway, a creak of floorboards. I leaned forward, tense, listening. There was a low whimper. Beatrice. I heard the sound of my mother: 'Shhh.' She was taking Beatrice, something she did sometimes, leaving in the middle of the night. She'd freewheel the car down to the road in the dark before turning on the engine. It was bad enough with Marie sneaking out the window and climbing down the wall, but my mother creeping out of the house with Beatrice half-asleep in her arms left me with a pitching feeling, as if the house were staggering sideways into the ground, everything sliding and falling, and I couldn't grasp anything I could hold on to. I lay back down, eyes open. When they reached the road the lights of her car switched on and hit the trees, splaying shadows backward across the ceiling of our room and down the wall toward me. They were going to meet Bill.

I tried to fall back asleep, willing myself to let go, but I woke with a jerk midway through falling. I never seemed capable of just floating or drifting down. I fell violently, from a bike, a branch, a building, the sudden drop jolting me awake before impact, leaving me with the sensation that the shock was still below, waiting to come. I tried counting sheep and imagining myself in a relaxing place, a forest looking skyward through the canopy. Now it was the Barbie Man whose blank face and sleek hair materialized above me. I gasped and sat up. I was sweating. We should have told my mother. She would never have left us in the middle of the night if she knew what had happened to Ellen. Not even for Bill.

None of us had even met Bill. Only Beatrice. 'That's why Beatrice has the box room instead of me,' Marie had said. 'So Mom can get her in and out of the house easier without waking the rest of us.'

'But Beatrice doesn't even like going. She's told me a hundred times.'

'So?' Marie had asked. 'Mom uses her. Beatrice is her Bill pawn.'

I'd imagined Beatrice as a chess piece on a board, being pushed around by adult fingers: her tangle of wavy hair, the freckles across her nose, her wide rosy cheeks and missing teeth, how she was always trying to please everyone, manoeuvred in a game she did not understand.

Marie sometimes expressed things crudely. She could see things from a detached distance, she said, because she had stopped liking our mother.

'Stop looking so shocked, Libby. It doesn't mean I don't love her. I don't have to like her too. Fucking hell.'

I can't remember when I first knew Bill existed. He didn't. And then he did. He was silent breathing on the phone, a pause, and then a voice that I knew but didn't know. 'Is your mother there?' Mom never denied his existence or that he might be Beatrice's father. It must have been Marie and Thomas who explained it to me. I don't remember. I knew not to say anything to anyone, especially my dad, even though I have no memory of anyone ever ordering this.

At home we'd made fun of Bill in front of my mother. We had guessed all sorts of occupations for him: trucker, plumber, milkman, travelling salesman who sold everything from Bibles to steak knives. We'd take out Thomas's walkie-talkies and perform 'Bill plays' when my mother was nearby.

'Breaker ten-four, this is Fat Man Bill. Can you read my handle? I am so doggone fat, I just can't get out of my truck and go see my daughter.'

'Roger, Fat Man Bill. You sure are ugly. I hear you're a no-good father too.'

We'd use hillbilly accents. Beatrice would watch and laugh with us, as if she didn't realize it was her dad we were joking about. When we drove past storefronts with a neon *Bill* blinking in the dark, we'd shout, 'Is that him? Is that Bill?' It could be *Bill's Carpets*, *Uncle Bill's Pancake House* or *Whiskey Bill's Bar and Grill*. Once, we passed a billboard that read *Bill Bowie for Sheriff*. We asked our mother, 'Is that him? Is Bill running for sheriff?' She didn't say anything, and we took her silence as a sign. We started a campaign for his opponent, making posters and slogans for him and marching outside her bedroom door, cheering on the other guy for sheriff. Beatrice did it with us. She didn't know if the Bill she knew was running for sheriff, but she didn't want him to win either.

Mostly Mom had ignored us. If we came up with a new Bill scenario she'd sometimes laughed at our guesses, like when Thomas had suggested Bill was possibly the guy who took our order at McDonald's. He'd noticed the name tag: *William*.

But we didn't guess about Bill any more, especially in front of our mother. She seemed too tired for it. I said Bill's name as little as possible, even to the others, because thinking about it or even acknowledging it made me feel like I was betraying my dad. He knew Beatrice wasn't his daughter, couldn't be his daughter, but he had never ever behaved as if she was anything but his. I knew he never suspected that we knew. Saying it out loud now, when he was gone, was like treachery.

'I have five sprogs,' he would say. 'Four strong women and a little man.' We would all straighten up a little under his proud assertion, be it to a waitress at the diner, a customer whose lawn he cut or a guy drinking beer at one of the Irish bars he took us to.

Marie and Thomas said that things had been bad between Mom and Dad long before Bill existed, that they had been separated, that I was wrong to confuse what happened to Dad with Bill. Dad had kept some of his machines in our garage and collected us some mornings to take us to school, but he didn't sleep at our house. Sometimes he washed up in the laundry room downstairs next to the garage, especially when Mom wasn't home. He kept cakes of soap wrapped in paper towels behind the seat of the pickup. He always used Coast, a bright-blue bar that smelled like him. We had a scentless

Dove. Some evenings when I came in from being outside somewhere on the mountain, I could smell his soap in the laundry room.

He moved around back then, and I don't know if he always had a regular apartment or place to go back to. He bought a camper top for the pickup and the foam mattress would still be rolled out in the mornings when we crawled in the truck to go to school. He said he'd bought the top to stop us getting soaked and wind-lashed in the open back. Now I wasn't sure. I found it too hard to even say it, to ask Marie or Thomas, 'Do you think he sometimes slept in his truck?'

My mother kept Beatrice close to her and somehow separate from us. Beatrice had never come when Dad took us in the back of the pickup to Burger King for giant milk-shakes or to the diner where we all drank coffee and got free refills. Beatrice had been too young to go working with him. The time we'd gone to New York to stay with him when he'd tried to start a new life there, Beatrice had been invited too, but we knew my mother would never have let her go.

Beatrice was treated differently, but we didn't hold this against her. We didn't envy her being shut inside our mother's room or being hauled out of bed to meet some man who was a stranger to the rest of us and who I couldn't stop blaming for everything bad that had happened. When Beatrice came back from visits with Bill, she was always quiet. Even after being treated to ice cream.

'I don't like his hands,' she whispered to me one night when we were lying in bed.

'Whose hands?'

'Bill's.'

'Why?' It disturbed me that she would say this. She'd crawled into my bed during the night, as she sometimes did, stepping across Ellen, asleep on the bottom trundle. She had snuggled in, facing me. She'd developed a habit of twisting sections of hair and looping them around her finger. We teased her that this was where her curls came from. Sometimes, without noticing, she did it to my hair when I was lying next to her. Marie said Beatrice was developing habits that displayed her worry.

'He's missing part of his fingers on one of his hands. They're just fat and round at the knuckles.'

'Oh.' I paused. I didn't like to question too much because Beatrice got upset when we started asking about her visits. Marie said it was messed up that our mom would force this secret on a child, tell her not to talk to her brother and sisters about it and drag her across the night to see someone she didn't want to. When Dad died, Mom stopped meeting Bill for six or seven months. He didn't phone our house, and she didn't sneak away. But it was like she wasn't there any more. Marie and Thomas made our food, and Mom was either in bed or pulling her shift at the hospital, just sleeping and working and sleeping for months straight. Her eyes were red-rimmed. Grief is exhausting, Gwen the counsellor we'd barely gone to had said. I'd wanted to correct her. She had it wrong. Our mother had divorced our father. She'd chosen someone else and kept him a secret from all of us. While she was better now and Bill was obviously back on the scene, it was like she couldn't look at us any more, the four older ones.

I tried to think whether there were any men we knew who had missing fingers. We didn't think Bill lived on the mountain because Beatrice said that most of the time they drove the same way we did when we went to swimming with Thomas: past the Guernsey Cow, the clog shop and the party shop, way further down that same road, past the people with the horse and buggies, which meant Route 30, heading through Pennsylvania Dutch country toward Wilmington, Delaware.

'Maybe Bill's Amish,' Thomas joked, and Marie laughed so hard that the milk she was drinking snorted out of her nose. I was still afraid that Bill might be someone we actually knew and that I might even have been nice to him, not knowing who he was. Marie said the only possible reason for him to still be a secret was that he was married.

'Do you know what happened to his fingers?' I asked Beatrice. I thought how he lost them might be a clue about the work he did. Lying next to me in the dark, she coiled her hair and looked up at the ceiling.

I must have fallen asleep because I didn't hear them come home. By morning my mother had already left with Thomas for swimming. The others were downstairs – Beatrice and Ellen on the sofa, Ellen stretched out, her feet touching Beatrice, who sat cross-legged reading *Tales of a Fourth Grade Nothing*. We'd told Beatrice that Ellen had a bad fall when she was walking home in the dark because she'd tried to go through the woods to get here faster. We'd said we didn't want Mom to know because she'd be mad that Ellen went into the woods. She'd sworn herself to secrecy. We'd told Thomas the same thing. Ellen was wearing a long-sleeved Tweety Bird nightgown that covered up most of her injuries except her face. So far, my mother hadn't seen Ellen, but if she asked about the cuts we had our story straight. Marie was reading a book in the beanbag chair. Ellen was pestering Beatrice.

'How was last night? Did you see Bill?' Her face was chalk-white and the gash under her eye had turned black.

Beatrice kept reading.

'What does he look like? Does he look like you?' Ellen was being mean.

'No. He looks big and wide,' Beatrice said.

'What kind of car does he drive? Do you go anywhere in his car?'

'I told you a thousand times. He's got a truck.'

'Does he wear a suit like Mr Walker wears to work or does he wear clothes like the plumber?'

'He wears shirts with squares all over them.'

'Checked? Like cowboys?' Ellen asked.

Beatrice shrugged.

'Where'd you go last night?'

'You know I'm not supposed to say I saw him. We just sat in the booth with our food, and then we sat in the parking lot.' She tucked her legs in under her.

'Jesus, Ellen, lay off,' I said. 'Aren't you supposed to be resting or something?' Ellen looked like she was about to cry.

Marie looked up from her book. 'Ellen, go upstairs. Take two of the baby aspirins out of the bottle in the medicine cabinet. The one with the pink cap.'

Ellen got up and walked slowly up the stairs, taking just one step at a time, using the banister.

I sat there in the rec room with Beatrice and Marie both reading their books. We had cream tiles that reflected the trees outside, so that the floor always seemed to be moving, shadows shifting light and dark from the swaying branches outside. The phone ringing jolted me.

'I'll get it,' I said, though no one else was moving. It was Sage.

'Charlotte's bringing me to work in a few minutes, but I have to tell you something first.'

I took the phone into the laundry room, where the others couldn't hear me. 'What?'

'Last night, up at the tower, Abbey said Wilson was there earlier trying to get a few boys together – you know, getting them to promise to go with him to take some pervert out. That the guy they were going to take care of had hurt a little girl from the mountain.'

I sank into the pile of dirty clothes on the floor in front of the washing machine.

'Oh my God.'

'I know.'

'Did he say who we were? Did Abbey know it was Ellen?'

'I don't think so. She would've said.'

'Did they go?'

'No. Well, not last night. Wilson said he was still finding

the guy. But asking would they help him. He'd give them dime bags of pot and he'd get a case of beer after.'

'Why's he doing this?'

'I don't know. Look, he'll probably never find the guy anyway.'

My mouth had gone so dry the words seemed stuck. 'Why can't he just leave us alone?'

'Tell your mom, Libby.'

I shook my head. 'Can't.'

When I stood to hang up the phone, I saw that I'd been sitting on Ellen's dirty uniform, which was covered with silt, blood and grit. She had just left it there. Everything seemed out of control. I threw the clothes into the washing machine and ran a long cycle and went back out to the rec room. The others were still reading, oblivious to all the trouble coming toward us.

I would tell Marie later and get her to get Wilson to back off, to stay away. I curled up on the sofa next to Beatrice, pulling my knees to my chest. I could feel the twill fabric against my cheek, lying there watching the patterns on the floor. I tried to slow my breathing. After he had left, Dad had stayed on the sofa once for almost a week when he was very sick. It pulled out into a bed and we had made it up with sheets and blankets for him. My mom had called a doctor. It was a time when everything felt right, my mother sitting on the edge of the pull-out sofa putting a thermometer under his tongue and cool cloths on his head, all of us taking care of him. Even then I knew it wasn't real.

Later that week, when he was better and sitting up, we had piled either side of him and he'd read to us. Even

Thomas, who was sometimes shy around Dad, lay on the edge of the sofa bed with us. Dad could recite sections of 'The Deserted Village' by heart. He'd often repeated those lines – '*Where wealth accumulates, and men decay*' – when we said something about someone being rich or someone's big house or another father's big job. That week when he was sick, he read 'The Song of Wandering Aengus', a poem by Yeats that he loved. The five of us were on the pull-out bed with him, as if it were a boat we were all clinging to on a pitching sea. He changed his tone of voice for the final lines, as if they always got to him. I could see the world described, the '*long dappled grass*', the silver and gold. I'd written the lines on the inside cover of my tree notebook. When I thought of those lines, I pictured him in a golden meadow, walking in the long grass, searching.

'They didn't even let us wake his body,' Aunt Rosie had said, with such pain that I knew we had done something terribly wrong, something we could never fix. I wished now, as I had a thousand times before, that I could have gone to him at that moment when he was dying, away from us and alone, and said something to him so he would have known how he was loved, even though we never talked like that in my family.

A cloud moved across the rec room floor and the room went dark. I looked up. Marie was still reading, Beatrice was leaning back with her book on her knees.

'Is it good?' I asked.

She moved her head up and down slowly without taking her eyes off the page. I looked out the window. The woods looked like rain.

7

On Friday morning, I woke to a lawnmower outside, a sound of order in the world, of adults taking care of things. A full week had passed since the night in the car. Mom had been working and Marie and Ellen had mostly stayed in our room, Ellen resting and Marie sorting through her stuff and keeping an eye on how Ellen was. The rumble of the engine rose and fell while the sun moved to light the wall beside me. I could almost smell the cut grass. The machine reached a crescendo, and I heard the jolt when it hit a rock. It was outside my window. I sat up. Someone was cutting our lawn. For a moment I felt happy. I stepped across Ellen sleeping on the lower trundle and looked out the window. I could see the line the lawnmower had made past the window and down at the end of the driveway, where the quartz boulders could be seen whole again. I thought my mother must have organized it.

Downstairs in the kitchen Thomas was hunched over his cereal at the table. He had broad shoulders from swimming and looked older than sixteen. He'd been shaving for a year. We had all stood around the sink and watched the first night he did it, Marie giving instructions.

'Fuck's sake, Libby. Did you do this?'

'Do what?'

'GI Joe out there.' Thomas pushed the cereal away. 'He's a creep. I told you I was going to ask the Griffiths

73

to borrow their lawnmower and just wheel it down. Why couldn't you just wait?'

I went to the front door and looked out right as Wilson McVay passed. He was wearing jeans and had taken off his white T-shirt and slung it over his shoulder. He looked like one of those men in the Levi's ads, rugged and beautiful. Except it was Wilson. He waved at me when he passed again, flashing a smile, and I felt sick. I went back into the kitchen.

'I have nothing to do with this. Has Mom gone to work already? Does she know?'

But Thomas slammed the plastic bowl and spoon into the sink and stamped up the stairs.

I ran up to Beatrice's room and looked out the window over the driveway. Mr McVay's Buick was parked there, with the trunk open and a can of gasoline on the drive. A rake was leaning against the passenger door.

I went back into our bedroom.

'Marie. Marie, wake up.' I shook her.

'What? Shit, what time is it?' Marie rolled on to her side and leaned up on her elbow and yawned. 'What?'

'Did you ask Wilson McVay to cut the grass?'

'No. Why?'

The sound of the lawnmower passed again, and Marie sat up fully and leaned against the wall.

'Whoa. Wilson is cutting our lawn?'

'Yeah. He's here with his dad's Buick. Did he wait for Mom to go to work? Is he watching us or something? Thomas is upset. He was trying to borrow a lawnmower.'

'So what if he cuts the lawn?' Ellen sat up on her trundle, her thin hair tangled and flat from sleep. 'It's nice of him.

74

Thomas should thank him. Now he doesn't have to do it.'

'Marie, make him go. Please. Please make him go.'

'What do you want me to do, go out there and say, "How dare you answer our call for help in the middle of the night and then kindly come cut our grass?" I mean, he obviously thinks he's doing a good thing.'

'He is,' said Ellen.

I hadn't told Marie yet about what Wilson was planning. Maybe she knew. 'Marie, just tell him to leave us alone. Now. Tell him to just go. Thomas wanted to cut the lawn.'

'You're being totally melodramatic,' Marie said. 'Thomas can cut it next time, and the hard work will be done for him.' She stood over by the window, looking out. 'It looks like shit, anyway. It's yellow.'

'Please, Marie. I don't want him here. He scares me.'

The back door slammed.

'Well, there goes Thomas,' Marie said, looking out. The three of us stood at the window and watched Thomas walk down the driveway. He kicked at the ground but squared his shoulders, staring straight ahead when he went past Wilson. Wilson waved but Thomas ignored him and kept walking. Wilson didn't seem fazed at all. He looked like he was singing.

Marie and Ellen made iced tea and took out glasses to the driveway when Wilson was finished. When we'd cut lawns with Dad, some owners would come out with drinks for us.

I watched the three of them from Beatrice's window, Ellen looking at him like he was a hero and Marie making

75

him laugh. I wanted to shout out the window for him to put his shirt back on, that it was obscene and all the neighbours could see. I wanted to scream, 'Get out and stop intruding.'

Later, hours after he'd left, I went and sat on the front porch and looked across the yard. He had done a good job: neat edges, and he'd cut it twice, creating a diagonal pattern. The grass was yellow but in the odd place there were narrow strips of green. The smell of gasoline lingered with the cuttings.

Thomas and I had worked with Dad the most. Marie wasn't the outdoor type and Ellen had been too small. I wondered if our machines were still in the Bronx or whether the cousin had sold them. They belonged to us. I knew where each of them had been bought, which lawns we'd cut with which specific lawnmower. I knew how to clean them and how to get them on and off the truck. My throat tightened. I breathed deeply again – gas, cuttings, summer heat. The past. Thomas still had not come home. Last summer he'd gone door to door asking to borrow a lawnmower. Wilson just had to take his dad's keys and throw their machine in the trunk. What were we going to tell Mom? I sat outside until I saw the first lightning bug.

Peter answered the door at the Bouchers' that night. 'Libby!' he shouted, and grabbed my hand, pulling me in across the threshold.

'Hey, Mr Peter Rabbit, how's the gangster-rabbit life? You eating lots of stolen cabbage and carrots?'

Peter laughed and ran around the kitchen. 'Bang, bang. This is a hold-up. Give me all your lettuce!'

'Hi, Libby,' Mrs Boucher said, coming into the kitchen as she fastened an earring. The scent of lemons drifted around her.

'Hi, Mrs Boucher' – and just as I said it, I saw the brown towel set we'd used the week before folded on the countertop. I had put them in Mrs Boucher's washing machine after Ellen and Wilson left but had never taken them out. I looked at the towels, the heat flushing my face, and then at Mrs Boucher, who was looking at me.

'Was everything okay last week, Libby? I meant to ask you.'

I was about to make up a story about knocking a cup of coffee over and getting brown towels so it wouldn't stain the kitchen rag, but I knew it would sound hollow.

'Hold 'em up, Libby,' Peter shouted. I put up my hands as if to give in. I would tell her.

'Last Friday, Ellen had an accident and she came here. I am really sorry. I should have told you. I've never had anyone in the house before when you weren't here.' I could hear the waver in my voice.

We sat at Mrs Boucher's long table. I told her almost everything. The art camp, getting kicked out of the car, hitchhiking. The man in the Camaro with white hair like a Barbie, Ellen jumping out and showing up at the Bouchers'. I didn't say how the man had touched all the way up Ellen's leg, how he wasn't going to let her out of the car. I made it sound more like she just got scared and she jumped when the car was going very slow. I didn't say how Wilson was organizing people to go find and hurt him. I told her Wilson McVay had appeared out of the dark to collect her, how I was confused about how Marie seemed to know him, how he had been hanging around since. 'He even came and cut our grass today.'

'Does your mother know what happened to Ellen?'

'No, Mrs Boucher.' I shook my head. 'Please don't tell her. Please.'

She squeezed my wrist for a moment. 'Your mother needs to know, Libby. Ellen should see a doctor.'

'She's fine, honestly. She's bossing Beatrice around, fighting with Thomas. She's completely like herself. My mother would just punish her. You know what she's like. Please.'

Mrs Boucher pushed her hands through her hair and looked at me. 'Leaving a child on the road. It's appalling, really.'

I looked at the grain of the table. Everything I did made things worse. 'Please don't tell anyone. I promise everything's okay now.'

I should never have told her anything. Earlier in the year, when I told Sister Benedict about my mom leaving sometimes for a few days and her not cooking, they'd called my mother in for a meeting. Afterward my mom had exploded. Sister Benedict had used the word *neglect*. She'd said she understood all we had been through and was very sorry, but she was concerned about our well-being.

'Do you realize what you've done, Libby?' my mother had shouted at me. The others, even Marie, looked at me like I was destroying us all. I had broken a code of silence we all kept about everything, and now here was another example of how, if I told our secrets to outsiders, bad things would happen to all of us.

Mrs Boucher sat there for a moment. Then she asked, 'Did Ellen get the licence plate number from the car?'

'No.'

'Libby, I need you to promise me that if you think Ellen needs a doctor or if you need any kind of help at all, you will call me. You can always call me.'

'I know. Thank you.'

'And one more thing. You're right to be cautious about Wilson McVay. He shouldn't be in the house when your mother isn't home. Nobody should be.'

Mrs Boucher worked in the courts and she probably knew more about Wilson than we did. 'I better get going. You'll lock the house behind me?'

'There won't be anyone here like that ever again, Mrs Boucher. I promise.'

I watched the tail lights of the Volvo blink through the dark wood, up toward the road, and then disappear as the theme music came on for *The Incredible Hulk*.

'Libby, *Hulk*, *Hulk*.' Peter was getting very excited. He stood in front of the TV as the theme music played, raising his shoulders and lifting his arms out wide. 'I'm the Hulk!' he shouted.

The episode was titled 'The Beast Within'. I knew it would give him nightmares. He'd seen *Hulk* once before when he'd gone for a sleepover at his grandparents'; every Friday for a month, I'd had to stay with him in his room until he fell asleep.

'They have no sense,' Mrs Boucher had said after the nightmares started. 'This is exactly why I've told their father I don't want them staying there. They'd think nothing of watching *The Exorcist* with the kids. I admire your mother for not having a television.'

'Come on, Peter. I'll race you downstairs to the bathroom and we'll brush our teeth.'

Mrs Boucher never told me where she went those Friday nights. I hadn't babysat for many families, but the other ones had always told me where they were going and given me a number for the restaurant or friends' house. Mrs Boucher only left an emergency number, which was Mr Boucher's. He lived with his soon-to-be new wife. My mother said Mrs Boucher was an *intellectual* and one of those *feminists*, like they were bad words. I wondered what had happened to her marriage. Like my parents, the Bouchers were divorced, but they were so different in every other way. I'd met Mr Boucher several times. Once Marie and I had bumped into him and his fiancée at the Acme. We'd gone in for donuts and watched them kissing by the seafood section, where whole fish were splayed out on ice, heads and all.

'Oh my God,' Marie had said, 'Barbie and Ken.' He did look like a Ken doll. 'He's so artificial-looking. I just want to run over and mess up his hair.' His fiancée, Angela, was as tall as him. Her blonde hair was cut and frosted just like Farrah Fawcett's. She was extremely tan and wore a bright-orange dress. She seemed young and silly compared to Mrs Boucher, who was small and dark but somehow more anchored and elegant than either of them.

I was pretty certain Mrs Boucher had started seeing someone. She'd taken extra care the last few months getting ready to go out. She'd be distracted when she came back and several times, when I got into the car to be driven home, I'd smelled something other than Mrs Boucher's lemony scent – some kind of cologne. But there were other things, things I hadn't told Marie or Sage. Lately, when the Volvo turned in from the road, the headlights would briefly hit the glass walls of the living room, only for a moment, and then cut. The car would stay there, sometimes for as long as an hour, and then the headlights would switch on again and the car would crawl down the drive to the house. The first time it happened I was terrified, wondering who was sitting in the car watching me inside the lit glass room. I sat still on the couch waiting, and eventually the car moved again. And it was only Mrs Boucher.

With the lights on inside the house, Mrs Boucher could see me but I couldn't see out. I wondered if I was being tested, to see what kind of babysitter I was. The second night I got up and tidied and made sure the dishes were done, seeing myself as if from the outside, like I was in a film and had an audience. But by the fourth time the Volvo pulled into the driveway and the lights cut, I was pretty certain that Mrs Boucher wouldn't be wasting all that time just to watch me. I wondered if she was sad and found it hard to come into the house, the way my mother sometimes just sat in the parked car in the garage after she had come home, as if she had to brace herself before facing all of us.

The last few weeks I'd been turning off the sound on the television, listening, and I thought I heard a car door shut before the headlights came back on. Was someone else in the car with Mrs Boucher? She told me once that she was never afraid living deep in the woods in a tree house, that it was the most private place in the world. I didn't want to spy on her, and I hadn't told anyone what I'd heard and seen.

Late the same night that I'd told Mrs Boucher about Ellen, I was standing at her sink squeezing a tea bag when the headlights swiped through the woods and across the windows. For a brief second my stomach lurched, thinking it was Wilson. But then the lights cut, and I knew it was only Mrs Boucher, home again.

8

I pushed my toes against the bald scratch of earth below the merry-go-round and started to spin again. Sage and the others were dark shadows across the Sun Bowl. I could hear the low murmur of their voices and every few minutes a burst of laughter. I looked up at the sky and felt slightly dizzy. The moon was visible behind a thin mesh of clouds like stretched cotton. It was fuller than half but not quite full. More laughter drifted from the others out in the field, sitting in a circle, passing a bong.

I was already tipsy. I'd taken some swigs of gin straight out of a Hellmann's Mayonnaise jar. Abbey had raided her dad's liquor cabinet. She said her dad had started to suspect his kids might be helping themselves so he'd taken to drawing lines with magic markers on the Seagram's bottles where he finished. The kids markered lines below his and he'd be uncertain which line was his and wonder had he drunk more than he thought. But they would never add water to bring the level up to his black line, Abbey said. He might be confused about which line was which, but he knew his drink and would know if it was diluted. Even though I was drinking Mr Quinn's gin, I thought it was depressing that his kids were still stealing it from him.

I heard Sage call my name, could see movement in the dark across the field as she came toward me, the clink of her bracelets. She sat beside me.

'Wilson went to Pottstown.'

'What?'

'Wilson went to Pottstown last night.'

'To find him?' I had heard of Pottstown, knew it was north of us, but couldn't remember ever being there.

'Yeah. Abbey and some of the others were just talking about it. He went around looking for the boys who'd said they'd go.'

'Are you sure they went?'

'Abbey says she saw Danny Shields with Wilson on Forge Mountain Drive.'

'What did they do to him?'

'I don't know. Maybe they never went or couldn't find him.'

'Oh my God. How does he know he's from there?'

'Beats me, except he knows a lot of strange people.'

'Did you tell them anything?'

'No. Abbey just said they were going to give a pervert a beating. That this guy had kidnapped a girl from the mountain and hurt her.'

'He told them she was kidnapped?'

'She kind of was, Libby. Barbie Man didn't let her out of the car. She's a kid. That's kidnapping. He should be punished. If Ellen hadn't jumped, what would have happened to her?'

I wasn't able to even think about that. 'I just want this to end.'

'I know.' Sage looked back toward the field. 'I'm going over for a few more minutes. You mind?'

I shook my head. 'I'm okay.'

Sage was going back to the others to get high. Most of them were older than me, and I didn't smoke pot. I didn't want to sit in a circle with them, passing a bong. I'd tried it once and spent the night struggling to shake away the floating feeling. I'd eaten toothpaste and slapped myself across the face, so that I could feel like my two feet were on the ground. I liked drinking better. The way it started in my body rather than in my head, that warm feeling rippling from the centre of my chest outwards. Abbey's mayonnaise jar was under the merry-go-round; I unscrewed the blue lid, took another long drink. It made me shudder and my eyes teared. I rolled the jar back. I tried to stop thinking about Wilson and Barbie Man, that Wilson might have gone up there. I leaned back and looked up to the night sky streaked with clouds, the few stranded stars. The air was warm.

'Well, Gallagher, shouldn't you be at home watching *The Brady Bunch* or something?' The voice came out of nowhere. I jumped from the merry-go-round and toppled back down. I was drunk and Jack Griffith was standing in front of me.

'Jesus. You scared me.' He was wearing a black T-shirt and jeans. His hair had gotten longer. 'You forgot. We don't have a TV. Shouldn't you be at home calculating algorithms?'

Jack laughed. 'Beer?' He held two bottles, one extended toward me.

'Yeah.'

He sat beside me on the edge of the merry-go-round. I looked at our feet on the worn dirt. We circled slowly. I took a swig from the bottle of beer.

85

Jack was one of the few people who had spent time in our house when my father was there. He and Thomas used to spend weeks creating elaborate maze-like obstacle courses with paper-towel rolls and uncooked spaghetti, which they rolled marbles across.

'So what's up?'

'With me?' How would I even start to explain my life in the last two weeks? 'Nothing. You?'

'Working mostly, tarring driveways with a guy down in Chesterbrook.'

'Oh.' I had never thought about Jack having a job.

'How's Thomas?' he asked. It felt awkward, like he should know because they had been friends for so long. We both pushed the earth with our feet. Someone in the distance screamed and there was a burst of laughter from the field.

'The same, I guess. He doesn't have a job. You know, with swimming and all.'

'And you're still into trees?' I didn't know if he was making fun of me. I'd seen him one other time after the night in the snow. A blizzard had hit us in March, followed by an ice storm, felling branches and trees across the mountain. I'd hiked down as far as Valley Creek to see the damage. The creek had frozen, a white sheet with a single dark seam threaded down the centre where water was still moving below the surface. Trees bowed under the frozen weight, and ice daggers crashed from branches across the woods. So much water was melting around me it sounded like rain. I was trying to take a rubbing from a black walnut that grew out of the bank, but it wouldn't

work because the tree was damp and the paper was dis-
integrating. I was leaning within inches of the tree when
I heard voices on the trail that ran alongside the creek. I
kept my hands on the trunk and looked over. Jack Griffith
and his dad. I turned back to the tree and put my forehead
against it, hoping they wouldn't see me.

'Be careful near that ice,' Mr Griffith called. 'It can be
very deceptive.'

'I will, Mr Griffith.'

Jack waved. 'I'm just looking at the bark of this tree,' I
said, to explain why my cheek was against its bole.

The merry-go-round had come to a stop. 'My dad
thinks you're a very strange girl,' Jack said. 'He means
that as a compliment.'

Across the field someone shouted, 'Pool-hopping!'
Cheers and whooping followed.

'Come on.' Jack stood up and held out his hand. I took
it. The shadows from the field were already running up
the path to the fenced perimeter of the Mountain Swim
Club, about fifty yards up the hill. 'Are you coming?'

'I better wait for Sage,' I said, looking around.

'Sage is probably climbing the fence by now. Come on.'

I stood and we ran toward the hill. It was only when
we were halfway up that I realized Jack Griffith was still
holding my hand.

The Mountain Swim Club was surrounded by a high
chain-link fence with foot-long barbed wire angled at the
top. I had been on guard before, sounding the warning
if the cops came – three hammer blows to the imitation

Liberty Bell that swung on a trestle outside the front gate. I had whooped with the others as we fled through the woods, the police lights bouncing off naked bodies as we ran. But while I was part of the escape, I had never climbed the fence and gone in.

One night two summers ago, Thomas and his friends had climbed over – Jack must have been there too. Sage and I stayed outside the fence on watch. The full moon lit the pool and Thomas started to swim lengths of butterfly up and down. Everyone stopped and watched him. He dolphin-kicked without making a splash and his upper body arced out of the water, his arms wide and his hands coming together just in front of his head. His body could just move through water soundlessly. 'God, that's beautiful,' Sage said.

Now Jack was walking ahead of me. 'Watch out,' he said as we stepped over a pile of cement blocks someone had put on the path. He waited while I climbed over, and we heard the repeated bounces on the diving board and the splashes as bodies entered the water.

At the far side of the pool, I could see five or six figures still clinging to the fence, like spiders dangling from a metal web. Every one of them looked naked.

'Find a tree you'll remember.' Jack had already started to take off his jeans.

I went to the far side of another tree and unbuttoned mine and took off my T-shirt. I left my underwear on. Jack left his on too.

'Here,' he said, stooping down and offering me his interlaced hands and a knee. 'I'll give you a head start.' He hoisted me up several feet.

I found my grip and started climbing. I went slow, squatting at the top with legs angled apart, trying to keep my skin wide of the barbs. My legs started to shake even though we were only about eight feet off the ground. I got my second leg clear and started down the other side. Jack jumped the lower half and stood reaching up, catching me by the waist and landing me on my feet.

'Race you in,' he said, and he ran to the deep end, cannonballing in. When he surfaced, he shook the water from his head and looked toward me. I followed, giddy with the thrill of having scaled the fence, breaking in, being half-naked in the dark. I cannonballed right next to him. 'Great form, Gallagher,' he said.

'I'm drunk.'

'Didn't anyone ever tell you never to swim while drinking?'

'I was told never to drink.' I wanted to laugh out loud I felt so good. 'Let's just float on our backs,' I said.

We lay still. The moon was exposed, the clouds drifting further away. The water was warm and lapped against the pool edges and for a few minutes I forgot about Ellen, Wilson, Barbie Man and Pottstown. We started an unspoken game, diving down to the bottom of the deep end where the drain was and pushing off. On my third turn I went down and started counting. I gave myself a minimum of one minute. I could make out the moon's light glancing off the surface of the water as it moved, the shadows of legs and bodies above me. Almost sixty seconds in, when I thought my lungs would explode, I crouched low and pushed off, my arms straight up. Before I broke the water's surface, I could hear commotion, muffled and distant. I gasped in air and heard the shouting.

'Cops, cops! The fuzz!'

Everyone was running to the fence by the woods; some were already halfway up. I panicked, looking for the ladder, trying to orient myself. Then I realized that the surface of the pool was shimmering with red and blue light. The police had pulled the car up across the lawn to the gate. They had another amplified light angled at the pool. The long side of the pool's L-shape was completely lit, and lawn chairs floated upside down. I was between the deep end and the main section.

I'm dead, I thought. *Mom's going to kill me.* I'd put my head down to swim to the side and turn myself in when someone grabbed me and pulled me further into the deep end, outside the light beams. I kicked and looked back. Jack's face broke the surface of the water. He brought his fingers to his lips and motioned me toward the ladder.

'Who's there?' a voice shouted. 'This is the Schuylkill Township Police. Come out now.' Two policemen were running toward the woods as the shouts of all the other kids went down through the trees. How had they got out so fast? Another policeman began to walk the perimeter, shining the flashlight on the water, the deckchairs and the decorative shrubs around the building where the office and changing rooms were. Battle cries echoed from the woods.

Jack pulled me behind the ladder so that our bodies were flush against the pool wall and the lip of the deck was above our heads, keeping us in shadow. He used the ladder to lower his body and hold himself so that just his face was out of the water. I did the same, trying to quieten my breath. Two sets of policemen were walking the fence from opposite directions, their lights scanning across the pool and hitting the deep end. When the line of light was almost on us, Jack slipped completely under, still holding the ladder. I did the same, grasping my hair so it didn't splay out on the surface above me. I could see the light on the water above my head, rippling in waves. I tried not to move. My lungs started to hurt. The light moved past us. I eased my face up to the night air and breathed in, trying to make it quiet. We were pinned there.

'Someone's left their clothes behind,' shouted a voice from the woods. I looked at Jack.

'Let's see if we can cut them off down on Jones,' said the first one, and the flashlight came swinging across the deck, near the diving board.

We stayed perfectly still, looking at each other. Jack was mostly in shadow. Water glistened on his face and shoulders. We heard car doors shut. The first car started and backed away from the gates, leaving us again in near-darkness. We heard the second car start and waited until both of them were distant sounds.

'Oh my God, I can't believe we didn't get caught.' I was euphoric.

'I just wonder which one of us is going home without their clothes.'

'Oh shit, I forgot.' I climbed the ladder in front of him, both conscious and careless of my body.

'I knew you were a bad influence, Gallagher.'

'*Me* the bad influence? You're older. You practically pushed me over the fence. You gave me beer.'

We were standing there dripping wet in the dark, facing each other. Jack went quiet. He took a strand of my hair that was stuck to my cheek and pushed it behind my ear. He sat down on a deckchair and pulled me down to lie next to him, his arm around me. I reached up to his shoulder. I was touching his skin. The kiss was slow and hesitant at first, nothing like the urgent tongue-flicking, mouth-to-mouth-resuscitation-type kisses I'd had before. I was lying back and all of his bare body was touching mine. I had a sensation of falling. Then he stopped and sat up. We stayed quiet.

'Tell me a good tree fact.'

'What?'

'What's a good fact about trees?'

I sat up and for the first time that night felt uncomfortable in my body. I pulled my knees to my chest.

'A good fact about trees is they breathe in pollution and breathe out oxygen.'

'Like us.'

'No. We inhale oxygen and exhale pollution. Trees draw in toxins and light through a thousand little mouths in the leaves and then breathe out oxygen.'

'Stomata.'

'What?'

'Stomata, from the Greek for mouth.'

'I almost forgot what a geek you are,' I said.

I thought he might kiss me again, but instead he stood up. 'We should get out of here.' I nodded and wiped my mouth with the back of my hand.

We scaled the fence on the woods side and fumbled around in the dark for a moment, looking for our trees.

Jack laughed. 'I think it's your clothes they got. Mine are here.'

'Oh shit.' At the base of my tree there was one sneaker, the one with a hole in the toe. Everything else was gone.

'Here,' said Jack, handing me his T-shirt. It only came down to the top of my thighs.

As we followed the path down into the Sun Bowl, Sage came running toward us.

'Libby? Where've you been?'

'They took my clothes.'

'Who?'

'The police.'

'Whose shirt?'

I looked down at the black T-shirt and my bare legs and pointed to Jack, shirtless beside me. Why was she asking?

'Ah, Jack – always a gentleman.' There was a pause. Then she said, 'Looking after his friend's little sister.'

We all went quiet and Sage stood there, hands on her hips, looking at us. I didn't know why she'd mentioned Thomas.

'I've got to go. See you,' Jack said.

We watched him walk off into the dark.

'Libby, what the hell's going on?'

'Sage, oh my God. We were in the pool when the police came. We had to hide behind the ladder in the deep end and go under the water when they searched there. And we kissed. And when we did, everything seemed to spin.'

'You're being dramatic.'

'No. I'm serious. The whole world was spinning.'

'It doesn't mean anything. Trust me.'

'Sage. I felt like I was falling.'

Sage held my shoulders. 'Shut your eyes right now.'

I did.

'Is everything spinning?'

I had the same sensation as earlier, as if the ground were pitching. I opened my eyes. Sage was looking at me.

'Well?'

'It actually is,' I said.

'See, sweetheart, you're drunk. You just shut your eyes when you kissed him.'

I was suddenly cold. A car crawled up Horseshoe Trail Road toward the Sun Bowl and everything I'd managed to put away from earlier in the night rushed in: Wilson, Pottstown, Barbie Man, Ellen. Both Sage and I instinctively stepped backward into shadow.

9

Sage's J. C. Penney's waitressing uniform was a checked peach cotton dress with a ruffled white collar and a white apron with a frilled edge. She wore white nylons with her Converse high-tops, carrying her white waitressing shoes in her hand.

'You look like a maid,' I said when I met her at the corner to walk her down the trail to the ARCO gas station.

Sage looked down at her outfit. 'That's the point. Make us look as servile as possible so men feel good when we wait on them with their coffee and slice of pie.'

I hadn't thought about this before. How almost all waitresses, especially in diners, wore outfits that looked like maids' uniforms, except in bright colours. That customers wanted this.

'It's hotter than Hades,' Sage said when we reached the mouth of the trail. It was the kind of thing Charlotte would say. 'Oh, why oh why did I put on the pantyhose?' She reached under her skirt and started to roll them down, unlacing her sneakers and slipping them off only when the hose were round her ankles. She used my arm to balance. The temperature had already reached the nineties even though it was only early afternoon.

We walked along the narrow section of the trail in single file, Sage in front. It didn't feel any cooler in the shade. The air was so heavy I felt like I couldn't get a deep breath. Sage had now slung her waitressing shoes over her shoulder by the laces. She'd wanted to talk but not on the phone, and I was waiting for her to start.

'You know Tony De Martino started working at the diner as a dishwasher?'

Tony De Martino was the youngest. He was Thomas's age and always out front working on engines. I wondered if he'd also taken pot shots at us with his BB gun. I didn't know he was working with Sage.

'Well, he has, and last night we were sitting in the break room just smoking and talking. He said he'd heard something about Wilson McVay beating up some guy.' I stopped walking behind her and she stopped too, and turned around. 'Tony said he heard Wilson beat someone so bad he might be dead. But he heard it was about a girl from Valley Forge Elementary who got attacked after getting off the school bus.'

'Wilson killed him?' I had an ache deep in my chest, like the time I had pneumonia and it hurt to breathe in.

'I don't know. Maybe not. I mean, they have other stuff wrong, like the school bus.'

'But the other night you said they were talking about a girl from the mountain.'

'Well, now they think somewhere else, which is a good thing, right?'

'How did Tony hear?'

'Danny Shields. But you know what he's like.' Danny was known to exaggerate. Once Sage had had a timed ten-second kiss with Danny in a game of spin the bottle.

He'd bragged for months about an all-nighter. He bragged about everything.

'But he went up there with Wilson?'

'I don't know who Wilson took.'

'Did you tell Tony anything?'

'No.'

We had started walking again; the path had broadened and we were side by side.

'Why's Wilson doing this to us?'

'Wilson's just doing what he thinks is right, crazy as it is. You need to tell your mom now. Or we tell Grady and get him to tell her.'

'No.'

'You have to. It's way bigger than us now.'

'No. We can't.'

The humidity weighed me down as if I were carrying a heavy load, my legs sluggish beneath it.

We walked in silence for a few minutes until Sage spoke. 'Do you still have Jack's T-shirt?'

'Yeah.' It was only five days since the pool but it seemed so far away now.

'It's probably got Hall & Oates on it or some lame group like that.'

'It's just a plain T-shirt. What've you got against him, anyway?'

Sage shrugged. 'Nothing. I don't have anything against him, exactly. It's just how . . . I don't know.' She stopped as if she wasn't going to say any more, and then started again in an angry burst. 'It's how he cares so much about what people think of him, how he's like all things to all people. Science nerd with Thomas, lacrosse star at Conestoga, bong hits in the Sun Bowl, girlfriends with frosted hair and Fair Isles. Why does he have to pick on you?'

It felt like a body blow to the very centre of me because I knew what she wasn't saying. She was trying not to hurt me. She saw him at school and parties and she knew another side of him around girls and there was no way he'd be interested in me. I felt rotten and small.

The weird thing was that the things Sage said about Jack you could almost say about her too. How she was popular at Conestoga, knew how to talk to adults and, like Jack, worked hard on her credibility on the mountain. Both their families did things like skiing and 'going to the shore'. It occurred to me that both Jack and Sage had made people in my family their best friends. Slumming it, Marie would say. I didn't want to think about Jack. My head was pounding. What had Wilson done up in Pottstown?

We crossed Oakwood at the bottom of the trail and below us was Route 23. The sky had darkened and the trees above us started to move in a wind we couldn't feel yet on the ground.

'I'm gonna head back now,' I said. We'd both gone quiet. What she'd said was wedged between us.

'Aw. Pleeease walk me down. I look so stupid in this uniform.'

Sage made a funny face and I knew she was trying to fix things. I walked down the street, kicking a stone in front of me. The delicatessen next to the ARCO station was empty. I could see Big Betsy, the only waitress who worked there, wiping the counters and arranging the laminated menus. The ARCO station was quiet too. A mechanic sat on a chair outside and considered the sky.

'Looks like rain,' he called over to us.

'Sure does,' Sage shouted back in a wide drawl. Sometimes she spoke like she was from the deepest part of the South. 'Can't help it,' she'd say if I teased her. 'The Charlotte and Grady effect.'

From the west, I could see the King of Prussia 102 lumbering toward us up Route 23. The big silver bus had a rounded front and reminded me of films from the 1950s and '60s. I couldn't see anything through the tinted windows except single silhouettes of other passengers. The bus made a hiss as it came to a full stop and the doors unfolded.

'Well, someone has to pour coffee for the blue-haired brigade.'

'And someone has to get rained on,' I said. We both looked at the sky.

'Damn, it's dark,' Sage said. A high-stacked dirty cloud with a purple-black underbelly hung above us. Sage climbed the steps of the bus, raised her shoes in a half-wave as the doors folded shut and she disappeared.

I set off back up the hill, walking fast. I didn't mind rain, but lightning terrified me. I entered the woods. It wasn't a safe place for lightning storms but neither were open fields; I couldn't remember which was safer. I started to run. This time of year, the trail got overgrown in parts, and I pushed through, turning my face away from stray branches and thorns. I heard a rumble and wasn't sure if it was distant thunder or a tractor trailer down on the highway. The air smelled like electricity, metallic and acrid; the temperature was falling and the wind started. Bundles of treetops swayed high in the canopy. I saw a flash and a few seconds later heard a roll of thunder. I kept running. On the next flash I counted the seconds between it and the thunder. Five seconds equalled one mile. It was close.

I heard the rain above me hitting leaves before I felt it. The sky opened then, not small drops but big heavy ones, raining sideways. In less than a minute my T-shirt was soaked through. Another flash forked through the darkened sky, followed by a clap of thunder – two seconds. It was right on top of me. I came to a bend and looked down into the ravine, at the old bottling factory, and remembered the cavern beneath the steps. I'd go in there for shelter until the lightning passed. I stumbled down the hill toward the stone ruin, grabbing on to saplings and laurel clumps to slow myself down. The creek had turned light brown and was capped white in the rushing water, thunder crashing and heavy rain sounding through the woods. Searching for a narrow place to cross, I moved toward the thicket of black locust trees in front of me. Then I remembered about black locusts – lightning strikes that tree more than any other. Why had I moved toward them? The creek seemed louder than it should. There was something else. I turned. A motorcycle was ploughing toward me, descending the hill I'd just come down. It skidded and zigzagged, revved and choked, the driver putting his foot to the ground to stop from rolling over. The visor was down and black. How could he see? It was so dark.

I panicked. It must be a Hells Angel, Pagan or Warlock coming for me. I thought of the Manson Family, but they were young women. He was shouting at me. I looked at the dark ground, the fallen locust flowers. The locust flower closes itself in rain. I had to hide. I had to run and hide. My legs felt powerless. I tried to move across the creek but couldn't decide – everywhere was too wide. The motorcycle was coming straight for me. I stopped. I knelt down on the ground, the locust petals all around me. Giving up. I heard my name shouted and looked up. The rain beat against my face. I could hardly see. I heard my name again. The biker. He lifted the visor and gestured toward me.

It was Wilson McVay. I froze. This frightened me more than if it had been a total stranger. He was yelling, 'Get on!' I was kneeling, shaking my head no. I wanted him to go away. I'd rather be hit by lightning.

He rolled the bike toward me through the rain. 'Get on the bike!' he roared. He was leaning forward and through the veil of rain I saw that his big hands gripping the handles were bruised purple and swollen across the knuckles. Both hands.

'Get on now!' he shouted. And I did. I stood and went to the bike and sat behind him. I had resigned myself to something terrible. It didn't matter anyway. The air was heavy with ozone and the scent of locust flowers. I gripped the sides of the seat. The motorcycle accelerated forward, and in a sickening moment I understood that he was going to go back up the hill. It was like climbing a vertical wall. I shut my eyes and leaned forward. Several times Wilson had to balance the bike with his feet as we swerved or stalled.

Then we hit the trail at speed and raced up the path, the heavy droplets drumming against my skin. Wasn't it more dangerous to be sitting on top of metal? I used to think that the rubber tyres grounded the electricity, but on a school trip to the Benjamin Franklin Museum we'd learned that that wasn't the case. The reason you were safe in a car was because of the metal shell you were in, which drew the currents to the ground. The motorcycle was a magnet for lightning. We came off the trail at the bottom of my street and revved up the road and into our driveway. Wilson pulled right up to the back door.

Lightning and thunder crashed together as I slid off the bike and lunged for the back door, trying to turn the wet handle. I pushed it open and went to shut it but Wilson was right behind me. He put his foot against the door and stepped inside. I crossed my arms and looked at the ground.

Wilson took off his helmet as Marie came down the stairs.

'Well, look what the cat dragged in.' I wasn't sure who she was referring to.

I looked at him: his smile, the bruised hands, the puddle of water forming at his feet. I'd left the trail. I couldn't figure out how he'd found me down there. Had he been following me and Sage?

Thunder exploded in the room. The lights flickered a few times and went out.

'There goes the electricity,' said Marie.

'How's Ellen?' he asked.

'She's good. Still stiff and bruised, but she's back to herself. Sullen and sketching.'

'It wasn't hard to find the guy,' Wilson said.

I hadn't told Marie what Sage had heard about Pottstown. I felt cold to the bone and looking down saw that my arms were goose-bumped, hairs on end.

'You found him? Who is he?'

'Some lowlife from Pottstown.'

'Isn't that like a hundred miles away?' Marie said. 'How'd you find him?'

'The Camaro. A friend of mine in Reading sells Camaros and I described the guy. He said he thought he knew of a guy like that and he called his friend up there. Anyway . . . he won't be bothering little girls again.' He said it with this serious look on his face and a voice like he was Kojak or Columbo. He really was crazy.

'Shit, Wilson. What did you do?' Marie was trying to sound calm, but I could tell that this information disturbed her. She must have seen his hands then. 'Oh God. Did you do something to him?' she asked.

'I had some help. Here, I brought some presents.' He reached into his motorcycle boot and pulled out a long piece of chrome. For a moment I thought it was a knife, but it was too bulky. He handed it to Marie: *Camaro* in metal. 'I got his fender emblem.' Wilson sounded proud, as if we would be impressed.

'How'd you take it?' Marie said, turning it over in her hands.

'With a hammer.'

He'd had a hammer. Had he used it on Barbie Man?

He reached into his jeans pocket and pulled out a ziplock bag. 'Here, this is for you.' He threw it at me and I caught it without thinking. It was so light I thought it was going to be more drugs, but it felt empty. Inside was something silvery-white. I opened it and pulled out long threads. Long white-blonde strands. A clump of human hair, just like Ellen had described.

'Oh my God.' I threw the bag back at him. I felt as if I'd touched something dead. 'What have you done?' I was shaking.

'I told you I'd scalp him,' Wilson said, looking straight at me. I looked back at him in horror.

'Come off it, Wilson. What'd you do?' Marie asked.

'He got a haircut.'

Ellen came into the rec room as he said it. 'Hey, Wilson,' she said. 'Who got a haircut?'

Wilson stuffed the sandwich bag into his pocket. 'Look who it is: Evel Ellen Knievel, daredevil herself. Did you come down here to do some more stunts?'

Ellen smiled up at him. 'Who got a haircut?'

'My dog. Samson. And just like the Samson in the Bible, he didn't like it. But the heat was getting to him, so I gave him a good trim.'

Ellen seemed to accept the explanation. 'Marie, the power's out,' she said. The house was dark even though it was only the middle of the afternoon. Rain was battering the windows. We could see sheet lightning in the distance, illuminating the dark trees.

'You should probably stay until the storm passes,' Marie said to Wilson.

'Mom's not home,' I said. I couldn't believe Marie would let Wilson stay in the house after what he had just shown us. 'He can't be here.'

Marie ignored me. 'Libby, get towels so you can both dry off.'

'Do you know how to play rummy five hundred?' asked Ellen, holding out a deck of cards.

'I know how to play any card game you can think of,' Wilson said.

Ellen sat on the couch and put the cards on the coffee table. Wilson plopped on the floor opposite her, took the cards and started shuffling.

'Now, who's the dealer?' he asked.

10

Climbing the stairs into Thomas's room was like spiralling into space; planets and stars spun from the ceiling, where the Milky Way seemed to recede into the distance. Most of the astronomical stuff was constructed from styrofoam balls, erasers, paperclips, clay and wire. We'd gone to see *Kramer vs. Kramer* the year before. The movie was soppy, he'd said, but he liked the kid's bedroom walls painted with clouds. Thomas wanted a ceiling that was the solar system in a night sky. He'd spent months looking at *National Geographic* and encyclopaedias, then drawn the solar system across the expanse of the bedroom. It took several weeks of planning and sketching before he painted it in. I was allowed to do base colours on some of the planets, but Ellen helped him the most. She'd known how to render the planets so they looked textured and real, as if they had weight.

I lay on Thomas's bed beneath all the celestial bodies. It was so dark that some of the planets were barely visible. He'd drawn them at an angle so they looked like they were spinning, suspended at different levels around the sun in the centre, a beautiful burning ball lit from within. Ellen had left some areas nearly white and daubed others in deep oranges, golds, yellows and all the glowing colours on that gradient. Thomas's room felt peaceful and ordered, and I cocooned myself under a blanket until I was warm again. I wished Thomas were home and could help get Wilson McVay out of our house. He was still downstairs, relaxed on our rec room floor, playing cards, acting like he was Ellen's big brother, doing crazy things to dangerous people. I had let him into the house even after Mrs Boucher's warning. And down by the bottling factory I had just given in, knelt on the ground, done exactly what Wilson said. Ellen had jumped from a moving car to save herself, but I couldn't even jump across a creek or say, 'No, I'm not getting on that bike.'

In biology, we had learned about the sympathetic nervous system, how the body is mobilized for fight or flight when there is a threat. While Sister Benedict had talked at the chalkboard, drawing diagrams to illustrate the responses, I'd thought about my own sympathetic nervous system's failure that night at Jessie Warren's house, when I hadn't been able to make my body move when I needed to the most. I hadn't been able to summon either response. I'd never been to Jessie's house before and we weren't friends exactly. In the seventh grade we'd been paired up in a history-class project where we had to act as the defence team in a mock trial of Marie Antoinette. Jessie was clever and her father was some big-shot lawyer, so she was good at making arguments and counter-arguments and knew how to object and redirect. We actually won the case, scapegoating the nobility. She invited me over to her house for a sleepover to celebrate. Her mother collected us from school in a convertible. She had a scarf tied under her chin and bright-red lipstick, and was glamorous in an old-fashioned way, as if she belonged in an Alfred

Hitchcock movie, whipping around cliff edges. Jessie was blonde too, tomboyish and gangly compared to her mother.

Jessie's house had white columns either side of the front door. She had a swimming pool that stayed covered until Memorial Day weekend. The garage had ski equipment and a boat, which we climbed into, and I sat at the wheel and pretended to steer.

'You're at the helm,' Jessie said, and I said, 'Yes, I am.' I had no idea what the helm was, but I was happy to be there. We played until we were called in for dinner. Jessie's parents were going out that night to a party, and they'd hired a babysitter, a college student at Penn, who read her book almost the entire time. Jessie's dad sat with us for a few minutes drinking his cocktail while Jessie's mom used a mirror in the kitchen to put in her earrings and apply the deep-red lipstick. Mr Warren had dark hair, slicked straight back, and wore round tortoiseshell glasses. He asked what my dad did and I told him that we had customers in this neighbourhood whose gardens and lawns we took care of. He said how cool it was that I worked with my dad and that I had been to Ireland.

That night Jessie and I watched *How the West Was Won* in the Warrens' TV room. When it was over, the Penn student said we should go to bed, and I asked if I could watch another show and sleep on the sofa. I wanted to keep watching TV; it was why I liked staying at other people's houses. Jessie went up to bed, and the babysitter went back to the kitchen and talked on the phone. I switched channels and the movie *Rebecca* was just starting. I had read the book. When the Warrens came home the movie wasn't over yet, and I could hear them talking to the babysitter in the kitchen, the car still running outside. I knew I should have been upstairs in the pink poster bed with Jessie and not in their TV room, and I wished then that I hadn't asked to stay downstairs. I could hear the babysitter gathering her stuff and saying goodbye.

Outside, I heard the car doors shut and the crunch of gravel under the tyres. Someone was still in the kitchen shuffling around, and now coming toward the TV room. It was Mr Warren. He stood in the doorway and then went over to the TV and turned down the sound. I pretended to be asleep and kept my eyes shut. He walked toward me. I could hear the clink of ice in his drink and could smell him standing over me. I tried not to squeeze my eyes shut so tight that he would know I was pretending, but not so open that he would see me awake. Then he moved away. I thought he was leaving, but instead he sat down on the sofa where I was, down by my feet. I heard him put his drink on the table and then he picked up my bare feet and put them in his lap. I tried to be absolutely still. He stayed like that for a few minutes, touching the skin on the soft underside of my foot with one of his fingers, then pressed my feet deeper into his lap and started to push against them. He shifted around under them, holding them with one hand suspended, and then another part of his flesh was touching me, between my feet which he held together. And all the time that he moved against my feet and exhaled and squeezed, I was motionless. Then he let out painful sounds and was gripping my feet hard, and I felt my feet wet, and still I just lay there, saying nothing, trying not to breathe. Then he wiped my feet with something, maybe his shirt tail, and stood up and lowered them gently, as if not to wake me, even though he had just been holding them so tight and pushing them down. He picked up his drink and left the room. I opened my eyes. On the screen, the housekeeper was standing behind the new wife at an open window. In the book, this is where she's trying to convince her to commit suicide, to jump. Then the flare signals from where the boat has crashed on the rocks.

When I think about that night at the Warrens' house, I don't think about what Mr Warren did; I worry about what I didn't do. Why I didn't just pretend to wake up and walk up the stairs to Jessie's room. Why I didn't just pull my feet away or kick him. How, before it even started, I already felt like I'd done something bad just by being there, by making myself at home in their house.

The following morning, I heard Dad's truck come down their driveway and turn in the gravel. I already had my bag packed and as I came down their curved staircase with the white carpet Mr Warren was opening the door and shaking my father's hand. They stood at the front of the house, looking up. Mr Warren had a question about the wisteria, which had started to look straggly.

'Prune it this summer,' Dad said. 'Cut it right back.'

My father was slightly uncomfortable making small talk with people like Mr Warren. He was more at home working for them and giving a bit of garden advice, and it was as if Mr Warren knew this was the best way to talk to him, something about plants. I looked at my dad standing there, his straight posture, his clean clothes, his truck tidied before coming to the big house to collect his daughter, and I wanted to shout at him that he was better than Mr Warren, a billion times better. I looked at Mr Warren, who was in the same dress shirt as last night, one shirt tail hanging out, and a pair of shorts, casual, slouched and at home while my father stood watchful, trying hard to make conversation, trying not to let me down.

I never told anyone – not Sage, not Marie, and definitely not my mother.

Outside Thomas's window, the storm had now subsided. I flicked through a *National Geographic*, using a flashlight he kept beside the bed. Finally, I heard the motorcycle start on the drive and take off up the road. A few minutes later Marie came up the stairs to Thomas's room and stood beside the bed.

'Libby, what's going on? Why are you being like this?'

'Like what? He brought back *souvenirs*? He's obviously crazy and you're acting like he's normal. I feel like he's a cat bringing his kill trophies to our doorstep. What's he done? Tony De Martino told Sage they've hurt him so bad he might be dead.'

'You knew?'

'Sage told me. I only found out today what Tony said, that they'd actually beaten him up. But I heard like a week ago that Wilson knew the guy was from Pottstown and that he was bribing a gang to go there with him.'

'Why didn't you say?'

I'd wanted to tell Marie but I was angry with her for bringing Wilson into our lives and then deciding to go live somewhere else, leaving me with the wreckage.

'I asked you over and over to make him go away and you wouldn't. I thought maybe you might even know.'

'I didn't.' Marie sat beside me on the bed. 'Look, I don't think he did something so terrible or else he wouldn't be showing us. He'd be scared.'

'I don't think he's scared of anything. I have a bad feeling, a really bad feeling. There's something wrong with him.' I told Marie that he must have followed me on the trail when I walked Sage to the ARCO. How when the storm was looking bad I thought I'd shelter at the bottling factory and I'd already gone down the hill and was trying to cross the creek when he turned up on the motorbike. 'How could he know I was there? In all the woods, in all the miles and miles of woods, how could he know where I was and how did I never hear him? How do you know him, anyway?'

'I don't know if he followed you,' said Marie. 'I met him after a show. I'd gotten a ride into Philly with Michael Miller. He was going to some basketball game or something. Michael said he'd bring me home if I stood outside the The Hot Club at twelve thirty. I waited for like forty-five minutes, and he never showed up. There's no trains or buses or anything to the suburbs at that hour. I only knew people vaguely at the show and most of them had gone and Rae wasn't there. I was standing on South Street in the middle of the night, thinking *What am I going to do?* I mean, everyone was gone. Then Wilson pulled up in the Buick. He said he'd seen me earlier and had wondered what was one of the Gallaghers from Valley Forge Mountain doing at a punk show, and he brought me all the way home to the top of the street.'

Marie lay back next to me on the bed and raised her hands together to cup a papier-mâché planet hanging on a string. She had on black lace gloves with all the fingers cut off. Her fingers were so small compared to mine.

'See, that's just strange,' I said. 'How did he know to check on you like that?'

'I think it was a coincidence,' Marie said. 'But he is definitely interested in us. When we were driving home, he asked about Dad. You know how no one ever talks about it, but he just said it. How everyone knows our mom's not around that much, working and everything, and our dad's gone.'

'I just don't understand what he wants. He's way older than us. None of us were ever friends with him. He doesn't even have friends.'

We both stayed quiet. I lifted my arm and tipped the edge of an asteroid so that it swung above me in slow circles. Thomas's little spinning projects made me sad. Since the funeral he seemed to spend all his time in his room, except when he was at school or swimming. He never saw Jack any more. I wasn't sure about his school friends. He went to an all-boys Catholic school.

I sat up suddenly, my heart pounding the inside of my ribcage. 'Oh my God, Marie, I've just thought of something. Ellen told that guy she lived on the mountain. She said she was going to Valley Forge Mountain and would take a ride to the covered bridge. She was wearing her school uniform.' I could hear the hysteria building in my voice. 'We're the only ones on the mountain that wear those uniforms. If he's alive, he'll find us and get revenge for whatever Wilson and those boys did.'

11

Sage and I sat on the floor of her bedroom with copies of the Pottstown *Mercury* spread out in front of us. She'd bought them at the newsagent's in King of Prussia over the last few days, and we'd scoured the pages for any report of a man being beaten or killed the week before. We were trying to figure out what had happened that night. Sage had taken Charlotte's map of Pennsylvania from her car and we found Pottstown. We traced the route Barbie Man must have driven the night Ellen got into his car and the one Wilson and the others probably drove to get him. Investigating helped me forget what Sage had said about Jack and we were almost like ourselves again. Sage had also been asking around. Tony told her that he'd heard now that the man had got a bad beating, was maybe hospitalized, but not dead.

'Oh God, look at this.' Sage pushed an open page toward me. An inmate at Graterford Prison had told a *Mercury* reporter that he had raped and murdered two women in French Creek State Park. He said he'd picked them up hitchhiking. We looked at the map, trying to find French Creek. It was south-west of Pottstown. Graterford was east. I felt sick thinking about what could have happened to Ellen.

'There's nothing in these about Barbie Man,' I said.

'He wouldn't report it, though, would he? They'd ask

him why he was attacked, and what would he say? "Be-cause I kidnapped a twelve-year-old girl"?' Sage was right. He wouldn't have told the police.

'What if he doesn't know why he was attacked?'

'Wilson told those boys why they were going up there. One of them will have said something to him. Probably Wilson. It wouldn't feel like justice unless he told Barbie Man why.' Sage folded the papers back up. Her fingers were black with newsprint. So were mine. 'We should just ask Wilson what he did,' she said.

I didn't want to have anything to do with Wilson. I worried that Barbie Man was organizing his own gang to come to Valley Forge and get revenge. Wilson's craziness had brought us a world of trouble.

Grady knocked on the door of Sage's bedroom and cracked it open. Sage pushed the papers under her bed, and we looked up at him in the doorway.

'Libby, Marie called. You need to head home. She said y'all are going out for her birthday. I can give you a ride,' he said. 'I'm on my way out anyway.'

I sat in the front seat of Grady Adams's Mercedes. We talked about nothing as we drove, just the weather, Marie's move to the city. We turned down my street and pulled into our driveway. Beatrice was standing at the front of the house in a pale-yellow sundress, waving at me. I said thank you and went to pull the door handle.

'By the way, how's Ellen doing now?' Grady looked straight at me, a serious and concerned expression on his face.

He knew.

'Oh, fine,' I said. Heat flushed my cheeks. Why hadn't I said *What do you mean?* or *I don't know what you're talking about.* I'd made it sound like I knew what he meant. I couldn't believe Sage had told him. After all we'd talked about, how she'd sworn she'd say nothing. I just thanked him again, pushed his car door shut and walked toward Beatrice.

Upstairs, the others were stuffed into the bathroom; Ellen was brushing her hair, Thomas was brushing his teeth, Marie was up close to the mirror, applying thick black eyeliner.

'You'll scare the Amish,' Ellen said to Marie as she added extra-thick layers of black under her eye.

'Oh God, it's not Plain & Plenty Farm, is it?' I asked.

My mother loved Amish country. Plain & Plenty was one of those all-you-can-eat family-style dining places where they'd seat you at a long table with other families and serve up communal bowls of food. She liked the country style, the ordinariness and sitting with strangers, who she seemed to like better than the people we actually knew. The other families were usually from somewhere in the middle of the state or Maryland and conversation was always awkward. But we rarely ate together in the house, never mind go out to eat, and we were all happy to be going.

We drove down Route 30 toward Lancaster, to 'Pennsylvania Dutch'. Thomas told us the Amish weren't Dutch, they were German, and so, technically, it should be 'Pennsylvania Deutsch'.

'Nerd fact,' whispered Ellen, sitting between us.

In Exton we passed the Guernsey Cow, famous for the gigantic billboard that was supposed to be the largest cow sign in the world. We'd been there before. You could get your homemade ice cream in a cone and then walk through the barns where they milked the cows. We'd all watched as the tubes attached to the cows' teats flowed white with milk. I'd concentrated on their faces, the bored impassive expressions looking back at me, then wondered aloud whether it hurt and cringed when my mother answered that it felt beautiful to breastfeed. We'd all looked away or at the ground. Marie said our mother liked having babies – the first part, giving birth and stuff and being embarrassing about it, but not the other part, like raising them.

I looked out across the cornfields as we drove further west, pastures and acres of wheat starting to brighten to gold. I was trying to push what Sage had done out of my mind. If Grady had said nothing so far, he probably wasn't going to. But she'd told. The fields outside were patterned and neat, the wheat spikes, farmyards and silos illuminated by the setting sun. We saw Amish buggies and clothes tacked to lines like paintings: blues, blacks, purples and greys. Marie and Thomas argued about whether the closed carriage meant they were married or not married.

'Do Amish horses get married?' Beatrice asked, and we all burst into laughter.

'The couple in the buggy, you idiot,' Ellen shouted. Beatrice laughed too. My mother laughed so hard she struggled to see the road.

The sun shone gold on Ellen's face and it hit me that she'd hardly left the house this summer. She was afraid.

'I hope we sit with a family that has kids,' said Ellen. 'We never get a table where there are other kids. It's always retired old people.'

'I've told you before,' Thomas said, 'this is a creepy world without children.'

'Well, they let *us* in,' said Beatrice from the back of the car.

Marie was sitting in the front. The dinner wasn't just for her birthday, it was because she was leaving. She was moving in with Rae the following morning and starting her job. I'd thought my mother might resist a little or tell Marie she wasn't allowed to go work in some punk record store in the city. I wanted her to do those things, but instead she acted as if it was the most natural thing in the world for Marie to do.

We drove past barns with stars and hexes, Pennsylvania Dutch folk art. Many of the designs had tulips and trees. We laughed at the place names along the route: Paradise, Intercourse, Fertility, Bird-in-Hand. We passed two boys on scooter bikes. They looked like regular bicycles but with no pedals.

'Why can't they have pedals?' Ellen asked. 'I mean, a bike doesn't use an engine – it's the human making it move.'

'Is it the gears or something?' Marie asked. 'The technology or machinery to make them?'

'I think it's actually to keep them from going too far, so they don't have contact with the English,' Thomas answered.

'It's wrong that their parents don't want them to be

with other American kids,' Beatrice said. 'They should be allowed to go where everyone else goes.'

'Yeah, but if you were trying to teach your children self-sufficiency living from the land and they came home demanding Luke Skywalker's lightsaber or Malibu Barbie and wanted to spend their chore time talking on a phone to their friends, you might not let them mix either.' Marie had an answer for everything.

'Or putting safety pins in their cheeks and painting their lips black,' Thomas shot back.

'Well, we're American and we don't have any of that stuff,' said Beatrice. 'I've never even had a Barbie.'

'Yeah, but we have a mother who wishes she was Amish,' said Marie.

'I do sometimes wish I was Amish,' my mom said.

It was something she said a lot, and looking out at the Amish world I could see why she liked it so much, everything looked-after and ordered and simple. But she'd never farmed or gardened and hardly cooked. She ran the washing machine and the dishwasher even with only a few socks or dishes. She wasted but didn't like waste. She was afraid of horses and loved driving. What she wanted to be and what she actually was seemed far apart. I didn't say that an affair with maybe a married man wasn't very Amish of her.

We ate with two retired couples from Delaware who all appeared to be wearing the same outfit, variations of blue polyester golf shirts and khaki trousers. We considered the four of them with disappointment as the waitress seated us; they watched Marie with dismay, her white powdered face, black eyeliner, black lips, vintage black dress, the pierced cheek.

'This should be interesting,' Thomas mumbled as we shuffled and shouldered each other, trying not to be the ones left sitting next to the geriatric golf team. Marie and Mom ended up next to them, the rest of us squished together at the bottom end of the table. Ceramic hens and cows hung on the walls behind us, the cloth on the table was checked red and white.

'Look.' Beatrice pointed. 'That waitress is Amish.'

'Shh,' said Ellen, elbowing her.

Thomas leaned in. 'She's Mennonite. It's not the same.'

'She's wearing a bonnet.'

'But her dress is bright green. I think she's Mennonite.'

I didn't know for sure, but I thought Thomas was right. Didn't the Amish just wear dark colours?

The waitress brought out rolls and apple butter followed by bowls of whipped potatoes, sauerkraut, canned string beans, applesauce, cabbage, pickled beets with red eggs and plates of meatloaf, pork and ham. None of us touched the beets or eggs but we ate everything else until we were full up.

Next to us, Marie had struck up conversation with the people from Delaware. One of them had a granddaughter starting college in Kutztown, where Marie had classmates also going. She talked to them, her face animated and polite. I knew by now that they saw her beneath the make-up – her intelligence and interest in people. I wished I could talk to her before she left, tell her what Sage had done, how afraid I was for her to leave us.

Dessert was shoofly pie with bowls of vanilla ice cream. Marie's had a lit candle and we sang 'Happy Birthday'. Everyone around us clapped. It was strange to have an audience.

Thomas pushed a small thin package wrapped in a brown Acme bag and masking tape toward Marie. 'Here.'

Marie opened it and pulled out a single.

'"Kill the Poor". I've wanted this all year. Dead Kennedys.' Thomas looked utterly delighted with himself, particularly for the effect on the Delaware couples, who were visibly appalled. 'How'd you get it?'

'Jack helped me.' The shoofly crust stuck in my throat, and I had to force myself to swallow. I didn't think Jack and Thomas talked any more. 'I gave him the money and he got it in Philly for me. I know you're about to start working in a record store but . . .'

'I'll be broke and working in a record store. Thanks.'

Mom's gift was a square box, perfectly wrapped with ribbons. Inside was an electric clock with an alarm – 'So you can wake up on time in your new life,' she said. My gift was wrapped in black tissue paper I'd taken from a shoebox. I'd gotten her fifteen punk pin badges: Ramones, Sex Pistols, The Stranglers, The Clash, Devo. Rae had helped me get them from people at her art college and from shows she went to. Ellen had done a pencil sketch of Marie, just her face, that she had rolled up and tied with a ribbon.

'Oh, that's incredible,' said the woman next to Marie. 'Just like you.' No one could believe Ellen had done it, and my mom held it for a long time.

'There's mine still,' said Beatrice. She'd gotten Marie a *Ziggy* mug. 'It's for when you have coffee in your new apartment.'

It was dark when we stepped outside. We walked down the lit path to the gift shop. They sold Amish hats, Amish aprons, bonnets, corn dolls, honey, figurines, patchwork quilts, milk soaps, candles, books. I felt sick in the gift shop, the scents of the lotions and soaps overwhelming on an overfull stomach. I went outside to wait for the others, walking round to the side of the small clapboard house in case I threw up. Two girls around the same age as me were already there, smoking. They glanced at me the way other high school girls did, up and down. They wore Mennonite dresses and had white caps pinned to their hair. For some reason it depressed me. I smoked too, but I wanted them not to. I wanted them to be wholesome and pure and to fulfil my idea of them.

We drove home, Marie animated and happy next to my mother, Beatrice asleep already in the way back, Ellen nodding off on Thomas's shoulder. All of us were together, maybe for one last moment. Marie would leave tomorrow.

Driving through Lancaster in the dark, I remembered my eighth birthday. I had begged to go to the Longhorn Ranch, a Wild West-themed restaurant down on Route 1 based on Buffalo Bill Cody's legendary place in Nebraska. I had asked for months that the three of us, me, my mom and my dad, would go, even though Dad hadn't lived with us for a long time. I remember driving into the parking lot where out front was a big-as-life plastic bull. The menu was huge and said everything was 'Texas size'. When they brought out my birthday cake with a single sparkler, they turned off the lights. All the waitresses and waiters, dressed as cowhands with imitation Stetsons and six-shooter cap guns in holsters slung around their waists, sang 'Happy Birthday' around our table. They roared 'Yee-haw!' at the end of the song, firing their cap guns in the air and then spinning them on their trigger fingers and putting them back in their holsters. I loved it.

Dad mostly stayed quiet. He said the whiskey menu was good, especially the prices, but the place itself was like a shrine to the worst part of American history.

'Look around you, Libby.' He gestured at the walls with his glass of whiskey. Indian headdresses and buffalo heads hung from hooks. 'They obliterate the land and a people and then display it as wall decorations.'

'Leave it, Martin. She just wants to enjoy this fiasco.'

Sitting in the back of the car that night, looking at the dark shape of my parents in the front, I felt bereft. There was something I understood. That the three of us, or all seven of us, together, happy, was as fake as the waitress with her Philly accent shooting her cap gun and shouting 'Yee-haw!' Nothing was real. Now, on the way home from Marie's birthday, I knew I should grasp this moment, with all of us together, and hold it. But everything spooling around me felt unreal, nothing was what it should be. Us, Marie leaving, me and Sage, Wilson watching us, Barbie Man still out there.

When I called Sage that night, it was late. I could tell she'd been out and was stoned.

'You told your dad. You promised you wouldn't.' I whispered it.

'What are you talking about? Speak up. I can barely hear you.'

'You told your dad about Ellen and the man in the car.'

'No. I didn't.'

'You did, Sage. He asked me how Ellen was doing now, and he stared at me, hard and, like, full of meaning. He knows.'

'He doesn't. I didn't tell him.'

'You must have. How else could he know?'

Sage started to laugh on the other end, and I wanted to slam the phone down. 'You're out of your mind. I never said anything, so stop accusing me. You are always so paranoid. Even if I did, which I didn't, it wouldn't be such a big deal.'

'It is a big deal and the only person who could have told him is you.'

There was a pause on the line. Why was she lying?

'Jack Griffith was in the Sun Bowl tonight,' she said. She was changing the subject and she was bringing up something hurtful to me.

I hung up on her. I sat there in the dark living room, my hand still on the receiver, and almost immediately it rang. I picked it up halfway through the first ring but so did someone else on another extension. My mother. Neither of us said hello. We just waited.

'You know what? Fuck you too.' Sage hung up. There was silence. I could hear my mother exhale on the phone.

'Who is this? Libby? Is that you? Marie?'

I pushed down the dial-tone button with my finger and put the receiver back on the cradle without making a sound. I heard my mother open her bedroom door. She walked toward the top of the stairs, and in the hall light her long hair was down and dark and silhouetted around her and the light hit her white nightgown as if it were illuminated from the inside. She looked like a ghost, sort of there and not there. I couldn't see her face. I stayed still, watching her from below, until she turned around, and I heard her bedroom door click shut again.

12

Marie left home the morning of the summer solstice, the first day of summer and the longest day of the year. Ellen, Beatrice and I sat on the top trundle while she packed. She had kept me and Ellen up most of the night after we got home from the restaurant, sorting through her stuff, her clothes and make-up, her books, photo albums, everything. The turntable and speakers were going because they belonged to her, and so all the albums we had inherited would now be useless. Even when we were all in bed and the light had gone out, I hadn't been able to sleep. Sage and I had fought on the phone, Marie was leaving, and I had that feeling again of everything pitching.

Now Marie pattered around the room while we waited for her to toss us a shirt or a skirt or an old pencil case, stuff she wasn't keeping.

'When will be the next time we see you?' Beatrice asked. She had stacked all her new things in a pile next to her but was worrying her fingers through loops of hair.

'When you come to the city on the train to visit me for a sleepover.'

'Really, Marie? Can we?' Beatrice looked at me. 'Will you take us?'

'You can come,' Marie said, 'but you'll have to bring your own sleeping bags and be ready to sleep on the floor.'

'When?' asked Ellen.

'When I get settled. On a day I don't have work.'

Marie was going through her school things, throwing stuff into a trash bag and setting aside a pile of textbooks and notes for me. Her blazer, sweater and kilt were still crammed into her canvas school bag with her books and papers. She pulled them out and folded them, presenting them to Ellen on the trundle: the grey, maroon and black plaid kilt, maroon sweater and grey blazer with the maroon and yellow insignia, the school motto wrapped like a banner around the Most Sacred Heart of Jesus. Marie made a mock ceremony out of it.

'*Cor ad cor loquitur*, heart speaks to heart.' She dropped her head in reverence. 'I give these garments to you, Ellen Gallagher, so that you too may walk the path of Jesus when in the wilderness that is Catholic girls' high school.' She passed the uniform to Ellen like an offering.

Ellen solemnly received the bundle of hand-me-downs as if it were a great gift that had cost Marie something. 'I will try to follow in your footsteps.'

'Yeah,' I added. 'Make as few friends as possible and at all times show general contempt for everyone around you, just like your big sister.'

'I pledge allegiance.' Ellen chanted it, her hand on her heart.

'That's the gene pool I love,' said Marie. 'It's because you're too tall and you already have one,' she said, turning to me, as if I had been wondering why Ellen got the uniform instead of me. I had already done my freshman and sophomore years.

Ellen hung the clothes on her side of the closet using a wooden skirt hanger. She had just one more year in middle school before she came into the high school and changed from the pinafore to the kilt.

Earlier, Marie had taken down her Siouxsie poster and rolled it up with rubber bands. Our room looked bare and somehow bigger, as though our voices would echo in it. She had swept all her jewellery into the metal Popeye lunch box she had kept since first grade. Her albums were alphabetically arranged in neat rows in a box, everything facing the same direction. From the shelves she had started selecting her books. The Jane Austen set my mother had given her went into the second box along with her copies of *A Clockwork Orange*, *Rabbit Redux* and *Slaughterhouse-Five*. I had tried to read all those books after her but had given up. I wasn't smart like she was. From the top shelf she took down *Rock On: The Illustrated Encyclopedia of Rock N' Roll* that Dad had given her.

'You can't take that,' I said.

'It's mine.'

'But it belongs here.'

'Jesus, what's wrong with you? It's mine, and I'm taking it. I'm not coming back.'

'You will. At Thanksgiving and Christmas and next summer and all the times you come back. And the book will be here. At home.'

Marie ignored me and kept sifting through the books and stacking hers into a box. The Nancy Drew complete set was pushed against the back of the bottom shelf, my quartz collection arranged in front. 'You can have my half

131

of the Nancy Drews. I bequeath them to you,' Marie said. Neither of us had read them in years.

'Fuck you,' I said, and stood to walk out of the room. 'And Nancy Drew,' I added, and slammed the door. The rhyme was an accident and ruined the impact of my exit. I could hear them laughing. I sat outside on the front doorstep. Three trash bags, two boxes and a little blue suitcase with red trim were lined up on the driveway. I wanted to take that suitcase back too, and hide it where Marie couldn't find it. I looked across at the Walkers' newly shorn grass and perfect flower beds mulched and layered with dark woodchips. Their grass was still glistening from the automatic sprinklers that came on each morning, quenching their deep-green lawn. Ours looked desperate, with bald patches, uneven spurts of yellowed growth and any possibility of green hidden at the root.

If one of the Walker kids was going away, they would have matching luggage and all the family would be outside helping and everyone would be happy because they would know it didn't really mean goodbye, that Harry and Minnie would make sure they saw their child every weekend. They would have barbecues out back to celebrate their kids' safe return each trip home. But not us. My mother hadn't even seen where Marie would be living. On the way home from Lancaster, when we'd passed Thrift Drug, she'd asked Marie was there something she needed for her new apartment. Marie had said no but my mom had insisted there must be something. We'd stopped so she could get Marie a tube of toothpaste, as if now Marie would be all set for life.

Marie often said, 'Indulge her, she's trying.' She said we'd made Mom feel helpless the past few years because we were all so capable. But I didn't feel capable and we weren't okay. Thomas was holed up in his bedroom growing further and further away from everything that was grounded on earth. Beatrice was sitting on Marie's bed inheriting T-shirts and dresses, completely unaware that the one person who made sure everyone had eaten, and had their work done, who checked if the doors were locked at night, who somehow understood what was wrong with us at any given moment and explained it, was leaving. Instead of being sad that Marie was going I was angry, angrier than I could ever remember. I wanted to kick something. I hated Sage. I hated my mother. I hated Jack Griffith. And I hated Marie for leaving me alone with all the worry of Wilson, Barbie Man and Ellen.

I headed for the woods barefoot. If I stepped on a copperhead it would serve Marie and all of them right. I walked past the clumps of fern toward the tall grove of birch, the straight dignified silver-white trunks, the shimmer of green between them standing there, guarding the entrance of the woods. I stopped.

Sound changes in the woods; everything diminishes to the hum of the ground and the slight rustle of leaves at the top of the canopy, the light gathered in isolated clouds, everything green and light and shadow. '*The green quiet,*' my father used to quote from a poet. I didn't know what it meant, but beneath the mysterious words was a feeling I understood. The green quiet, that still calm in the woods.

I turned on to the trail and headed down toward the Kingdom. Inside, I smoked one of Charlotte Adams's menthol cigarettes from our stash at the base of the red oak. The cardboard matches kept falling apart when I tried to strike them. I finally hit the match against the flint half-heartedly, and that one lit. I inhaled and leaned back against the oak. I thought the cigarette might be stale – Sage often said that with absolute authority when they'd been buried in her bag or in the tin in the earth for a long time – but I didn't know for sure.

Sage and I hadn't been here together since that first day of the school vacation, the morning after Ellen jumped from the car, and it was as if nature had reclaimed it, the laurel and rhododendron pushing further into the space, erasing our time here together. I stood up and tried to break off the branches with the cigarette just hanging from my mouth, the smoke wafting into my eyes. I sat down and kept smoking. It made me feel sick and light-headed. Sage had started buying Marlboro Lights. Menthol, she said, was for old ladies. I reminded her of this when she continued to steal Charlotte's menthols and smoke them. The sticky sap from the rhododendron on my fingers had grubbed the cigarette paper, and I wondered if it was poison to inhale. The nectar of the rhododendron, laurel and azalea are all toxic. I smoked anyway, even when the sapped paper sizzled against the ember tip.

The rhododendron blossoms around me were dead and hung in bowed clusters, their vibrant purple faded, pale in death. Seven or eight pods hung from the tips of thread-like stalks. Each pod, I'd read, contained over five hundred seeds. I tried to calculate what that meant per cluster and for every bush. Millions. I looked at the petals all around me on the forest floor; I was sitting on the possibility of billions of future rhododendrons.

I needed to get home, so I didn't miss Marie leaving. Instead of walking back along the trail toward my house, I walked further down and cut through the Hunters' property. I clapped my hands to scare away copperheads as I moved off-trail through the laurel and trees, barefoot down toward their backyard. The Hunters were away on their summer vacation in Ocean City, New Jersey. Meredith Hunter, who was two years younger than me, mentioned it every time Ellen and I met her coming down the street from the Mountain Swim Club in her bathing suit, a towel slung around her shoulders. She was deeply tan and blonde with those stiff highlights only chlorine in the sun can make.

They had a deck at the back and a small pond with goldfish and koi. There were wildflowers growing around it, day lilies, violet and heartsease. Dad used to say that Americans had the seasons wrong, that summer started on May Day. When he was growing up they had a tradition of picking spring flowers – cowslip, butter-cup, bluebell – and bringing them back to the house to scatter across thresholds, doors and windowsills, so that nothing and no one would be taken from them that year. I looked at the Hunters' flowers and picked six of each, rolled them in the bottom of my T-shirt and tucked it into my cut-offs.

As I came back up the street, I could make out two cars

in our driveway, a blue Oldsmobile I didn't recognize and Wilson McVay's dad's Buick. The trunks of both cars were open. Marie's trash-bag luggage was in the trunk of the Oldsmobile and the bike that we shared was in the trunk of Wilson's car, along with the turntable. My mother, Wilson, Marie, Marie's friend Rae and a man I had never seen before were all standing in a circle talking and laughing. Rae waved at me as I came up the driveway and my mother turned.

'Libby, where've you been? We've been waiting. Marie has to go.'

'You're taking the bike?' I asked her, but I really wanted to say *You've brought him here, again?* After everything she knew, I couldn't believe she had asked him to help her move.

'It's mine. So, yeah,' said Marie.

Everybody knew Wilson McVay was a headcase and yet my mother was completely untroubled. She was making introductions. 'Libby, this is Rae's father, Mr Dixon. He's helping Marie move.' Mr Dixon put out his hand. 'And Wilson's helping too. I think you know him.' What was wrong with her?

Wilson stuck out his hand, the knuckles still visibly bruised, as if to shake mine. I stepped back from his out-stretched hand, repelled. They all laughed, like I was making a joke.

'Really, Wilson, we are so grateful. It's so good of you.' My mother was gushing. She had a strange imbalance of being rude when it counted – like to teachers or other parents or neighbours – and effusive when it wasn't appropriate, like to the local delinquent who was wrecking our lives.

'I'm happy to do it, Faye, and when we get there I can help Marie move the boxes up the stairs.'

I nearly choked. Had he just called my mother by her first name? Had she told him to call her Faye instead of Mrs Gallagher? What was wrong with everyone? A deranged psychopath was driving Marie to her new life and everyone was behaving like this was normal.

'And Wilson,' my mother continued, 'Ellen tells me that you were the one who cut the grass a couple weeks ago. I really must ask you to take some money.'

'I was glad to do it. I couldn't accept payment. It needs another cut. I can come down when I'm back.' Wilson smiled. Rae's dad looked pleased. Marie was smiling. Ellen and Beatrice clearly thought all this was wonderful. Even my mother was smiling.

'Actually, the grass is my job. Mine and Thomas's. We don't want you to cut it again.'

'Libby!' I had embarrassed my mother. Marie shot me a look as if to say *Please don't do this.*

Wilson looked straight back at me. 'I wouldn't want to upset you or Thomas. I could bring down our lawnmower if you want to borrow it.'

Fuck him. He was saying all the right things. My mother's face softened. I hated him.

'We've already borrowed one. From someone else.' Everyone was silent, my lie hanging there.

I looked over at Marie. She was wearing a vintage black lace dress and her Doc Martens with bare legs. She was tiny but strong-looking, her hair on the side that was long hanging across her eye. She already looked like she belonged somewhere else.

'Well, I guess I'd better say goodbye, then,' she said, and went to hug Beatrice first.

'Well, okay then, Marie,' I interrupted. 'I have to go rearrange my new room. Hope you enjoy your new life in the city.' I didn't even look at her when I said it.

I slammed the back door hard and ran to our bedroom. I looked out the window. Rae's dad was shutting the trunk and my mother was hugging Marie, something that we didn't do very often. But it only made me angrier. Why wasn't she taking Marie to the city? Why was it okay for strangers to take her? How did she get like this – or was she always this way? I couldn't remember. I decided she probably was. Even before Dad left.

I had ruined the goodbye. I'd wanted to punish both of them. I heard the slam of car doors and the acceleration away as the cars climbed our road. I reorganized our shelves and closet. Marie had left the Marksman hidden in a B. Altman box. She'd taken everything else, so I wondered why she'd left that. Mom went out and Thomas, Ellen, Beatrice and I ate SpaghettiOs in the kitchen. Then I lay on my trundle. I'd told Ellen she could have Marie's single bed.

On the longest day of the year, I waited for everyone to fall asleep. Mom still wasn't home when I went round all the doors with the flowers. I crawled back into bed, Ellen asleep across the room and the bed below me empty for the first time, and waited for the sound of my mom's car coming home. She left it on the driveway and came in through the back, so silently I could hear the hum of the crickets when the door opened. There was quiet then. A few minutes later I heard the sound of the vacuum cleaner starting up in the rec room, and I knew the flowers and all their possible protection would be gone. Something would be taken from us, again.

13

I found *Harriet the Spy* under my pillow, Marie's favourite book from childhood. I remembered the first time she read it, one of my few memories of Marie crying, sitting on the stairs, trying to tell us how Ole Golly was leaving and now Harriet would have no one because her parents weren't like real parents. Something about Harriet and Ole Golly had hit her in a place where there was no armour. She was eleven; I would have been eight. I later read it too, at about the same age, and expected a burst of emotion that never came. It was sad when Ole Golly left, but not devastating. I didn't know why it had upset Marie so much.

I sat on the front step the morning after she had gone and read, skipping ahead to that part when Ole Golly goes. I'd forgotten about the illustrations. The writer had done them herself, sketches in black pencil. Ole Golly looked almost monstrous, a mix between Morticia Addams and a linebacker. In Sage's basement they had paintings – or prints, as Sage called them – by Modigliani. The people in them were elongated and out of proportion. Ole Golly looked like a Modigliani painting, except in crude black pencil. I could remember exactly where I was when I'd read it first – in our closet with a flashlight, thinking that I was a bit like Harriet. I had even started a notebook for spying on others.

When Ole Golly leaves, Harriet wishes she could still tell her the things that were happening. She imagines it must be even worse when someone dies. I felt differently. I didn't want my father to know the things that had happened after he'd died, what our grass looked like, what had happened to Ellen, what was happening with my mom still sneaking out to meet Bill, how when she was home her door was closed, how Thomas was becoming the same way. I didn't want him to know things that had happened in the past either, the things that would cause him pain, like Mr Warren. I wanted to go into the past and say things differently. I wanted to go back and tell him the things I never did or change the things I did say, or say them better. I wished I had called him more when he was alone.

I wasn't bookish like Marie, but we'd just read *The Catcher in the Rye* in sophomore English. Holden Caulfield talks to his little brother who is dead, and he changes the things he said to him in the past, to make up for the times he left him out. He tells Allie it's okay, he can come with him now, to go get his bike and meet him outside Bobby Fallon's house. When Suzie Sheerin read it aloud in class my throat hurt. I understood how he wanted to go back to fix the things that could never be fixed. I felt like that every day.

I heard laughter in the distance and looked up. At the top of the street, two figures turned the corner. One of them was Sage in her J. C. Penney's uniform. She had to come down our street to take the trail to the bus. Abbey was with her. Sage had her head down, but Abbey saw me and waved.

'Hey, Libby,' she called. I half-waved back but pretended to concentrate on my book.

Sage didn't say anything until they were almost past the house. 'Did Marie leave?' she called out. She had stopped and was looking back up toward me. She was wearing her sneakers and holding her waitressing shoes. She had her hand over her eyes to shield them from the sun. Even in her ridiculous outfit, she looked cool.

I wanted to tell her *Yes, and it's awful*, but instead I got up and went inside the house and shut the door behind me. I watched them through the window as they walked down the street, catching glimpses of Sage's peach-and-white uniform through the trees. She had tried to make it up with me. She was always like that, being fair and kind and seeing the other person's side. It was something about her that I admired and hated. It was like having a friend who was a reasonable adult while I was a childish brat. The only other time we'd had a fight like this was after she had met Bill, and I'd been so angry with her I hadn't spoken to her for weeks.

Sage had met Bill in a snowstorm. It was during the unexpected blizzard earlier that year. She was at the mall, working, when the snow started. By the time she got on the bus for home, the roads were nearly impassable, and the snow was still falling in a whirl of thick flakes. Her bus crawled up Route 23 to the base of the mountain. The driver let her off. There was no one there to meet her, so she started the climb by road in just her uniform and a thin coat. Night had fallen and there were no tyre tracks; no car had even tried to make it up the hill.

She had walked for nearly an hour, she said, when she started to get scared. Her legs were soaking wet and freezing. The snow had reached her knees and was still falling. She had another two miles to go and had started to think she might just have to find a house for help when she heard a low thrum and saw headlights in the distance. There was a truck making its way up through the snow, spinning some but never stopping. She stood to the side of the road and watched as it approached, hoping the driver could see her in the dark through the blue haze of snow. She could hear the heavy chains wrapped around the wheels, giving it traction. It pulled in beside her and the passenger door opened. She didn't recognize the truck – she said it was red and oversized, one of those king cabs – and she looked in. My mother was sliding over to make room and a man Sage didn't know was driving. They continued up the hill. Sage said she had been so cold and it was so dark, she never got a good look at him. They ploughed up through the snow in silence. She saw him in profile when she got out: he was broad, wore a brown suede coat with sheepskin lining and collar, and his hair was brown and curly.

Sage called our house the second she got inside, her voice shaking with cold and excitement.

'I met Bill. He drove me up the mountain with your mom. They're on their way to your street.'

I hung up the phone, shouting for everyone to come quick, Bill was on his way. In a minute, we were in the rec room pulling on our Irish wellington boots underneath nightgowns and over pyjamas, all five of us, Marie, Thomas, me, Ellen and even Beatrice, who had probably just seen him a few days earlier. We galloped like lunatics down the drive, falling into the snow with no coats. Struggling up, we staggered forward, lifting our legs high. The snow was too heavy and deep to kick through, and it fell into the open tops of my boots, freezing my bare feet. Several times I walked right out of them. We ran and fell, elated that we might finally catch sight of him.

'Shhh . . .' said Thomas.

We stopped. It was so quiet and still. Snowfall at night casts its own strange spell, and the streetlights glittered across the white drifts and the whole world, as I knew it, was erased by this beauty. When I looked up toward the lights, I could see the thick flakes still falling.

'I heard a door slam,' Thomas whispered.

And then we heard the rumble of the truck starting up at the top of the street and watched as a streak of red tail lights disappeared in the haze of snowfall. A dark figure was trudging down the road toward us – my mother. We turned to get back inside the house before her. We had missed him. We had missed the best chance we ever had.

I was staying at Sage's house a week or two after she met Bill. I quizzed her endlessly about the truck, about him, details she noticed in the truck, anything in the back of the truck, tools, machines, and was it a Pennsylvania licence plate. She'd listened while I complained about my mother and Bill and the secrecy. When we were falling asleep, she said something else.

'Libby, maybe Bill makes your mom happy.'

It sucked the air out of me. I was stunned that she would say something so treacherous.

'How can you say that? How can going around behind everyone's backs be anything good?'

A while before, Marie had told me to stop going on about Mom and Bill, that I was turning into a weird Hamlet. 'I don't even know what that is,' I told her, and she said Hamlet obsesses about his mother's affair with his uncle and thinks about them together. 'That's sick, Marie.' But I did worry about why they met at truck stops and diners, that Marie was right: Bill was probably married or else they would just go to his house or apartment and we'd have met him by now.

Sage kept talking to me in the dark. 'I'm not saying they're going about it the right way. But your mom obviously likes him and wants to be with him, and she probably deserves that – you know, after your dad and all that.'

'You mean she deserves Bill because my dad is dead?'

'No, you know: before that, the way he was with your mom, the stuff you told me.'

'Please shut up now.'

'I'm not trying to upset you, Libby, but maybe she loves Bill. Don't you want her to be happy?'

I lay in the dark on the other bed in Sage's room. She had matching twin beds with matching green bedspreads that matched her drapes and carpet. She had what Charlotte called a vanity and an overstuffed armchair with throw cushions that also matched the bedspreads. It all suddenly seemed vile. I put on my sneakers and jacket over my nightgown and stood over her bed, where she was lying on her side.

'I'm going home,' I said. She didn't say anything back.

Sage's bedroom was on the ground floor, and I opened her window and crawled out. There was still snow and ice on the ground and the moon was full. I ran home in the bright cold, angry. I would never forgive her. I ran and stopped only when I reached my own driveway. I sat there on the quartz boulder in the freezing cold in my nightgown and hated myself. I had told Sage too much. Did I not want my mom to be happy? Did I even love her? I wondered, if it had been me instead of Sage on the road that night in the snow, would they have stopped? Would my mother have left me there on that road?

Watching Abbey and Sage through the window now, a glimpse of Sage's bright uniform disappearing through the trees, I had that same sense of my dishonour, spilling secrets nobody else in my family spoke of. Why had I ever breathed a word to Sage about my mother or father or Bill? I had told Sage almost everything. I had called her that night about Ellen. I knew Grady and Charlotte Adams didn't like my mother, that Charlotte thought she was irresponsible. When Sage knew all this, why would she tell him about Ellen?

I didn't realize Thomas was home. I was still staring out the window when he came into the living room.

'I heard you told Wilson we had borrowed a lawn-mower to cut the grass.'

'Did Mom tell you that? Was she mad?'

'Ellen told me yesterday, after. She said you told Wilson to stay away from our grass.'

'Yeah, well, I don't know why he thought he could cut it in the first place.'

'Maybe because you and Marie let him.'

'Trust me, I don't want him here. I don't like him. Marie met him at a punk show or something.'

'And then suddenly one day he's in your bedroom and another day he's cutting our grass.'

Ellen must have told him about Wilson being in our room. We hadn't told Thomas about Barbie Man and now it felt like it was too late.

'I know. It's weird. But I swear he just did it. Marie didn't ask him to do those things either.'

He didn't believe me. 'Wilson's trouble. Stay away from him.'

'That's like a daily goal.'

'I'll try the Griffiths tomorrow for a lawnmower.'

I wanted to say *No, don't, anyone but them.*

'Okay,' I said. I looked back out the window and watched a blue jay shoot across the sky toward the evergreens then tilt backward into a stalling angle, the wings beating forward. We'd learned something about it in biology, how they have a bone or an extra wing that can help them brake.

After I left Sage's that night in winter, I'd avoided her for almost three weeks. But I'd replayed our conversation in my head. Maybe Bill did make my mom happy. I had never really considered my mother's happiness. I didn't want her to be unhappy exactly, but I certainly didn't want her to be happy with Bill. I wondered if I wanted to punish her and whether this was what was wrong between us. That she knew. It was Sage who had fixed things. She called our house and spoke to Marie. Marie said to go look in the

Kingdom, 'whatever that means', that Sage had left me something. I didn't go for days, even though I was curious, and I missed her. Desperately. At school, I had friends in my classes but on the mountain, it was always Sage.

I waited until dawn on a Saturday morning, when I knew she would still be in bed and there was no chance of meeting her. I didn't know what to expect. The snow had melted and the air had warmed, but the woods looked bare in that stark late-winter way. If whatever she had left was still there, it must be in the hiding place. I pushed away the leaves and the board and there above the tin was a parcel wrapped in brown paper shopping bags. I unwrapped the paper to find another package in bubble wrap. Inside was a black picture frame. A few summers earlier, Dad had said Sage could come with us one day to cut grass. Sage had brought her camera and treated it like a field trip, taking pictures and asking him about everything he planted or pulled. She'd framed a black-and-white photograph of us from that day, standing by the pickup truck, him in his white T-shirt and work trousers, me in jeans and a T-shirt. We were both smiling, looking sort of proud and shy. My head was tilted toward his shoulder and he was looking toward the camera. We looked happy. In the bubble wrap was a small white card. I opened it.

I'm sorry. I loved him too.

In the picture we are both smiling with our mouths closed. I looked like him.

14

It was Thomas who ended up meeting Barbie Man on the mountain first, even though he didn't know who he was. We'd made a deal. I'd edge what were supposed to be flower beds and pull weeds and Thomas would walk up to the Griffiths' to borrow the lawnmower. I used a spade, angling it to create a clean edge of earth between the grass and the beds that had no flowers. I had almost finished the first one when Thomas came around the corner and down the street, pushing the borrowed lawnmower.

Thomas and I were the two who had cut grass and worked with my dad the most, ever since we were small. Thomas had always tried to prove himself through hard work. I watched him coming down the road and I knew it had humiliated him to ask. I remembered a day at the Cat Lady's when we were working with my dad. She lived alone in an old Victorian-style house with at least forty cats. My dad had looked after her garden for over fifteen years, since before I was born. She had been trying to sell the house for a long time and a few summers ago it had finally sold, even with all the cats hanging around, lying on counters and sitting in sinks. When she was moving, she hired my father to do some work inside, pulling up carpets and taking old furniture to the dump. Marie, Thomas and I all went to help with the job. It was late July and hot, well into the nineties. We'd peeked through her windows before to look at the cats but had never been inside. The heat and stench were stifling. The ammonia from the cat pee burned our eyes. We choked and the air squeezed out of my lungs. It was a three-storey house, and the cats had been everywhere. To make it worse, she had turned off the air conditioning.

'The mean bitch,' Marie muttered.

We started on the third floor, where it was hottest, and tried to pull out the small carpet nails at the edges. Dad told us to go back to the truck and get gloves. The fumes were in my mouth and throat. When we rolled up the first carpet, which was damp, the floorboards were rotten underneath.

'Get out of the house and wash your hands and faces at the outside spigot. Get the soap in the truck,' Dad told us. 'Thomas, you stay with me.' He said that the odour would never come out; the new owners would have to take up the floorboards. Marie and I sat outside for hours, saying very little, while Dad and Thomas finished the work alone, carrying rolled-up rotten carpets and heaving them into the back of the truck. Thomas worked intently, staggering under the weight and smell, never wanting to let my father down. He was fourteen.

I sat on the kerb with Marie and looked over at the garden that my father had planted for the Cat Lady years earlier. That year's tomatoes were ripe and red on their vines against her deck. Dad had canes supporting them with soft string so as not to damage the tender stalks. The Cat Lady had a Venus de Milo statue in the garden, a naked woman about as high as my hip with missing arms. Marie walked over and kicked her to the ground and came back and sat next to me on the kerb. Her face was dirty and streaked.

'Fucking people think they know something about culture,' she said.

Now, Thomas wheeled the Griffiths' lawnmower into the drive and stopped where I was working with the spade.

'Were they nice about it?'

'Yeah. Jack's going to collect it later after work. They invited me to go to the shore with them tonight.'

'Oh. You should go.' I tried to disguise the pang in my voice.

Thomas started to push the lawnmower up the driveway and stopped. 'Hey, doesn't that Kowalski kid drive a green Impala?'

'What?'

'A green Impala? Some weird guy was just asking.'

I could feel the thuds of my heartbeat in my stomach. 'What do you mean, "weird guy"?'

I knew the kid he was talking about. Craig Kowalski drove a green car and he hung around with Danny Shields.

'What weird guy?' I repeated.

'Some guy just stopped me on the road and said he was looking for a kid with a green Impala, that he had something belonging to him and did I know who he was.'

'What made him weird?'

'He was a freak. Long hair. I don't know. Scary. Even if I knew where the Kowalski kid lived, I wouldn't have said. His face was all messed up.'

'What?' I looked at the top of the street to see if there were any cars, if he had followed Thomas. I tried to think.

Where was Ellen? She and Beatrice had both gone with Mom this morning on her way to work. They were with school friends.

'His face. It was all bruised and swollen.'

A grenade was exploding in my head. He wasn't dead and he wasn't so hurt that he couldn't drive. And he was here. Thomas moved the lawnmower further up the drive and leaned over, setting the choke and pulling the starter. The engine kicked in. Barbie Man was up here, and he was looking for the people who had done this to him. He had come alone in broad daylight. I tried to pull a clump of weeds but my arms were powerless. I sat on the front steps watching Thomas cut the grass. Barbie Man was up here and who could I tell? Marie was gone. Sage and I weren't speaking. Wilson was the one who had brought this trouble to us. I kept looking toward the top of the street to see if a car – Ellen had said he drove a black car – passed or turned down toward us. Thomas came and sat beside me when he'd finished the grass.

'You didn't finish spading.'

'I'm tired. I will, though.'

'The grass still looks shit.'

'It's a lot better than it was. A few more cuts.'

'Yeah.'

I wished I could tell him everything, how the weirdo in the car could be coming for us, what had happened to Ellen. But we were so far in and I didn't know how to undo not telling him in the first place.

'Mom will probably kill me if I take off for the shore without asking her first. I should call her at work.'

'Don't. It's not an emergency. Get Mrs Griffith to call her tonight. Swimming's finally finished. You haven't been anywhere. You should go.'

Marie said Thomas was one of those people who was funny when you got to know him. Smart-funny, Marie called it, which she said was wasted on people our age. He seemed lonely to me.

'It'll mess up my study schedule.'

'What study schedule?'

'SATs.'

'Are you kidding? That's what you're doing up in your room? You hopeless geek.'

Thomas pushed me on the shoulder. He had achieved a near-perfect SAT score the fall of his junior year. He was insisting on taking them again. I thought how sensible both Marie and Thomas were, studying hard. We all worked hard at school. Sage was always messing up, not turning stuff in and missing tests. She was smart, smarter than me, but she didn't care as much as we did. Marie said the difference between us and other people was that we didn't have the same safety net. We couldn't afford to fuck up.

'A few days isn't going to blow your SAT scores.'

When we went inside, I walked through the house locking all the doors, then lay down on the couch in the rec room, where I would be able to hear any door or window open.

I must have drifted off and I woke with a start. Thomas was standing over me with his school bag. For a moment I was confused, thinking I had overslept for school.

'What?'

'I'm leaving. Jack's here and we're going to the shore.'

'What?' I rubbed my eyes. Jack Griffith was standing at the door of the rec room, looking at me. I sat up, wiped the sleep-drool from my cheek and pushed my hair back. He must have rung the bell or knocked and I hadn't heard. I had fallen asleep when I was supposed to be on watch.

'Do we have a beach towel?' Thomas was talking to me. I was still half-asleep.

'One of Sage's is in the linen closet.'

Thomas dropped the bag and went upstairs. I looked down at my legs, streaked with dirt, grass blades stuck to them. I tucked them under me.

'You good?' asked Jack, looking around the room but not at me.

'Yeah. Good.' I would have loved to tell him how shit everything was.

'I saw Sage the other night.'

'Yeah?'

'She didn't say?'

'No,' I lied. He didn't seem able to look at me. I couldn't think of anything to say. 'Do you want your T-shirt back?'

Jack glanced toward the stairs. He didn't want it mentioned.

'No. Keep it. I don't want it.' It was awkward.

'Pink fucking flamingos?' Thomas walked back into the rec room holding Sage's beach towel. I'd forgotten how pink it was. We all laughed.

Jack took a few steps toward me and reached out his hand. *Oh my God, he's going to pat my head.* He pulled something from my hair. My hand instinctively pressed against the side of my head. I almost said *What the hell was that for?*

He was holding a leaf in his hand. He had taken a leaf out of my tangle of hair and he turned to Thomas, still holding it. 'Libby in her leaf world,' he said. I knew that there was some kind of rejection happening, that the gesture of pulling the leaf from my hair was supposed to make it like before, when he was just my older brother's friend. The gesture was for Thomas, sort of a joke at my expense.

'Okay. We're heading. You'll tell Mom? Jack's mom is going to call her later in case she's upset or whatever.'

I said okay and watched as they walked toward the door. Jack was still holding the leaf. It was from the magnolia tree.

They were gone. I was alone in the house. I checked again that all the doors were locked. If Barbie Man was up here looking for the boys that had hurt him, I needed to tell somebody. I took out the phone book but there was no listing for any McVays on Valley Forge Mountain. The Mountain Directory had a list of families but my mom kept it with her papers in the locked chest in her bedroom closet. Sometimes, when just Marie and I were home, we picked the lock with a bobby pin. I got one from the medicine cabinet in the bathroom and went into her bedroom. Her room was sparse: a queen-sized bed, two bureaus and a chair. There was a picture on the bureau of the five of us. Beatrice was only about one. Marie was holding her and I was standing next to them, looking as if I were the attending nurse, just in case Marie dropped her or something. Beatrice was holding my finger. Looking at it, I thought

157

I would do anything on this earth for her. Thomas, about age nine, was looking off to the side. Ellen was staring straight back at the camera, intensely. I couldn't remember a photograph where she was smiling. Marie had a joke that Ellen was practised in the art of scowling. The picture was us. Beatrice holding us together; Marie pragmatic and mothering; Thomas thinking about astrophysics or the universe; me worrying, being vigilant; Ellen angry and looking straight out at things.

I knelt on the floor in front of the wooden chest, spread the bobby pin open, laid the flat side down and turned, slowly applying pressure. The chest latch popped, and I lifted the lid. Inside, all the documents were organized into neat bundles and sectioned into packs by rubber bands. There were photographs and letters and certificates and the Mountain Directory with the Valley Forge Mountain Association information. I opened it and looked up the McVays. The family was listed. They lived on Paul Lemen Drive. Wilson was an only child. Born October 1961. That made him almost twenty. Next to *Phone* it read *Unlisted*. I put the directory back.

I reached for the bundle that held my father's things. His birth, marriage and death certificates. His passport. His green card. The divorce decree. I started with the birth certificate. The last time we touched it, Marie had said it smelled like Ireland. I don't know why we'd started doing this, looking at the documents. Maybe it was just finding proof of things that were never talked about. I unfolded it carefully and held it up to my face and breathed it. His birth was entered in handwriting. Black fountain pen.

Father and Mother: Sean Gallagher and Bridget Fox. It was a last name I loved and sometimes pretended was my own. *Libby Fox.* I imagined his mother and father, Sean and Bridget, travelling into town to register the birth of their newborn son. I saw it in black and white, a long, long time ago. They had written their occupations. *Farmers.*

I'd met my grandmother, Bridget Fox, just once that I could remember, when I was ten. We'd been to Ireland before, but I was so young I didn't remember her from those earlier trips. I only remembered her from the time that just Dad and I went. The day we were leaving to go home, she held on to my father and wouldn't let go. Her black skirts reached the ground and she had a grey bun and hairs growing from her chin. She was so small she didn't reach his shoulder, and he wasn't a tall man. She cried little sounds and clung to him. She spoke to me, but I couldn't understand her; I had hardly understood a word she said the whole visit.

It was the last time my father saw her. She died the following winter during a snowstorm. We had been home from school for a few days, and the morning school re-opened the phone rang very early. I knew it was Ireland calling because the phone always beeped at the start of the call. A voice that sounded far away asked for Dad, giving his full name. I said he had gone to shovel driveways because we were never to tell them in Ireland about his not living with us. He had no phone in his apartment. When he arrived in the pickup truck that morning to take us to school, we sat in the truck while he went inside to make the phone call home. He walked back to us in the truck, his black wool hat pulled low. He put his two hands on the wheel as if to drive and just kept them there.

'What is it?' I asked.

He didn't answer. A few times he cleared his throat as if he was about to speak. He coughed out his first word and then tried again. 'I can't speak right now; my mother died this morning.' He looked out the driver's-side window, away from us.

Marie handed him the roll of paper towels on the floor of the cab and he pulled off a sheet and blew his nose. He drove us to school through the snow in silence. Outside, branches hung toward the earth, wheels spun and cars crawled, and all the strangeness was magnified by the news that Dad's mother was dead. I looked up at him and saw a trail like a snail leaves on the carpet tracked down the side of his face.

When we left Ireland that last time, my grandmother had sobbed in the doorway of the house as we walked down to the road where the car was parked. Even then it had gripped me that she didn't know the truth about her son's life in America. That he didn't live with us, that he lived alone, that he pretended everything was fine for her.

He arrived in Ireland for her funeral during the heaviest snowfall they'd had in thirty years and was stranded in Dublin waiting for the trains to run again. He'd told me that when he was ten, the same age I was then, his mother's father had died. She hadn't been able to go to his funeral because of her duties on the farm. He and his brother got on their bikes and cycled up the country forty miles to be there for her. The morning my grandmother Bridget Fox was buried, I went into the woods and made a snow angel and lay there and listened.

I folded the birth certificate and slipped it back into the rubber band. I skipped the petition for divorce. *1973.* My mother the petitioner. My father the respondent. I opened his certificate of death dated *1980. Country of origin: Ireland.* Under *Education* there was a place to tick the highest grade completed. My father had never been to school beyond elementary; *5th* was ticked. The names of his mother and father appeared again on the certificate of death. Under *Marital status, Divorced* was ticked, but in the next section it said *Surviving spouse (if wife give maiden name)*, and my mother's name was there: *Faye Royston.* If she was no longer his spouse, I wondered why her name was on the certificate, how this had been allowed. Our names weren't on it. There is no space for the deceased's children on a death certificate, even though I knew he would have said we were the most important detail of his life. I looked down to the end of the certificate, the parts filled out by the certifying physician and coroner.

Death was caused by:
immediate cause: cardiopulmonary arrest
due to or as a consequence of septic shock
due to or as a consequence of sepsis

And in the column to the right of each of these the time frame was indicated: *Approximate time between onset and death.* The arrest was listed as *sudden.* The shock, the time during which he was semi-conscious, his organs failing, struggling to breathe and alone in his efficiency apartment, was listed as *day(s)*. He was presumed to have had sepsis for *five days* between onset and death. The sepsis was a result of an injury working on a building site for his idiot cousin, who brought him to a questionable doctor who my mother said probably gave him the infection while stitching him.

It was the five days that I couldn't get over, what I couldn't accept. For several days my father lay sick, and for the last of those days so sick he was dying. He always called us on a Saturday morning from a payphone after he moved, but he hadn't called then. 'He was so proud,' Marie had said the first time we looked at the certificate. 'Too proud to even ask anyone for a small bit of help.' She was furious with him. I blamed everyone else. His cousin, America, my mother, us, me – because he shouldn't have died alone in a room on a treeless street in a city where he had no one.

15

For the rest of the week I was in charge of Ellen and Beatrice. I hadn't told anyone that Barbie Man had been here, that Thomas had spoken to him. I wanted Ellen in my sight, and I didn't want to have to tell her why. By Thursday afternoon I was half out of my mind with worry and I decided we would take the bus to the King of Prussia mall the next day: me, Ellen and Beatrice. I needed sneakers and I wanted us to get off the mountain. Beatrice had never been to the mall by bus, and she was bursting with excitement and questions. I gave her the coins for the fare the night before, to put in her pocketbook.

'What if I put them in the wrong slot?'

'I'll put my money in first and you do what I do.'

'Are you sure the bus is definitely coming at nine thirty?'

'Yes, it comes that time every day. And every two hours. There's a seven thirty before it and an eleven thirty after.'

'What if I get lost and I don't know where to catch the bus home?'

'You won't get lost.'

We set off down the trail toward the stop just after nine. Ellen was wearing a white short-sleeved top that Sage had given to me. 'Broderie anglaise,' she'd said, a fabric Charlotte loved with cut-out patterns and eyelets. It was the first time Ellen had shown her arms since that night. There were still raw spots, flat pink areas of new skin, but she had healed. Beatrice was wearing a pair of Ellen's shorts and a striped T-shirt. Her hair was pulled back in a braid, and her pocketbook had a strap that went over her shoulder and across her chest. She held it with both hands anyway. As we walked down the trail, Beatrice chatted about the Fourth of July parade that was coming up and how she wanted to decorate her bike. Ellen was quiet while Beatrice talked about getting crêpe paper and streamers.

'We'll do something better than that,' Ellen said eventually. 'Let's try to make something completely different. Something good.'

There was still a week to go, enough time to pull an idea together. Beatrice was our last chance. By next year even she wouldn't want to do it. Every Fourth of July, a fire engine led a procession of kids on decorated bikes around the mountain. There was a competition for best bike. Last year a girl dressed in a sequined red, white and blue leotard, nude stockings and white cowgirl boots on a bike with training wheels had won. Every few hundred yards, she'd hopped off her bike, smiled and spun her baton and done cartwheels. Marie had said it was disturbing for a group of middle-aged men to award highest points to a little girl all made up and dressed like she was in a Junior Miss beauty pageant in Texas or some place and call her cute.

Along the trail, the early sun broke through in flecked light, the saplings, weeds and wildflowers luminous green and almost as tall as us. The trail narrowed as we neared the bottling factory and even from the ridge, high above the gorge, I could smell the locust.

As we came out of the woods and started down the hill to the main road, a motorcycle passed. Wilson. And behind him a passenger holding a pair of white waitressing shoes in her right hand, blonde hair blowing from beneath the helmet. Ellen was waving absurdly and started running after them. I shouted at her to stop.

'What?' she said.

'We have to stay with Beatrice. I don't want her to run down the hill – there's gravel everywhere.'

'But it's Sage and Wilson.' Ellen looked at me.

'Just slow down!'

She must have heard something in my tone. 'Are you fighting?' she asked.

'No,' I lied. 'Not really.'

'What happened?'

'I'll tell you later,' I said. Beatrice was walking in front of us, clutching her pocketbook and checking her wristwatch. I wanted to slow us down so we didn't have to wait with Sage, and possibly Wilson, at the bus stop. I needed to think. Why was Sage with Wilson? It was dangerous and I had to warn her. I knew I should chase after them and tell Wilson about the guy being on the mountain. But I didn't.

'Beatrice, do you want to get a soda when we get to the ARCO?'

'Will we have time?'

'Yeah.'

We went straight into the gas station and I gave Beatrice the money to drop into the machine. She got a Coke for herself and Ellen, and we walked to the bus stop about a hundred yards up Route 23. The bus with its black windows was coming toward us, and Sage and a few others waiting stepped forward.

'Sage!' Beatrice ran ahead and hugged her. 'Libby's taking us to the mall.'

'Hello, Miss Beatrix Potter. Are you writing more stories?'

The bus stopped and the door fanned open.

'You first,' I said to Sage.

Beatrice had her coins ready in her hand. Ellen followed Sage up the steps. I told Beatrice to follow Ellen and do what she did. She dropped her coins in carefully and waited until the driver nodded to her to go ahead and take a seat. She walked down the aisle, past Ellen, and sat in the empty seat next to Sage. I sat next to Ellen and listened as Beatrice told Sage how Ellen was going to design her bike decorations and costume for the parade, how I was getting sneakers and she was going to get Marie a gift for her new apartment. When the bus pulled in at the mall, I told Ellen we'd get off at the first stop by the Wanamaker's entrance. I knew Sage would get off at the next one by J. C. Penney's. I wanted to tell her, but I didn't know how.

'Have a great day, Beatrice,' Sage said when we stood to get off. 'If you come to my diner, I'll give you a complimentary ice cream. You too, Ellen.'

A fountain trickled over a plastic waterfall and spotlights lit the pool below from underneath. At the top of the fake falls, plastic foliage was clumped in bunches to suggest something lush and verdant. Muzak played over invisible speakers and the air was cool. Lighting in the mall always seemed dimmed, maybe to keep the temperature down, but any time I entered it I felt as if I had stepped out of the brightest sunlight into shadow, and I had to readjust. Marie said malls were designed to disorient you. That's why, like casinos, they never had clocks or windows. They wanted you to enter this fake world and lose track of time and reality.

Beatrice wanted to throw a penny into the fountain to make a wish. A group of teenagers had taken all the benches in front of it and were setting up their boom box. Mall rats. Marie had once asked Thomas what the collective noun was for rats. 'A plague or a swarm,' he said. *A plague of mall rats* described them perfectly, Marie had said. Cassette tape in, the boom box blared AC/DC's 'Back in Black' while a girl around my age played air guitar with a cigarette between her lips. She looked like she couldn't lift her eyelids up enough to see. It was only ten o'clock in the morning; the mall was just opening.

'Stop staring,' Ellen said to Beatrice.

'C'mon, Beatrice,' I said, taking her by the arm. 'Throw it in, make your wish, and let's get what we came for.'

I bought white Converse high-tops. Ellen and Beatrice spent nearly an hour in the craft and hobby shop discussing Beatrice's bike decorations and finally selected crêpe paper, pinwheels, big sheets of blue poster board, masking tape and face paints. In the fabric store, Ellen bought cheap yards of red and blue cotton, needles and thread. Beatrice picked out Philadelphia-themed dish towels for Marie's new apartment in Wanamaker's home goods section. We passed the Space Port arcade and stood at the door, looking in. The whole interior was painted black, even the floor. At the far end, they had ultraviolet lights that lit up psychedelic swirls on textured surfaces. Beatrice wanted to play a racing video game where you drove a car. I told her it was a waste of time, that it just stole your money, but I agreed to go in. 'Just pretend you're driving.' I leaned against her car door while she spun the wheel and crashed. Beside us, a full row of boys faced Space Invaders machines. I could only see their backs as they leaned, first one way and then another, ducking as Space Invaders, white blobs that looked like marshmallows, fell to earth. Amidst all the noise I could hear the bass beat of the Space Invaders sound, like a fast heartbeat, underneath the staccato of players shooting and player death explosions. I looked over at Ellen, who was standing there watching the Space Invaders, and got a fright. Her white shirt was completely illuminated, and she glowed purple in the UV light, even her white training bra underneath.

J. C. Penney's was at the far end of the mall and Beatrice wanted to take Sage up on her offer of an ice cream so that she could watch her take orders and put her slips on to the line and serve food. I suggested a compromise. I would take them to Friendly's for ice cream sundaes, much better than the metal bowl of vanilla, chocolate or strawberry that you'd get in Sage's diner. Beatrice agreed.

The Friendly's waitress seated us in a booth that looked out on to the parking lot, the only place in the mall I knew of where you could see the outside world. Beatrice sat beside me and Ellen opposite us, and we ordered our ice creams. I started to ask Ellen what the plan was for the bike, but she was looking at something behind me, over toward the bathrooms, her face frozen. She shrank in the booth, head down.

'He's here,' she whispered. I knew without turning.

I stayed very still, expecting to be struck from behind. I didn't turn my head but waited for the blow as a shape passed me, then stopped and turned. I didn't move. I could smell him, a smell like patchouli. Marie had used it once or twice in her Grateful Dead phase but had stopped because it was overwhelming us all in the car to school every morning. He slid into the booth behind Ellen, where another man was already seated. Barbie Man was facing me, but I was too terrified to look up. Ellen lowered herself further in the booth, leaning over the table.

'The booth behind you,' I whispered. 'He didn't see you.'

'What?' asked Beatrice.

'Nothing,' I said, and right then the waitress arrived with our ice creams, which came in tall sundae glasses with long spoons. Beatrice started on hers right away. Ellen and I just stared at ours. Ellen picked up the spoon but her hand was trembling and she put it back down. I didn't know what to do. Beatrice was oblivious. Ellen and I were looking at each other. Tears welled and fell from the bottom of her eyelids in plops on the Formica.

The waitress was passing. 'Everything okay, hon? You don't like your sundaes?'

'Oh no, it's good,' I said. Ellen and I immediately started to spoon into the ice cream.

I felt like I couldn't swallow, as if my throat had started to close. I kept my hand at my forehead, elbow on table, and tried to steal a look at him. He was exactly as Ellen had described: hair almost white-blonde with a sheen, as if he had ironed it flat and then added something to make it shine. He was wearing a blue bandana from the top of his head down over his forehead, covering his hairline. I felt a sickening thud in my stomach. He was covering up where Wilson had scalped him. There was bruising along his cheekbone and one eye was black and blue with streaks of pooled red blood. His eyelashes and eyebrows must be so blonde that he looked like he had none. They were nearly done with their food. I tried not to stare.

'What's wrong?' Beatrice asked, looking at us both.

'Shut up,' Ellen said under her breath.

Beatrice looked at me and put her spoon down on the table.

'What? What did I do?'

'Bea, eat your ice cream.' I was never stern with Beatrice, and she heard it in my voice and did what I said. Sage and I had measured Valley Forge to Pottstown on the map. It was about twenty miles, not a hundred like Marie had said. The Mall was under six miles from the ARCO station. Was twenty-six miles a bit far to go for a mall? Why was he here?

The waitress was talking to Barbie Man and the guy with him. She was writing their check. 'You look like you've been through the wringer,' she said.

'Yeah, his plastic surgeon's on vacation.' Barbie Man said it, pretending she'd spoken to the other guy. His voice rasped, a gravelly sound as if he smoked four packs a day. They all laughed like he was funny.

The waitress put the check on the table. 'I'll come back when you're ready.'

Ellen was listening too. I knew she was trying to understand what was being discussed. She must have seen the bruises. We didn't move in our booth.

I watched them each put money on the table and stand up, and I felt vomit rise in my throat. He was a giant. At least as tall as Evi van der Graff's dad, and he was supposed to be six-five. He had on a black leather vest over a white T-shirt, a thick black belt, blue jeans and black boots. A sling was draped over one shoulder holding his left arm in a cast. They'd broken his arm. I felt a quick surge of panic. The other man looked ordinary and middle-aged, a bit like Mr Walker. We stayed sitting in our booth. I watched them leave while Beatrice ate her ice cream and Ellen looked at the table. We sat until the waitress came with our check. I left the money and a tip. Neither Ellen nor I had finished.

'We're going to use the bathroom now,' I said.

'I don't have to go,' said Beatrice.

'The rule is we go together.' We went to the back of the restaurant, and I stayed outside by the phones where I could keep an eye on the restroom door. 'Go inside,' I said. 'I'll be right there.'

I dropped in coins and dialled.

'Hello. Directory services.'

'Can I have the number for Rage Records on Third in Philadelphia? It's a record store.'

'Would you like to be connected?' asked the operator.

'Yes, please.'

I waited. The phone rang twice and Marie picked up and practically sang, 'Rage Records on Third.' When I heard her voice, I started to cry.

'He's here, Marie.'

'Libby? Is that you? Who's there?'

'Barbie Man.'

'Where? At the house?'

'No, here. The mall.'

I told her we had seen the man, how he'd been in the booth next to us, how Thomas had met him on the mountain the day after she left; how he was looking for Craig Kowalski, that I didn't know what to do.

'Did he see Ellen?' she asked.

'I don't think so.'

'Libby, calm down. There's a bus at two. Go through the mall to the bus stop. Don't go outside into the parking lot. I'm going to call Wilson and see if he's home and get him to meet you at the ARCO.'

'No. Not Wilson. Please, Marie. That's who he's looking for. We have to stay away from him.'

'Well, get off the bus and go straight to the trail. Don't hang around on Twenty-Three.'

'Okay.'

'Calm down. He didn't see her. And it's Wilson he wants.'

I nodded and tried to stop crying. 'Marie, I'm sorry.'

'For what?'

'How I was when you were leaving.'

'Don't be stupid. Call me when you get home. If I don't hear from you, I'll be worried and probably call the National Guard. Get the bus. You have fifteen minutes.'

I went into the restroom. Ellen and Beatrice were both standing there by the sinks.

'We're going to go now and get the bus,' I said, trying to sound cheerful.

'Libby, what's wrong?' Beatrice asked. I ignored her question.

We walked out into the mall. Across from us was J. C. Penney's.

'Hey . . . Let's go say goodbye to Sage.'

The girls followed me. Sage was at the diner counter when we walked in. She must have seen it in my face because she came straight over.

'What's up?'

I pulled her away from Beatrice and told her that we'd seen him. 'We have to get back on the bus. Please, Sage. Walk us as far as the Wanamaker's stop?' Ellen was watching us, and Beatrice was looking at the customers seated around the counter, which was shaped like a kidney bean.

Sage undid her apron and leaned across the counter, putting it on a shelf on the other side. 'I'll be right back, Gretta.'

We went out into the mall again, up the escalator to the next level, and walked down the concourse toward Wanamaker's.

'You need to stay away from Wilson,' I told her. 'Barbie Man is looking for him.'

'I was only on his bike because he saw me on the road on the way to the bus stop.'

We passed Chick-fil-A, where Marie had her first job, filleting chickens and squeezing lemons for the homemade lemonade, and past a men's suit store. Next was Space Port. Ellen had her head down, afraid to see or be seen. As we passed the arcade, I glanced in. A black hole in the middle of a sunny day. The video players looked like black silhouettes against the dark. At the back, just one person stood out. His arm in the sling was extended like a webbed bat wing and was glowing purple in the ultraviolet light. I took Beatrice's hand. Ellen was still looking at the floor.

'Sage.' I nearly sputtered her name. 'That's him.'

Sage looked over into Space Port and then at me.

'Run,' she said. Not even Beatrice asked why. We just sprinted through the mall, all the way down the concourse, past fake oases, into Wanamaker's, past perfume counters, ladies' lingerie and bathing suits, all of us running as if for our lives, out the back entrance and into blinding light.

16

Lightning bugs were out. Thomas told me once that lightning bugs – what some other states called fireflies – were Pennsylvania's official state insect, and that it had been a bunch of schoolkids near us who'd campaigned to have them picked. It made me oddly proud. A faint smudge of gold was just visible against the clouds to the west as I went up our street. I still had to walk to the Bouchers' despite seeing Barbie Man a few hours earlier at the mall and knowing that he could very possibly turn up on the mountain. Going past 'the Manson House', I decided to trigger its lights in case there was someone behind me. I had on my new Converse and sprinted. I couldn't stop looking over my shoulder. If I saw headlights from a car, I would step into the woods and hide.

When we'd sat down on the bus earlier, Beatrice at the window, me on the aisle and Ellen on the seat across from me, Ellen had said one word: 'Wilson?'

'Yeah.'

She had puzzled it out. We listened as Beatrice pointed to things out the window, but we couldn't talk about it in front of her. We got off the bus at the bottom of the mountain and walked straight up the hill, not wasting any time on the main road.

The house was empty. Ellen and Beatrice went upstairs to start working on the Fourth of July outfit. They spent the rest of the afternoon on the floor, tearing the new fabric into long sections. Ellen stuffed Beatrice's white stockings with newspaper and started the tedious task of sewing on the blue and red strips. The newspaper was to prevent sewing the stockings shut. I sat with them on the floor and sewed one blue strip. My stitching was all over the place, and I kept unthreading my needle. Ellen worked quietly but her fingers were deft and fast, her stitches neat. Both Beatrice and I gave up, but Ellen kept sewing. I knew she was trying not to think about what had happened earlier. Beatrice chatted away, suggesting ideas. She took a red strip and a blue strip and looped them through the tops of her sneakers to make large bows.

'That looks good,' Ellen told her. Beatrice glowed.

By the time I left to babysit, Ellen and I still hadn't talked about seeing Barbie Man in the mall and what Wilson had done to him.

At the Bouchers', Bruce and I waltzed through the kitchen, his feet on mine, while Mrs Boucher gathered her things for her night out. I sang 'I Could Have Danced All Night', and he could barely stand it made him laugh so hard. 'What kind of dancing partner is this who keeps his two feet on mine the whole time?' Peter kept pulling on Bruce, saying, 'My turn, my turn.' Later I sat on the sofa and watched TV. I tried calling Sage to talk to her about what had happened at the mall, but Charlotte said she had gone out.

At a quarter to one, headlights lit the huge windows and then cut. I waited a few minutes and went into Mrs

Boucher's bathroom without flicking on the light. I put my face against the window and looked out but I couldn't even see the outline of the car. I went back to the living room and watched TV with the sound off. I didn't hear the car door this time, but the headlights turned on at one thirty and the car rolled down the long driveway toward me.

Mrs Boucher came into the kitchen, filled a glass of water, and leaned back against the sink and drank it. She had on a red wraparound dress that plunged at the front, but tastefully. She wore a long chain made from wide interconnected circles of hammered silver. Her high heels had straps that fastened round her ankles. Her hair fell down her back, sleek and dark. She was beautiful. I thought she was probably the prettiest adult I knew.

'How was everything tonight?' she asked.

'Good. Fine,' I said. I had taken a message from her ex-husband to say he wouldn't be able to collect the boys till noon the next day, and all she said was, 'Good – we can sleep in a bit . . .' The boys went to their dad's every other Saturday.

She opened her pocketbook and counted out $10. I always felt funny putting it into my pocket, in case it seemed like I was being greedy. I waited until we were outside in the dark before I pushed my hand into my cut-offs.

We climbed into the Volvo. There was a faint waft of alcohol mixed with cologne. Mrs Boucher smoked in her car, so there was always a stale smoke smell. She drove and neither of us spoke. As we came down Horseshoe toward Forge Mountain Drive, there was something ahead of us on the road. A car. Could it be the Camaro? Everything blurred for a second. The car was stationary, the door left open, and a man, made large by the headlights of his car, was standing in the middle of the road. I made myself breathe in. My Swedish PE teacher had told us that when Americans meet something stressful they breathe out, whereas Swedes breathe in. She'd said it was a difference in attitude about what was before us. We needed to inhale and believe in ourselves. Be ready for the battle.

'Uh-oh,' Mrs Boucher said, and she stopped a distance from the car. She rolled up her window. 'I hate meeting things on the road at night. Lock your door.'

I locked mine and the one behind me. We both peered out into the darkness. The man looked huge and I was trying to see if it was Barbie Man.

'Has he hit something?' she asked. 'I don't know if I should keep driving toward him.'

I was scared. I didn't know what to do either. I imagined creepy lowlifes from Pottstown hidden in the woods around us.

'Keep driving. Go fast,' I said. 'We can go past him.' Mrs Boucher turned to look at me. She could hear I was scared.

The man had seen us and was sort of waving, as if to say *Go around.* Mrs Boucher put the car in gear, and we went toward the man and the car with the open door, driving much slower than I would have liked.

'Go faster. It's a trap. It's the man that picked up Ellen.' I realized I was almost shouting in the car.

She accelerated forward. We'd only gone a few feet further when I realized who it was.

'Wait. Stop. I know him. It's okay. I'm sorry.'

'I think we should keep going,' she said. She was gripping the steering wheel with two hands. I had terrified her.

'It's okay. It's Dr Adams. My friend Sage's dad. We should stop.'

Still she seemed to speed up for a moment before braking. We sat in silence. Grady Adams was coming toward us and she hit the wiper blades by mistake and fussed trying to turn them off. He was next to her window then, and she rolled it down just a bit and looked up. He leaned down to speak through the tiny gap.

'I'm sorry if I scared y'all, but I've hit a deer.' I could see he was shaky from it. He ran his hand through his hair and shook his head. 'Damn,' he said, slow and dragged-out and almost under his breath. Sage had that same Southern slowness in her speech. We idled there for a moment with him at the window.

'I'll get out,' I said.

'Libby, wait.' Mrs Boucher reached toward me, but I was already on the road. I walked around to the front of the Adamses' car. Charlotte wasn't there; it was empty. I looked at the deer on the road. Grady came and stood next to me.

'He just came out of nowhere and came right into the car.'

Behind us Mrs Boucher reversed, pulled in behind his car and put on her blinkers. She walked up to us and stood there in her high heels.

'I hit a deer,' he said to her. He'd already told us. I wondered if he was in shock. He seemed so upset and unlike himself.

'Is it dead?' asked Mrs Boucher.

'I'm not sure.'

I wondered if I should introduce them or if that would be inappropriate given the circumstances.

'Can you check to see if the deer is dead?' Mrs Boucher sounded impatient.

Grady knelt down next to the deer in front of the head-lights, creating distorted shadows up the road. The animal was a dark shape on the ground, and a darker pool of blood seeped out in a circle around its head, like a black halo. The body didn't look right, the way it had twisted back on itself. Grady had his hand near the deer's face.

'I can't feel any breath,' he said, as though he was surprised.

I took a step closer and leaned down next to Grady. The deer's eyes were open and fixed on me. For just a second, I thought I saw a flicker. I moved back and saw that it was just me reflected in her eyes. A young white-tailed deer. Female. She had thick lashes and was thin around the neck. We used to watch deer in the woods from the rec room window and Dad had taught me that the slender neck and high stomach indicated youth.

'He's definitely dead. I need to get him off the road.' He stood back up. 'Someone else could hit him.' There were no streetlights on the mountain.

The three of us stood there looking at the dead animal. For a moment, I thought how quiet everything was, but I heard the crickets then, a sound so loud I couldn't understand how I hadn't heard it earlier, like all of nature was grieving.

'I need to move him,' Grady said again. He stepped over the deer, straddled her and grasped the two front legs at the thin part just above the hoof. He tried to drag her but stumbled back and lost his grip. 'Good God, it seems sacrilegious,' he said. 'I'm sorry.'

'I'll help you. I'll take this one,' I said, taking the right leg. 'If you take that one, we could pull together.' I knew how to lug stuff. I counted us in, already pulling slightly on each count. 'One, and two, and three—' We both pulled and the deer moved about six inches on her back. I counted again, and this time we moved her several feet. I felt terrible dragging her, dead, across the road grit, disturbing her peace. We were nearly at the grass verge between the road and the woods, and we tugged one more time, pulling the doe up on to the grass.

Grady sank down on the ground, leaned his body forward on his bent knees and breathed hard. His hands hung down, his wrists limp, in front of his bowed head, and I noticed the silver chain he always wore that made him different from the other dads, even out here in the dark. 'He just ran right out in front of me as I came around the corner,' he explained again.

I was looking at the front of his car. There was a big dent and dark streaks near it, and I wondered if it was the deer's blood.

'It's a doe – a she,' I said.

'Is it?' he asked. Maybe they didn't have deer in the part of Mississippi he was from, but he had lived here a long time, longer than me. It seemed like he should know.

'Yeah, a white-tailed doe. Bucks have antlers. She's

young.' Then I wished I hadn't said that because I didn't want to make him feel worse.

Grady reached out and put his hand on the deer's hindquarter and left it there for a moment. 'I feel real bad about this. Sorry, girl.' He was talking to the deer. I loved him right then, out there in the dark, devastated about the deer. Sage said her dad was likeable because he had extreme humility, that he was almost sorry for existing, and that that was why patients liked him. He made people comfortable because there was something slightly uncomfortable about him in himself. It was so strange sitting with him there, the car headlights on us and none of us acting like ourselves.

Mrs Boucher, who had said almost nothing the entire time, finally broke the silence that had fallen between us. 'Libby, I'm sorry, I think we should go now. I'm worried about my boys alone in the house.'

I stood up and brushed down the back of my cut-offs. 'What will happen to the deer?' I worried about dogs or foxes coming, and I didn't want to leave the doe out there for them to scavenge.

'I'll call the township in the morning,' said Grady. 'They'll come take it.'

'Okay, then. Well, goodnight, Dr Adams,' Mrs Boucher said. We climbed into her Volvo, which was still running. Grady was standing again, but he wasn't moving to get into his car. He just stood there on the road in the headlights, looking at the mess at his feet.

Mrs Boucher put her car in gear and we drove past him. She glanced at me but didn't say anything. She rummaged in her bag with one hand, pulled out a cigarette and lit it. I nearly asked her for one. I was jittery and began babbling. I asked her if she knew the man on Yellow Springs who had hit a deer the year before and gotten killed. The deer had come straight through the window and split his skull. She had heard about it, she said. She dropped me at the top of my street.

'Libby, wait,' she said before I could close the door. 'Why did you say the car on the road could be the man that picked up Ellen?' She was looking up at me.

I could see the lit lamp post at the end of my driveway, which Ellen had remembered to put on for me. I could tell Mrs Boucher now and the fear wouldn't be just ours any more. It would be other people's problem. But it seemed like every time I told people things it just brought more mess.

'I was just scared. I don't know why that came out.'

'You're sure everything's okay?'

'Yeah. I'm sorry.'

I closed the door and sprinted toward the light on my driveway, still frightened of what might be in the woods.

I washed my hands at the laundry room sink and went upstairs to my bedroom. I could hear Beatrice's soft snore from Ellen's trundle and see the shape of Ellen in Marie's bed. Beatrice still liked to spend nights in our room. I left the light off and tried to change in the dark, sitting next to Beatrice on the trundle, taking my sneakers off first. My hand touched something warm and sticky on the top of the right sneaker and without thinking I put my hand toward my face. It smelled of earth and metal. I carried the sneakers into the bathroom, turning on the light. The right foot of my new white Converse was smeared in blood that had already started to brown. I looked at my reflection and saw I had a streak on my cheek from where I had lifted my hand. I turned on the hot tap and wiped my face and hand repeatedly. I put the shoe into the sink and started to rinse it with hot water that steamed, and then remembered that it's best to use cold water to get blood out. I had a strange feeling in the bathroom, like this was happening to someone else at nearly three in the morning, standing there at the sink with a strong scent of iron or metal from the deer but also something else, a smell like pine needles.

I climbed across Beatrice into my own bed and lay down in the dark, Beatrice still snoring just a few inches below me.

'Libby?' It was Ellen. 'What did Wilson do?'

17

I had slept in. The girls' voices and my mother's drifted up from the kitchen. I opened my eyes and it took me a minute to focus on the shape across the room from me. I leaned up on my elbow. Ellen had nearly finished Beatrice's parade costume. She'd created a headless life-size mannequin by stuffing newspaper into the legs and pillows into the torso. It was propped up on Marie's bed, facing mine. The legs were striped in circles of red, white and blue. Its blue denim cut-offs and white T-shirt were Ellen's. She'd stitched a vest to wear over it from the red and blue strips of fabric. Ellen must have been sewing half the night. On top of her dresser sat a giant blue top hat made from the poster board; she'd rolled it into a cylinder and stuck it into a cut-out circle of cardboard. Against the wall was a huge sign on white poster board, the text done exactly like in the Dr Seuss books: *I Am Sam, Sam I Am*. Beatrice was going to be a Dr Seuss Uncle Sam on her bike.

I went down to the three of them seated around the table, Ellen and Beatrice eating Wheaties and my mother sipping a cup of tea.

'Ellen's going to art camp!' Beatrice shouted when I came in.

'Really?' I asked, looking at Ellen and then at my mother.

Ellen never got overly excited about anything, but she was brimming with happiness. 'Mom signed me up. I have to stay with the Gambinos for the two weeks so I can walk back and forth each day.' She eye-rolled on *Gambinos* but couldn't disguise her pleasure. I crossed myself as a joke. The Gambinos were the most Catholic family we knew. Their son Gabriel, who was my age, wanted to become a priest. After the Gambinos visited us, Marie and Thomas would go around the house lifting their hands and talking like Vito Corleone from *The Godfather*. Lorenzo and Sofia Gambino had come from Italy on the boat. They were older than my parents, but Dad had worked with Lorenzo in construction when he first came to America. Sofia worked in a soup factory.

'God, two weeks with Gabriel Gambino sounds like punishment,' I said. Gabriel was strange. He wore suits around the house with his shirt buttoned up to the top, and he did everything with his mother. I'd never seen him in colourful clothes, always black and white. Even though his father was a labourer like ours, Gabriel had always looked at us as if we were feral beasts. He was immaculate.

'Don't be smart, Libby,' my mother said. 'They're doing us a favour.'

'And guess what?' said Beatrice. 'I'm going to a sleepover camp for two weeks.'

'What camp? Where?' Beatrice had never been away from home before and she had never been to a camp, never mind a sleepover one.

'It's in North Carolina. In the mountains where you sleep in a cabin. It's a really good one and Mom's coming down there too. She'll see me on Sundays.'

'They take moms at the camp?'

'Noooo.' Beatrice laughed at me. 'She'll stay nearby.'

'Camp Arrowhead,' said Mom. 'In the Blue Ridge Mountains, not far from Asheville.'

'Isn't seven young?'

'They take campers from six. Beatrice will be absolutely fine.'

'What about us?'

'You and Thomas are going to be here on your own, unless you can stay with Sage?' She said it like a half-question, like *Can you ask the Adamses because you know I can't?*

'No, I can't stay with Sage. She's working. I'll stay here with Thomas.' It annoyed me that she was throwing it back on me to ask. 'Where are *you* going to be?'

'Nearby.'

'Where nearby?'

'Asheville.'

'But where exactly? A motel? Log cabin? Pig farm?'

'There's a place that's not far.'

She was evading the question. She wasn't going to tell us and there could only be one reason. He was going. The camps Ellen and Beatrice were suddenly allowed to go to gave her the space to do this, to have freedom away from us with her boyfriend, and it made me angry. I wanted to demolish her lies. We all knew what she wasn't saying. Beatrice started looping her hair; Ellen stared at the pattern on the tablecloth.

'I'll go with you too.'

'You know that's not possible.' My mom looked tired. She fiddled with the label at the end of her tea bag, preoccupied and worried, and I felt miserable. *It's true*, I thought. *I don't care about her happiness. I get in its way.*

'Please, Libby.' It was Ellen. She was siding with Mom? I turned to snap back at her and saw her face. She had the chance to be away from here and Barbie Man, and I was threatening it. It wasn't just about the art camp. She'd barely left the house the past four weeks. She was afraid. Being away would solve the problem. For me too. I wouldn't have to worry every minute. She'd be safe. I was blowing it. I had to back down.

I sat next to Beatrice at the table. 'I have to babysit anyway. Camp in the mountains sounds great. When's everyone going?'

'Next Saturday,' said Mom. 'Early.'

'But the bike parade. Ellen's made Beatrice an outfit.'

'I'm sorry. They can't. I'm dropping Ellen first to the Gambinos' and then we have the drive to North Carolina, which could be at least nine or ten hours.'

The parade didn't start until midday. There was no choice. Ellen was getting art camp, Beatrice was heading off to overnight camp, where she would share a cabin with other girls and spend days canoeing and horseback riding and having campfires, telling stories. This was good and the costumes didn't matter and my mom was trying to do something, giving Ellen the camp and trying to make up with her, whatever her other reasons.

'Ellen,' I said, 'I thought of something. We could give the costume you made to Peter Boucher. He loves Dr Seuss.'

'Really?' She thought about it for a moment. 'The face paints are important, though, for it all to look right. Paint his face with the white face paint first and then for the cheeks I was going to do the American flag inside heart shapes.'

'That's a great idea.' Mom looked grateful.

'Yeah, well, I'll ask Mrs Boucher first. I don't even know if they're doing the parade.'

Everything settled, as if the room had taken a deep breath and exhaled. We were all calm again.

It was high summer now. The sky was almost shrouded by the canopy except for the trace of the trail I could see where the trees didn't quite meet. I always liked to look at that line, like a bright river above me to follow, how the path was written in the sky. Everything was lush and alive. I should have been happy. My mother would be gone for two weeks. Thomas and I would be home alone. Ellen would be safe. But instead I felt something I couldn't name, like grief.

I looked at my feet. The trace of blood was still there, a dark smear in the creamy white of the shoe. One of the last times Ellen had come working with us, it was a job for people we'd never worked for before, just a one-off, in a rural place. In a weird way, it had made Dad more uncomfortable, like these were people that should be turning their grassland for hay and why were we there cutting a big lumpy meadow for them. The woman who came to the door was young and she had a pile of children around her. She reminded me of Laura Ingalls's mother in the *Little House on the Prairie* series. Even though it was the late 1970s, this woman at the door looked like she belonged to another century.

Dad had gotten a seat for the Gravely. It didn't have a steering wheel, we had to turn the machine using levers on the handles, but it had a seat that hooked on and it was the first and only time we ever had anything resembling a sit-on lawnmower or tractor. All day Ellen begged him for a ride on it. The handles were thicker than her wrists but she kept asking. Dad and Thomas were running it across this huge field, maybe five acres. The grass had yellowed and thinned and gone to seed. Papery spears reached my thighs. We didn't even try to catch the grass; the woman just wanted it cut. I was going around large oak trees and their bumpy roots with the edging mower. Ellen wanted to try the big one and eventually Dad let her sit up on the seat for a few rows and walked alongside her as she drove it. She was halfway up the second row when he reached over and hit the ignition off. He told her to get down and step back.

She'd hit something.

Ellen climbed down and looked behind her at the path she'd cut through the grass and screamed, jumping back. Thomas and I came over. It was a nest of baby rabbits. Parts of them were dispersed across the gold stubble of the field. We all stood, horrified. Ellen turned white with shock. I'd always seen her as being tougher than me, more abrasive and thicker-skinned. After hitting the rabbits, she was wounded. Even days later, she'd swear to me she wasn't thinking about it or remembering it, but her body would still have that feeling, and when she'd try to think what it was, what was wrong, she'd remember.

After Dad died, I knew that feeling too, how sadness

could be in your body even when it wasn't in your head. Maybe that's why she didn't work with us as much after that. I was saddened by the rabbits and really sad for the weight on Ellen for what she thought she'd done, but I reacted differently than she did. More detached. The same with the deer the night before. I was sad that it had happened but not distraught. Maybe that was the difference – when you were the cause of the catastrophe. Maybe if it had been me sitting on the Gravely or driving Grady Adams's Mercedes, I would have been devastated.

Inside the Kingdom, I pulled an oak leaf and lay on my back, stretching my legs against its trunk. I had bruises on my right shin and raw scratched mosquito bites. I held the leaf toward the light. Red oak. Its underside is a paler green. Toothed lobes, slender stalk and very fine tufts of hair along the midrib. Its leaves can grow ten inches long and seven inches wide. The bark of the red oak looks like it has bright shiny silver stripes running down it. It was the most common tree in this part of the woods. Ancient cultures believed that the oak was sacred, and they interpreted the messages of Zeus and other gods through the rustling of the oak's leaves. Suddenly, nearby, I heard a rumbling. I dropped the leaf and listened. I knew it was Wilson McVay.

I lowered my legs and rolled on to my stomach, keeping my head down. The motorcycle downshifted, slowed, the throttle dropping. It stopped.

'Hello?'

I kept my face down in the soft moss and didn't move.

'Libby?'

I stayed perfectly quiet, not scared so much as resigned to the fact that he was following me, maybe all of us, and it was weird. He brought danger wherever he went because people were looking for him. It wasn't his crimes now that bothered me as much as knowing that he was someone who was confused and could also be violent. I couldn't lose the picture of him terrorizing people, punching out their windows and then standing there naked and bleeding in the dark.

The motorcycle started up again and moved further down the trail. I stayed where I was, waiting for it to sound further away, but instead he sounded closer.

'Libby? Marie called me. About the mall.' Shit. Marie had said she was going to call him. I'd said not to. He knew I was near. There was no point in hiding.

'Here. I'm over here.'

Wilson pushed through the understorey, crashing in rather than coming around to the gap at the back. He nearly stepped on me as he entered the clearing.

'What the fuck are you doing on the ground?'

'I was looking at the sky.'

'You're facing the wrong way.'

'Yeah. I ducked when I heard your bike.'

'You're like a kid who covers their eyes and then thinks you can't see them.' He dropped his helmet as if he were in someone's living room and plopped down on the moss carpet next to me. 'Wow. Good find.' He leaned back and looked up. 'Like a little fort.'

'It is our fort. Or was. Mine and Sage's.'

'I was waiting for your mom to leave and she hasn't.

Usually on a Saturday she's gone by now.'

Oh great, he knew her schedule, even at weekends. 'Swim season's over. So you were watching our house? You actually do that?'

'I guess so. Yeah.'

'Do you realize just how creepy that is?' I knew I should feel more terror or anger, but deep down I already knew he'd been watching and that there was something wrong with him; he probably watched other people too.

'Yeah, well. You made it clear you don't want me doing your lawn or helping out, but Marie called last night and said you had some bother at the mall yesterday.'

'Please leave us alone.'

'Marie said the guy was up here?'

'Thomas saw him. He was looking for whoever owned a green Impala.'

'Fucking Kowalski. Idiot.' I didn't ask what he meant but he offered anyway. 'Drove right by him when he was still on the ground, shouting out the window. That's how he saw the car.'

I didn't want to know the information. It made me feel sick. Teenage boys hunting down a psychopath and then going back while he was injured on the ground to taunt and provoke him further.

'It's not Craig's car that led them to Valley Forge Mountain. Ellen said in the car that's where she lived.'

'Oh.' I could tell Wilson didn't know this, and that it made sense now that Barbie Man had shown up here. 'I was wondering because an Impala's a pretty generic car to have chased down.'

'Anyway, if Marie called you it was only to warn you that he's looking for you. We don't want to be caught up in this.'

'Well, you are,' Wilson said.

'I don't want to be. Please.' I looked at him when I said it.

'Where's Ellen?'

'She's at home but she's going away to camp next week, so she'll be gone.'

'Good.'

I had a sudden sensation of the sky spinning. I sat up. Wilson was stretched out next to me, relaxed and leaning back on his elbows. I pulled my knees in toward me.

'New Converse?' Even my mom hadn't noticed.

'Yeah. Except I already messed them up.' I pointed to the stain. 'Blood.'

'Whose?'

'A deer that got hit last night.'

'You've been out examining roadkill? Or took one out with your brother's Western Flyer?'

'No. Someone hit it on Horseshoe. We saw it on the way home from babysitting.' I told him about meeting Grady Adams on the road.

I didn't know why I had started to have a regular conversation with him. His craziness was wrecking our lives and he had just confirmed that he was watching us.

'I have to go,' I said. I left him in the middle of the laurel and rhododendron, lying on our moss carpet like it was his kingdom.

18

Sage had called and said to come up. I hadn't been to her house since Grady Adams drove me home and mentioned Ellen. Most summers, I'd have been there until late at night, playing kick-the-can in the dark with Sage and her brothers and other Valley Forge Mountain kids, or in her basement eating Charles Pretzels from large tins they bulk-ordered, watching *The Love Boat* or *Fantasy Island* and sneaking out to smoke Charlotte's Kents, and listening to Rolling Stones eight-tracks. I walked to Sage's at dusk, vigilant. Wings whirred at my ears; I brushed them away and felt the clammy touch of skin against my fingers. There was no visible moon. Before I'd left the house, Thomas had pointed to the moon calendar above the kitchen table. There was a black circle positioned on Wednesday, July 1st: the new moon. 'It's the first day,' he said, 'so you won't see it.' He had come back earlier that afternoon from the shore, tan and healthy-looking. He said it had been great and I didn't ask too many questions.

Thomas made a moon calendar every year. Dad had told us that when he was growing up they always knew the phases of the moon and how the tides would change according to what the moon was doing. They needed to know for fishing and harvesting shellfish, he said, not like here in America where no one knew where anything came from any more.

In the last year or two before he died, when he would go on like that, complaining about 'America' and 'Americans', it embarrassed me. He seemed angry a lot of the time, angry that Americans didn't know geography or where the olive in their martini came from or how to grow things. They just consumed, he said – consumed and discarded. When he was like this, and maybe had been drinking, and was collecting me at someone's house or from a hockey game, my friends or my friends' parents or whoever we were with would be uncomfortable. I knew they were because they would say nothing or just sort of agree with him about Americans to make it stop. They wouldn't argue with him, which would have been better, at least to show his views some respect. They just shut down. I felt shame in those moments, and I think he knew it, sensed it in how I looked away, interrupted to say we'd better go or just fell silent, leaving him alone, adrift in the conversation.

Not long before my dad left for New York, Sage had told me that she thought he had changed, that she used to think he was always smiling and happy but not lately, not any more. 'Maybe he's unhappy,' she said. 'Maybe he should go home to Ireland.' Even the memory of it hurt. Sage's honesty. I knew that I'd held these things against her, had resented her for being there, for being so close that she could see the things I couldn't or didn't want to. I hated myself for having told her anything, and her for listening, for witnessing things and sometimes saying them back to me.

There are superstitions about new moons. It's important to see them in the open air outside. On our last trip to

Ireland we'd waited for the sun to fall – which was nearly midnight because the days are very long in the summer where it's so far north. We had gone outside and stood in the back field to look for the waxing crescent because seeing the new moon through glass was unlucky. It was there just as the sun dropped, a thin silver arc on a dark shape. We stood and watched as it faded and then disappeared. I started to walk back to the house, but Dad said to stop and listen. At first I didn't hear it, but then I did, a rumble from far away.

'That's the sound I miss the most when I'm away from here,' he said.

'What is it?'

'The sea.'

We listened, and after a while we heard another sound from the long grasses near the pines where the pheasants roosted, a grating squawk. I thought it was the female pheasant that he'd pointed out to me over and over, a sound almost like a hoarse bark. I was wrong.

'The corncrake,' he said, so low I barely heard him. It sounded again, like a raspy quack, but I knew how happy he was to hear it and to be able to name it.

As I walked toward Sage's, I listened to the click of crickets at the wood's edge, the slight whisper of trees, the sounds of the mountain, as if there were another frequency to hear and to be moved by. I wondered if one day I would have that same wrenching longing for this place, the way my father had had for the sounds he'd heard growing up.

*

I hadn't seen Sage since the mall on Friday when she walked us to Wanamaker's glass doors for the bus. Her lie still hung between us but I needed and missed her. I started to run toward her house. At the top of her driveway a pile of bikes had been dropped on the ground. A group of boys were playing basketball outside with Sage's brothers. The boys barely noticed me as I walked through their game to the back door. Grady and Charlotte were inside watching TV.

'Hey, Libby – stranger.' Charlotte stood and gave me a hug with one arm, the other holding her cigarette away from me.

'Hi, Mrs Adams. Hi, Dr Adams.'

Grady glanced up. 'Hey there, Libby.' He turned back to the television. The news was on: Charles and Diana and the upcoming royal wedding at the end of July.

'Bless her,' said Charlotte, gesturing at Diana on the television, all bashful, looking at the camera from under her hair. 'So sweet. But him . . . Prince or no prince, he's got a face only a mother could love.'

It was the kind of thing I'd have repeated to my father. He loved to hear Charlotte's irreverence and her Southern sayings. 'I'm as full as a tick,' she'd say, leaning back after a dinner she'd hardly touched, or 'She's so stuck-up she'd drown in a rainstorm', turns of phrase he thought weren't that different from the Irish – 'He's enough neck for two heads.' And he loved anything said against the British monarchy. When talking about the royal family, he referred to them as 'a bad clique', which made me and Marie laugh, the monarchy reduced to a petty in-group.

'I feel like we haven't seen you in so long,' Charlotte said. 'Where've you been all this summer?'

I was about to say *Oh, I saw Dr Adams the other night* but something stopped me from saying anything, or asking Grady about the deer. He was sitting there, focused on the TV, not looking at me. Sage hadn't mentioned it on the phone either. Maybe he didn't want them to know he'd killed something beautiful or that he had been so rattled by it.

'Sage is in her room,' Charlotte said. 'Go on ahead down.'

'Wild Horses', Sage's very favourite song, reverberated down the hallway from her room. It was supposed to be about Marianne Faithfull waking up for the first time after an overdose and saying those lines to Mick Jagger when she opened her eyes. But there was another story that it was Keith Richards who had written it. We didn't know which one was true. Sage couldn't say why it was her favourite, except that its emotion caught her, forgiving and still loving someone even when they've really hurt you. We'd both read *Up and Down with the Rolling Stones* that spring. Sage had started to dress like Marianne Faithfull and Anita Pallenberg, tops with billowing sleeves, hip-huggers and feathers. But for me, the book was terrifying. Brian Jones, warlocks, drugs, black magic, Gram Parsons dying in a hotel room and his friends stealing his body and trying to cremate him – it said that chaotic and dark forces were spinning around us; one foot wrong and you'd be sucked into the vortex.

I knocked three times on her door and went in. Sage

sat up on her bed and reached over to the stereo to turn it down.

'Libby, finally. Come on, we're going up to the towers.' Sage was wearing a red tube top and faded denim cut-offs frayed to white threads in places. Silver earrings dangled to below her chin, the layers of silver leaves making a small rippling sound. I looked at my Converse, at my legs covered with scabs, bruises and scratches from the woods. I had still never shaved them. Marie had said that once I started, the hair would turn black and become like stubble. Sister Benedict wore nude pantyhose and her leg hair was so wiry that it poked through the sheer nylon. Her legs looked like a mass of spiders squished against mesh. It put me off letting a razor anywhere near my legs. I looked at Sage's; even her thighs were smooth.

I didn't want to go to the towers. I'd thought Sage and I would stay in her room, talk and work things out. I wanted to tell her I was sorry, not just for the phone call, but for everything.

'Come on,' she said, grabbing my wrist and pulling me toward the door. 'Someone's getting kegs. Loads of people will be up there.'

I shook off her hand and stopped to look at myself in her mirror. My hair wasn't washed or brushed. I ran my fingers through it to straighten it. In front of the mirror Sage had jewellery and make-up arranged in little baskets. I took a tub of lip gloss, dipped my finger in and leaned forward, close to the mirror, spreading its clear shimmer across my lips. It tasted like strawberries. I stood back. I had on one of Marie's T-shirts she'd left behind – Talking

Heads, *Remain in Light*. She had worn it so often that the red masks across the four faces had bled pink across the white. My hair had grown so long it nearly reached the bottom of my shirt now, and strands of it around my face had been lightened by the sun.

'You look beautiful, Libby. Wild and sleek. Like one of those mountain cats. What is it? A bobcat.' Sage was able to say these things, to compliment; Charlotte did it too. In my family we didn't know how to do that, saying those good things to each other. I think our faces would have contorted and our sentences fallen apart if we'd tried. It was hard for me to imagine my mother saying *You look beautiful in that.* I'd thought Sage looked stunning when I walked in but I hadn't said it, and if I did now it would seem as if I was only saying it because she'd said something nice to me. I tried to say something else.

'You always make me feel good, even when I know I look like a feral racoon.'

When we reached the top of her driveway, Sage stopped me and held my wrist. 'Libby, I didn't tell Grady anything about Ellen.'

'Okay,' I said. I didn't want to bring it all up again. I missed her.

'The other day, I went back to Space Port. I meant to tell you.'

'Why? He'd notice you and remember. In there with your waitress uniform.'

'I know the manager. He's a regular in the diner. I stood there talking to him for a bit. Barbie Man was playing some of the games but mostly he was looking around, like he was looking for someone.'

'Maybe teenagers from the mountain hang out there when they go to the mall? Maybe he was hoping he might recognize one of them.'

'That's what I thought. But it was only Upper Merion kids in there anyway. I left before he did. Poor Ellen. I can't stop thinking about her in the car with him. The way he looks.'

As we came through the woods toward the tower lot, we could hear laughing and cheering. Sage and I stood for a moment at the mouth of the trail, taking it all in. Across the clearing they had made five or six small fires, which they were feeding from a mountain of branches and sticks at the edge of the lot by the woods. One of the De Martino brothers was standing on top of it, hurling down branches to others waiting below, who were dragging them to the fires, dried pine exploding in sparks through the air. Three boys were rolling kegs across the loose stones; there was one already tapped along the water tower's perimeter fence on the eastern side, the furthest away from the road. Groups of teenagers were gathered around the scattered fires.

Abbey came toward us, holding a plastic cup of beer. 'You're here. I thought you might not come.' She kissed Sage on the cheek, then looked at me and touched my shoulder. 'Hey, Gallagher, you out in the world again?'

I nodded half-heartedly and realized I was practically standing behind Sage, like a shy child with its mother. I stepped out and tried to hold myself tall, and not cross my arms, a dead giveaway that leads to unfavourable shifts of power, according to Marie.

They had blocked the service road with a barrier made from branches and tyres. Police cars wouldn't be able to drive down.

'It'll take them a long, long time to move it, and by then we'll all be spirited into the woods. Like ghosts.' Abbey made a motion with her hand to show how we would all vanish into the dark. 'That's us. Shwoop. Gone. Like that.' She stared at us for a moment for effect. She looked wasted. I wanted to ask her what was stopping the cops from just getting out of their squad cars and walking around the heap and up the trail?

'You won't be vanishing anywhere fast if you keep going like that,' said Sage. 'You'll just be sitting on your ass in the dirt, legs useless in front of you, waiting for the kind policeman to take you home.'

Abbey laughed and pushed Sage. 'Go get beers. There's plenty for everyone.' She gestured toward the kegs. 'And then come sit by that campfire.' She pointed to the furthest one, closest to the service road, and wove her way back toward it. Sage and I went down to the keg at the fence.

Older boys were standing around in groups. Sage filled her cup first and a guy with greasy lank hair started singing 'You Shook Me All Night Long', apparently to her, but he only knew fragments of a line about thighs and kept singing them over and over. I tried to fill my cup but just foam came out. I opened and closed the lever, opened it again, but nothing. Someone leaned over from a group behind Sage and the AC/DC guy and pumped the keg.

'It just needs more pressure,' he said. 'Hold your cup lower.'

I knew before I looked up that it was Jack Griffith.

'Once in a lifetime,' he said.

'What?' I looked at him. Up here, in the middle of the Valley Forge Mountain crowd, he looked clean-cut and tidy, while most of the other teenagers had Harley badges and wore denim or army jackets with cut-off arms, their hair long and wild. I had no idea what he was talking about. It sounded deep, like something I should understand.

He pointed at my shirt and I looked down. 'Oh. Oh, yeah. Talking Heads. It's not mine, it's Marie's.' My cup was full and I took a clumsy mouthful and coughed because I had swallowed too much. I wiped my mouth with the back of my hand.

Sage was watching us. 'Come on, Libby,' she said. 'Abbey's waiting.'

'See ya,' I said to Jack, and I walked toward the black line of trees on the other side of the clearing, the tower lights intermittently blinking red across all the gathered faces.

19

Sparks from the burning branches leapt and floated in the night air and the lights from the towers flashed in steady rhythm; above us in the open sky the absence of moonlight magnified the endless stars. Someone had taken out a guitar and the tune drifted across the tower lot. I was conscious of Jack at another fire, people from his high school sitting around it, kids Thomas used to hang out with. At our fire, Tony De Martino was playing Boy Scout, hauling over branches and logs and making skewers for us with a knife. I was baffled. I only ever saw him with a greasy rag, working on Honda 50s and lawnmowers or cleaning the barrels of BB guns. I didn't know what we were going to skewer on our sticks but we all held them at the fire. Sage had brought me another cup of beer.

'Does anyone have a ghost story?' Abbey asked. 'Like the haunted house on High Point?'

'Oh, don't tell that one,' Sage said. 'We have to walk home that way later.' There was a house that everyone said was haunted, and even before I'd heard the stories I'd always had a bad feeling when I passed it. Coming off the trail from the tower lot, it was the first house, a standard 1950s shingle-clad one, no different from any others. Except it *was* different. I had never seen anyone in it and even on Halloween none of us dared ring the bell. There was one story that a man had killed his wife in the house, another that a man had kept women in the basement as prisoners; they were never found until after he died and a new person bought it and discovered a false wall. On the other side were the dusty remains of five women. My mother had said there was no truth in these stories, that they were just tall tales told because the house had been owned by a man who was a recluse. 'Like Boo Radley,' Marie had said. 'You can't choose to be alone or quiet up here without being turned into a monster.' (I would look for trees with knotholes when passing, imagining I was Scout down there in Alabama, wondering if someone inside was desperate to make a connection but didn't want to be seen.) The house's windows were always dark; a house that could only look out. The grass, like ours, stayed uncut. It sat on a plot that the sun never seemed to hit, the woods shadowing it from every angle.

'You guys know this mountain was a sacred site to the Indians.' Abbey was storytelling. 'It was their graveyard for the dead, a holy place.' I had heard this before, how our houses were on top of ancient burial sites. People on the mountain had reported unusual noises and blinking lights in the woods, and some people heard screaming voices. 'Then, about a hundred years ago, white men came and started mining and quarrying and building houses. They were drilling and bulldozing into the ancient underworld, upsetting the spirits and pushing them out of their resting places.'

Abbey was drunk but the effect improved the telling. The words came slow off her tongue, she took her time and spoke low. We were all leaning in to listen, our faces lit and shadowed by the fire, which snapped and sparked into the night air.

'You know how there's quartz all over the mountain? That's probably why the Indians brought their dead here. You know how it sparkles? It was to help the dead find their way and also to light a trail for the living so they could return and visit their dead. But then white men came and started to dig the quartz out of the earth, blinding the spirits, who could no longer see their way through the underworld.'

Abbey paused and looked at all of us sitting by the fire. 'See, Sage, that's why on your stretch of road the electricity is always going out. The spirits are lost and are interfering with everything.' On that side of the mountain people said that there was some kind of electrical field that caused lightning to hit repeatedly. Sage's family always had candles ready in the summer for when the lights went out. 'And Tony, where you live almost every family has someone who's a little sick in the head.' Abbey didn't try to say it in a polite way and she didn't hold back. I thought maybe she was going too far, because it was true. On the De Martinos' road there were only about seven houses and around the same number of psychiatric cases, including in the De Martino family. One of Tony's brothers was damaged forever from a heroin overdose, but people said he'd heard voices before he ever started taking drugs, it was why he took them in the first place. Tony just nodded at Abbey, like he was agreeing with her.

I shivered. *Please don't let her say anything about us, about our road.*

'Did you hear that?' Tony De Martino stood up, alert, looking toward the woods where they'd built the blockade. There was a growl and a crashing sound in the thicket. Both Sage and I screamed without knowing what we were screaming at. Everyone around the fire stood up. 'Shhh,' Tony said.

'What is it?' someone whispered.

'The cops?'

Everyone stayed silent. The singing at the other fire near us stopped and they stood too, and looked at us looking into the dark wood. I saw the flicker of lights blinking through the trees. I was about to turn and run – some already had. There was a light weaving through the woods toward us.

'Fuck, you scared me,' said Tony as Wilson appeared through the trees, pushing the Yamaha. He had on the suede leather-fringe jacket and black jeans and boots. 'Why didn't you just come up the trail, man?'

'It's blocked,' said Wilson.

'Yeah, to keep out cars. You could've just gone around it on the bike. Not sneaking up on us like this.'

There was a group of people who'd come forward. Jack was with them.

'Your boyfriend checking up on you, Libby?'

I looked at Abbey. She meant Wilson. Why would she say something like that in front of everyone? Why would she say something like that at all? 'What's that supposed to mean?'

I hated Wilson all over again. That his name was even associated with me. I hated that she'd said it in front of Jack. Had Sage said something to Abbey about Wilson hanging around?

'I'm just messing,' Abbey said.

I pushed through the people gathered round and headed down toward the other end of the lot. I found an empty cup on the ground, swilled some beer around to clean it, then filled it. I moved a few yards down from the keg and sat on the gravel, my back against the chain-link. Tony De Martino and his brothers were back at the woodpile, conducting and orchestrating the delivery of branches to fires. My cheeks were burning. I hated what Abbey had said and I hated that Wilson was here. The afternoon when he was in our house during the thunderstorm, I'd told Marie how it bothered me that Wilson hung around teenagers way younger than himself, showing up at parties, being awkward. Marie said there was an obvious reason. I didn't get what she meant. She looked at me like I was dense.

'He sells,' she said.

'Wilson actually sells drugs?'

'*Clearly.*'

Abbey had implied that people on the mountain knew Wilson was hanging around us. And that bothered me not only because he was a psycho who sold drugs but because I didn't want any of us to be associated with him when he was on a hitlist.

A few yards away, the third keg had been tapped. One of Abbey's older brothers was standing on it, making a war cry and pounding his bare chest. He was even older than

Wilson. He was nearly thirty. He'd been to Vietnam and in and out of prison ever since. He always wore his army tags around his neck and his army jacket with the arms cut off and nothing underneath. He had shoulder-length brown hair that girls would envy. Marie said he was the image of Jackson Browne. But something had happened to his left eye when he was on his tour of duty so that the pupil was always dilated, like David Bowie's, except on Abbey's brother it looked crazy instead of interesting.

'Libby!' Sage was standing at the corner of the fence, shouting down to me. 'Libby! Come back.'

I could see the shadows of the others as I walked toward them: Wilson standing there on the margins instead of sitting like a normal person; Tony De Martino like a fire god, dancing around, pushing in branches; Abbey stoned and storytelling. Jack was there now too. Sage sat near where Wilson was standing. The only place left was between Jack and Sage.

'Abbey's still on her ghost stories, how we're living on Indian graveyards,' Sage said.

'Like the Amityville Horror,' Tony said.

'That wasn't about an Indian graveyard, was it?' I whispered to Sage. 'Wasn't it because there were people murdered in the house?' Sage had the book and had seen the movie.

'It was a family that got murdered,' Wilson said. '112 Ocean Avenue, Amityville, on Long Island. Six of them. Mother, father, two brothers and two sisters. All murdered by their twenty-three-year-old brother. Ronald DeFeo Junior.'

'Why do you have to creep us out by knowing information like that?' I blurted it out because it bothered me that other people, especially Jack, would think he was a freak memorizing those kinds of details.

'It's in the book, which I read. And it's in the movie, which pretty much everyone here but you has seen.' The others were agreeing. They knew those details too.

'People say that the stuff in Amityville – how Ronald went crazy and all – was because the house was built on an Indian burial ground.' Tony seemed determined that there was a link.

'Abbey, what happened to the woman you were talking about that was ill?' Sage asked. 'Keep telling that story.' She must have finished the one about High Point.

'Well, after months of the banging and noise and voices, now she was really sick and weak. She went out back and into the woods in her nightgown. She hadn't been out of bed in weeks. And she sat down on a stump and spoke to the spirits out there. She said, "I am very sick, and I think I am dying, and I am asking you please to help me do this, to do this the best I can, and I can't with all this racket." And she asked them to stop. Her husband found her as she came back out of the woods and she was shivering and pale and soaking wet, but she was smiling. "They're going to stop," she said. "They told me they would stop." And they did.'

'Who was the woman?' Sage asked.

'The Carlsons near Hamilton, you know that house with the really long driveway into the woods?' Everyone was quiet. I knew the Carlsons. Mrs Carlson had been really sick and had died. When I raised money on Daisy Day for cancer, Mrs Carlson had bought a daisy. She came to the door in her robe, and she was so thin that her face looked like it was caving in. When I told Marie, she said I should never have gone to their house, getting her out of bed and asking her for money. 'That woman is sick with cancer. What'd you go there for? Of all houses?' But Mrs Carlson had thanked me – really thanked me – and I knew she meant it because she was sick, and she thought what I was doing was in some way for her, and I felt then that it was.

Abbey went on. 'But I also heard that when she was out in the woods with the spirits and talking to them, they said something to her.' She paused and we all waited, rapt, waiting to hear what the Indian ghosts had told Mrs Carlson in the woods. Abbey leaned forward and spoke low. '"Don't be scared." That's what they said to her. And she said that helped her. It really helped her.'

I shivered again.

'They're my neighbours,' said Jack next to me.

No one asked him if it was true or whether he'd heard anything, as if we didn't want the story contradicted because it made us feel better, that the spirits of the woods could be spoken to and could be merciful if we just asked.

'What kind of Indians were here? Was it like Sioux or Cherokee?' Tony asked.

'Delaware,' said Jack.

'No,' Wilson said, cutting in, 'that's what white settlers called them because they couldn't say their name. They were Lenape.' I had never heard of them.

'What happened to them?' asked Tony.

'They got wiped out. They got disease and most of them were pushed west.' Wilson had finally sat down at the fire next to Abbey.

We were silent for a moment and then Wilson spoke again.

'They have a cool creation story, though. Their creator had a dream of earth and he created a special tree. From the roots of that tree the first man was born. Then the man born from the tree kissed the earth and that's how woman was made. So the whole of human creation came from the roots of trees.'

I doubt anyone sitting at the fire had ever heard Wilson McVay say so much.

'Who'd have taken you for all this hippy talk,' said Sage. 'Where'd you hear all this?'

'He's making it up for the tree girl,' said Abbey, looking over at me. What the fuck was wrong with Abbey and why did she keep saying these things to me about Wilson? And especially in front of Jack, who might also say some of this back to Thomas.

Wilson stared back at her. 'I didn't make it up. My mom's an anthropologist. She's always talking about this stuff.' I remembered the bag of drugs he'd brought down to our house, saying his mother's medicine cabinet was so full she wouldn't miss any of it.

Nobody said anything, and they were all probably thinking what I was: how strange to imagine Wilson McVay with a mother, never mind sitting down with her, listening to her tell creation stories.

'So why are all you pioneers sitting around with spears?' Wilson asked. 'You plan to fight the police with your sharpened sticks?'

'Oh wait, I forgot!' Tony said. He leaped up and ran back over toward the woodpile.

'Maybe he killed a squirrel with his BB gun that he wants us to cook,' said Sage.

'Or snake,' said Abbey.

'Copperhead or garter?' Sage and Abbey cracked up.

Tony came back with a grin on his face and an Acme brown paper bag. He pulled out small plastic packets, flinging them at us. One landed in my lap. Marshmallows. I looked over at Sage and we both burst into laughter. It was unbelievable. Tony looked so pleased with himself, and he sat back down and put two marshmallows on the end of the stick he had made into a spear and handed two to Sage next to him. I opened my bag, took one and put it on the stick. People were passing them, so I passed my bag to Jack.

'Tony made us skewers,' I said.

'I can see,' he said. He seemed annoyed about something. He leaned forward and said, 'Can I talk to you? Like, apart from everyone?'

'Yeah, okay.' I got up and walked away before Sage had a chance to say anything to us. I could feel Wilson watching as we walked across the lot. I led us toward the mouth of the trail and I remembered the night we had watched the snow up there with Thomas and the night at the swim club, and how, despite what Sage had said about him, there had been something between us.

20

I moved quickly through the dark, surefooted despite the beers. I could feel the trail beneath me, roots like bent arms in the path that could catch your foot, the spine of angled rocks, and I knew without looking where they were. The yellow rectangles that some nights blazed on trees were barely visible. I had the sensation of something behind both of us. Abbey's stories about graves and upset spirits didn't scare me. If the spirits were here and all around me, they knew I wouldn't tear up the ground or level trees. I believed Mrs Carlson's story. She seemed like that kind of person, someone who would go out there alone and explain herself and listen.

'Whoa. Slow down. I can't see anything. It's pitch-black,' Jack called behind me. I kept walking. 'Jesus, Libby, just stop.'

I turned and waited for him. 'Let's sit here.' Just off the trail was a flat-topped boulder. He sat next to me but shuffled to sit further away. He was breathing fast, as if he'd been running, and seemed different from the Jack I'd been with at the pool. He was rigid and upright, his relaxed confidence gone. The night was dark, and the air had become very still. I turned to face him, but he was looking straight ahead and I knew he hadn't brought me down here because he liked me.

'What's up with you and Wilson McVay?'

I suddenly felt cold away from the fire. Why was everyone so obsessed with me and Wilson?

'Absolutely nothing.'

'Thomas told me he's always hanging around your house. And Abbey said stuff.'

'No. Oh my God, no.'

'Wilson's like twenty.'

'I know . . . It's not like that. I don't know why he's hanging around. He's sort of friends with Marie. I think he thinks he's helping watch over us or something.'

'Well, that's ironic. Complete headcase now the Gallaghers' guardian angel.'

'He's not our guardian angel. And he's not a complete headcase.' I surprised myself with how I was speaking. I didn't know why I was suddenly defending Wilson McVay and meaning it. But Jack's judgement and sudden big-brother attitude pissed me off.

'Most people on the mountain think he is.'

'He helped my family with something. That's all.'

'Cutting your grass?'

'Why do you say that?'

'Thomas said he did.'

'Well, anyway, it was something else. And we can mow our own lawn.'

'I'm just saying you should stay away from him. He's coked-up half the time, going around headbutting people.' I wondered if this was true, if Wilson did those kinds of drugs. Had Jack heard about Pottstown? He must have.

'Are you serious? You dragged me out here because of Wilson?'

'No. I don't even know why I mentioned him. He's an asshole.'

'Okay, then. So what did you want to talk about?'

'It's nothing. Never mind.' He stood up. 'I have to go home.'

'Okay, be like that,' I said.

He paused for a moment, standing in front of me, his hands now deep in the pockets of his jeans, shoulders hunched.

'You good to get back to the others?'

Again the concerned big brother. I didn't say anything back.

'Okay, then. I'm heading.' He turned and started to walk down the trail.

'By the way,' I said to his back, 'you're the one who said you wanted to talk. So fuck you.'

'Now I don't want to.'

'What did I do?'

Was it because I'd defended Wilson? I'd half thought that maybe we had come here to be alone.

He started again. 'Did you talk to Thomas?'

'Yeah. Pretty much all my life.'

'I was wondering, did you say anything?' He paused. 'I mean about me?'

'No. Like what?'

'You know.'

'No. Did you?'

'No. Of course not.'

I couldn't believe it. We were in the woods so he could tell me never to tell my brother we had kissed. It made me feel stupid for ever having liked him and even worse because it had embarrassed him so much.

'Look, are you okay to go back up?'

I turned without answering and walked up the trail, back toward the towers. Only a few hundred yards up, I could hear the party and see the beating lights. I found another empty cup and filled it from the keg, not even bothering to rinse it this time. Our fire was still going. Tony De Martino had his arm around Sage, who was letting him, and Wilson was sitting back, legs crossed, looking way too at home. I sat down, trying to make eye contact with Sage, but she was letting Tony feed her a marshmallow from his stick. It was as if reality had been rewritten while I spent a few minutes in the woods.

'You missed marshmallows,' said Abbey.

'Here,' said Wilson. He leaned forward and handed me the stick Tony had given me earlier. There was a white marshmallow at the end. 'I saved you one. These stoned savages devoured them all.' I held my marshmallow over the fire, watching the sugar skin tinge and bubble.

I tried to chew the marshmallow, but my mouth had gone dry and it was like trying to eat sticky putty. I threw the whole stick into the fire.

'That's ungrateful,' said Wilson.

'Too sweet,' I said. I looked over at Sage again, willing her to look back, but she was still being stupid with Tony De Martino. I could hear them talking about the Stones concert in Philly in September. He was going too.

'The roots of education are bitter, but the fruit is sweet.' Wilson was looking at me.

'What's that supposed to mean?' Did Wilson think I was learning some lesson here? Was I learning my place?

'Aristotle said it. In military school, our classics teacher was always saying it.' Another trickle of information about Wilson. So that's where he'd disappeared to those years.

'What's my bitter education?' I stared hard at him.

'That's what you have to find out.'

I wanted to go home but I was afraid to go by myself. I felt like there was nothing to look forward to.

'You guys marching in the parade Saturday?' Abbey was talking to me.

'No. Beatrice is going to camp. Ellen made a costume and a sign for her but she's going to let Mrs Boucher's little boy wear it and do up his Big Wheel.'

'So cute,' said Abbey. 'Little patriots on their bikes.' She and Wilson had obviously been smoking while I was gone. Wilson was grinning at the fire and Abbey's eyes were nearly shut she looked so stoned.

'D'ya still babysit them?' Abbey asked.

'My sisters?'

'No, the spawn of the lovely Mrs Boucher.' I remembered what she had said that night at the start of the summer about Mrs Boucher, how someone thought she was beautiful. What had that meant?

I looked over at Tony and Sage. He was whispering something to her and she was laughing. In the firelight Tony looked half handsome, and all his Boy Scout of America effort had clearly paid off because Sage was leaning on him and had her hand on his thigh.

Abbey poked Wilson in the leg with her skewer. 'Hey, Wilson, why didn't you just go around the blockade? Why'd you come through the woods like a ghost to scare us all?'

Wilson just laughed. It was strange how he sat with us when across the lot at other fires there were people his age that he should be hanging out with, that he must have been friends with when he was younger, before he became different. If he was the oldest at this fire circle, I was the youngest and probably only tolerated because I was friends with Sage. I looked at Abbey, her wild curly hair glinting in the firelight, her eyes still shuttered. She looked like a fortune teller. Sage and Tony had started making out; he had cupped her face toward his. I looked away.

I wondered if Mrs De Martino was afraid of her boys, who drank beer in their yard and took pop shots at passing kids with BB guns from their lawn chairs. I had seen her with her eldest son earlier this summer, the one who'd taken the overdose, leading him by the arm to the car, his feet unsteady, his skin pallid and fleshy. Only two summers earlier, the first time I had waited outside the fence while people broke into the swim club at night, I had seen him and his friends jumping naked off the diving board, young powerful bodies arcing through the air, whooping, shaking their long wet hair as they re-emerged, breaking the surface of the water. It was like they belonged in a movie. Now, even though his mother was probably only five feet tall, he'd seemed small beside her, unused to light and air, dependent on her small self.

Marie said Sage had a class complex, that she was drawn to the working classes. She said it was to defy her family, to go against the grain. I didn't think that. Sage just preferred people like Tony and Abbey and our family. I felt sorry for Tony, who must have been collecting wood for a week and had gone to get marshmallows, thinking Sage would be there. He'd obviously been waiting for her to arrive. He'd probably get his heart broken.

I had started to feel woozy from the beer. I'd lost count of how many. Four or five. I wanted to go tap Sage on the shoulder and tell her to walk home with me, to ask her what the hell was wrong with Jack. Wilson must have sensed it.

'Come on,' he said. 'I'll give you a ride home.'

'On the motorcycle?'

'Yeah.'

'No. You're completely stoned.'

'Correction. Only a little bit stoned and completely capable of steering. I'll go slow.'

I wanted to go home. I didn't feel well. Sage wasn't going to be done any time soon, and I didn't want to be up here any more. There was no one my age and my head was spinning.

'You won't do any stupid shit like taking jumps or popping wheelies?'

'Definitely not. Especially when you're drunk sitting behind me. I like this jacket. I don't want anyone to throw up on it.'

We got up on Wilson's Yamaha. He kick-started it standing, then sat down, the heft of his body in front of mine. He turned on the gravel and we moved into the woods, whooshing past the leaves and branches on the dirt track, past the blockade they had built and on to Horseshoe Trail Road. Wilson downshifted as we glided down the hill and rounded the corner where just a few nights earlier Grady Adams had hit the deer. The disturbed gravel at the side of the road was still visible. Sods of earth were upturned. The township must have used some sort of machine to lift her. I looked the other way and for a moment let my cheek rest on Wilson's back. We turned left on to Forge Mountain Drive and I leaned with Wilson and the bike, looking ahead. The thrum of the engine beneath me, our headlight finding the road, a slight breeze on my skin and through my hair, Wilson's sturdy presence in front of me – I felt wrapped and good. For a few minutes we launched through the night, holding the road and the air and the dark. As we came around the corner after Rock Hill, a few hundred yards from my street, I tapped Wilson on the shoulder. He downshifted and pulled in, steadying the bike with his feet on the ground. He leaned his head back toward his shoulder to listen.

'In case my mom hears. I'll get off now.' I knew I probably needed to walk the last bit before going into the house. If she woke up and saw me like this, she would know I'd been drinking and I'd be dead.

I tried to get off the bike as if I were experienced but I had to hop on one foot as I swung the other leg over the seat, my skin unsticking from the leather. I stood next to him on the bike.

'Thanks.' I thought for a moment and then added, 'I forgot to say something. That guy was in Space Port and he was looking around, maybe for one of you.'

'I know. Sage said.' I tried to remember if I had seen them talking at the fire.

'Tonight?'

'No. The other night. On the phone.'

'Oh.'

'Later,' he said, and he leaned forward on the bike, pushing off, freewheeling down the hill. I couldn't see him but only heard the sound of the tyres picking up speed. I walked fast. As I turned on to my street, I heard the Yamaha engine kick and accelerate, a sound muffled and remote as it moved into the distance.

My house was dark. At the end of the driveway, I chewed a stick of Wrigley's gum. I smelled like beer. I tried the back door – the knob turned. Unlocked. Thomas had left it open for me. It meant she wasn't at home; she would have locked it. I moved through the rec room and opened the door into the garage. There was just emptiness where the shape of the car should be. In the kitchen, I flicked the light on for a second; the clock over the sink read one ten. In my room, I stepped out of my Converse and climbed over Beatrice into bed.

I lay on my side, facing the wall. Everything was confusing. Jack was embarrassed by what had happened but was he also somehow jealous of Wilson? I thought I hated Wilson, but I had defended him to Jack. Sage had called Wilson and never told me. She had his unlisted number. She knew I didn't want him involved, that I had wanted him to get away from us. Why were they talking so much? There was something else I couldn't place. A realization I was trying to grasp. Thomas had told me once that this feeling, like a sixth sense, wasn't ESP or any of that pseudoscience crap. It was another part of the sympathetic nervous system's fight or flight response. It happened, he'd said, when your body knew something before your head. If you were an animal in the jungle and there was a crack of a twig or a movement in the bush, your body would perceive those things and react before your head had even processed them. It was how you survived. Like when there's danger and your body senses it and you have a gut feeling or a bad feeling before your head understands what it is. Your body is hearing, smelling, sensing, and your instinct, based on real information, gives you the feeling you should have. Lying in bed, thinking about the night, was when this other thing took a shape I could understand. Even though I was alone in my bed in the dark, I covered my mouth with my hand. I understood now about Mrs Boucher.

21

Thomas had helped Beatrice pull suitcases down from the attic. Beatrice was leaving the following morning for camp and she was choosing which one would best hold her things.

Thomas looked up at me when I came into the living room. He was trying to free the zipper on the smallest of the cases, which had gotten caught on the lining. And before I could say what seeing the suitcases reminded me of, he responded as if he'd heard my thoughts. 'Yeah. I know.'

The only time we'd ever had them laid out was before trips to Ireland. Dad would usually take just one of us with him because we couldn't afford for everyone to go at the same time. When the suitcases came back from the trip, we'd put our heads inside and breathe in the smell of over there – peat fires, clothes wind-dried in sea air, freshly turned hay. The large blue-and-green plaid one was his, the one he always took, filling it with cotton sheets, coveralls, socks and underwear he bought in Sears for his brothers and sisters, big tins of Folgers coffee, and reading glasses for half the village. The weeks before he was going home, he'd always be busy shopping for everyone he could think of. Tool kits for a brother, full dish set for a sister. The suitcase had carried so much.

It was usually this time of year he'd be going over, when the sun was so hot that it stunted the grass and he could get away from the lawns for a week or two. Whenever I thought we had nothing of his, I was forgetting the suitcases in the attic.

'Look what else I found.' Thomas nodded toward a small case, plastic but with a pattern that was made to look like it had a weave. It had a handle at the top and a flap that snapped at the bottom. Dad's Sony reel-to-reel tape recorder. It must have been seven or eight years since I'd seen it. He'd bought it in the early 1960s, maybe when Marie was a baby. Every New Year's Eve he would bring it out and at midnight we would each say something into the microphone. We hadn't done it since Beatrice was born. 'The tapes are there too.' There was a pile of square boxes that held the reels of tape. Each was labelled with names and dates in Dad's scrawled cursive.

'Is Mom home from work yet?' I asked.

'No. And after she's getting stuff on Beatrice's camp list.'

'A flashlight, batteries and insect repellent,' Beatrice started listing. 'A canteen for when we hike in the mountains. Did you even know there were mountains in the South?'

'Where do you think the Appalachians and the Blue Ridge Mountains go, you idiot? Isn't your teacher teaching you any geography?' Thomas slid the suitcase back toward Beatrice, who was sitting cross-legged, watching him. 'Try that now.'

Beatrice slid the zip up and down and then stood, walking the perimeter of the living room carrying the empty suitcase, which was nearly the size of her.

'Have you listened?'

He shook his head.

'Should we?'

Thomas clicked open the case. It looked old-fashioned and huge compared to cassette tape recorders or even eight-tracks. He picked up a box labelled *December 31st 1972*. I had no idea how to use the machine, but Thomas put the reel on and threaded the tape through a slot at the bottom, then drew the tape up the other side, spinning it on to an empty reel. He clicked the switch. Nothing happened.

'It's not plugged in,' said Beatrice, marching past the couch, luggage in tow.

Thomas plugged it in and clicked the switch again. The reels began to turn. I looked at him sitting on the floor in front of the machine, his head down, waiting. I lay on the carpet and looked the other way, so I didn't have to watch him hearing it. At first there was nothing, and then the crackling of the record button being pressed and some whispering. A child's voice, very young, asking 'Is it on? Is it?' My father cleared his throat, making it formal as he talked to the future.

'Hello. This is Martin Gallagher speaking from Ardmore, Pennsylvania on the thirty-first of December 1972.' The sound of his voice in the living room reverberated against my ribs and stomach, the voice tinny and far away and more Irish than I remembered him sounding.

'It is a mild day for this time of year. Raining and sixty-two degrees. It is eleven thirty p.m., not long before we ring in 1973. I am here with my wife, Faye, and children

Marie, Thomas, Libby and Ellen. Each one of them is going to say hello and we'll start with the youngest, Ellen Gallagher.' He was shy and serious. There was a pause and a muffled sound as the microphone was passed to Ellen.

'Hello. I . . . My name is Ellen Gallagher. I'm three and.' There was a pause. She must not have known what to do. 'Happy New Year.' There was whispering behind her: 'Tell them what you wish for.' She must have been holding the microphone to her mouth because you could hear every breath. 'I wish . . . I can't remember.' There was another pause and then the tape switched off. I would be next. Again, the sound of the recording button being switched on. I lay with my cheek on the carpet and listened.

'Hello. I'm Libby Gallagher. I'm six and a half. In the first grade. My teacher is Miss Collins. She's very nice. You'd like her.'

Thomas snorted. My mom said I never shut up as a child.

'We are learning about the planets. We have to draw our favourite planet and write a page. I picked Pluto because Thomas says that is the furthest away from the sun, and I thought that was sad, and I chose Pluto because everything is frozen there and it is cold. And because it's the smallest.'

'Oh my God, you're giving a school report, you freak,' said Thomas, but we were both laughing; tears were running down my face.

'I want to wish everyone in the world Happy New Year. My wishes are that I will get to ride a horse, get a bike, the

Vietnam War would end and that my grandmother's cataracted eyes would get better.'

'You're next, Thomas,' said Beatrice, who was now sitting by the machine too.

The young Thomas cleared his throat just like Dad had. While I had practically shouted down the microphone, Thomas was whispering, and we strained to hear him.

'My name is Thomas Gallagher from Ardmore, Pennsylvania. I am eight years old and am the only boy in my family. I am in the third grade at St Colman's Catholic school. In 1973 I wish for a telescope and in 1973 I also wish to go fishing with my dad and maybe catch a fish or to go in a boat with him in a lake or the ocean.'

I wanted to make a joke but didn't trust myself to speak. His wishes made me sad.

The tape kept rolling and Marie had already started her recitation. 'I'm Marie Gallagher. I'm nine and the eldest of all the children.'

'So *there*,' said Thomas now.

'I'm in fourth grade. I like art and music and gym class. My wish this year is that my younger brother and sisters would behave and stop annoying me but most of all that I would get to meet the Beatles.'

'So Marie,' I said.

'I am now going to sing a song with my dad, Martin Gallagher.'

I don't think we'd ever listened back after the day itself. I remembered the ritual but not the recordings. I'd never heard my dad sing.

'This song is called "In My Life" and it is the only Beatles song that Martin Gallagher even half likes and was willing to learn. Faye Gallagher isn't joining us because, as Martin would say, she hasn't a note in her head.' And they started and sang the whole song together. We were all stuck in our separate places on the living room floor, not facing each other, listening to our father and Marie sing. His voice was like those Irish singers who sound as if they're singing through their noses, nasal and slightly shaky. It sounded like it was from a very long time ago. Marie's small choir voice next to his was sweet, and I could hear how happy she was to be singing this song with her dad, how serious it was because it was into a microphone and being recorded. And I had no idea when they'd learned this or how. Where had I been when that was happening? Marie must have memories of us all together, and of having something like a family life, things Thomas and I were too young to remember. Her ease talking about Mom and Dad, and how Martin teased Faye. I had no memories like that. Not even one.

Thomas switched off the recording. 'Shit, I wasn't expecting that.'

My back was still to him. 'I know.'

'I wish I could tell him stuff,' he said.

'What stuff?' asked Beatrice. I rolled over then to look at her. She was still holding the handle of her suitcase, looking at Thomas.

'I wish I could tell him he was a good father,' said Thomas. 'I don't think he knew.'

I felt the same.

'We should put them back before Mom gets home,' I said. Thomas started rewinding the tape, spinning the reel backwards with his finger. 'Bea, don't tell her we were listening to them. I don't think she even remembers they're up there.'

'Can we listen to the others? Another day when I get back from camp?'

I looked at Thomas.

'I guess,' he said. 'That's why Dad made them.'

I sat on the front steps, looking toward the top of the street, any minute expecting to see a black Camaro creep down the road. Sage had told Wilson about Space Port behind my back. She'd known before I did that Jack would want the whole night forgotten, knew other stuff about him at school. I felt left out, small and resentful. Everyone was full of secrets. Sage, me, my mother. And now I knew Mrs Boucher's. But I wanted to be sure.

At the top of Paul Lemen, I hesitated but kept going. I had never been on the McVays' driveway. Even when I was selling daisies for Daisy Day, I hadn't gone up because Wilson McVay lived there. The driveway and house were shaded by giant cottonwoods. I picked up a fallen twig as I walked toward the house. Through the glass extension I could see a large television and a fireplace and nice furniture with cushions. But outside, something about the place felt like it wasn't cared for, a neglect not that different from our own, the way weeds grew up along the house at the back of the bedded gardens and crabgrass had overwhelmed the mulch. Impatiens had shrivelled. Grass pushed through cracks in the asphalt driveway. It was Friday afternoon, and I wondered if his parents were already home and how I would explain what I was doing there. I looked at the front door. There was a large knocker but no bell. I had come this far. I lifted the knocker and rapped three times and waited. No one answered.

I snapped the twig in my hand as I stepped away and looked at the star pattern in the pith. It only appears in fallen cottonwood twigs or branches, not living ones. There is a story that the night wished for stars and asked the wind for help, and the wind shook the cottonwood and the twigs fell, releasing their hidden stars.

'What're you doing here?' The voice came from behind, startling me. Wilson was standing there with a cloth and a tub of wax. I saw the outdoor shed with a carport, and the Yamaha. He'd seen me go up to the door.

'Jesus, you scared me.'

'You're here to see my parents, then?'

'No, obviously.' I held up the two ends of the twig. 'You have cottonwood twigs on your driveway.'

'Is there something that you want?' He seemed irritated that I was at his house, even though he repeatedly intruded in ours.

'No. I need a favour.'

'Did something happen? Did you see him?'

'No, not that. I . . .'

Wilson just stared at me, wiping grease from his hands with the cloth.

'Will you check something for me tonight?'

I asked him if he'd drive up Horseshoe Trail Road from the Nike Site and past the Sun Bowl and see if there were any cars parked there or anyone walking on the road. It had to be at one, not before or after. But not to go down the Bouchers' driveway or even look down there. Sometimes she parked at the end of her driveway at that time. And could I trust him not to say any of this to anyone, ever?

'So you're, like, doing the Libby *Rockford Files*, spying on people?'

'Isn't this the kind of thing you're good at?'

'Maybe what people do up there at night is none of your business.'

'That's rich coming from you.'

'There's some stuff you should stay out of.' And I knew that he knew what I was looking for, and that he already knew the answer. But he was advising me on people's privacy when he violated everyone's privacy every day, mine especially.

'Okay, I have to go.' I walked down his driveway and picked up two more twigs. One to show Beatrice and one for her to take to camp. I wondered where Wilson's dog was. 'Where's your dog?' I called back.

'Who?'

'Your dog. Samson.'

'I don't have a dog.'

'Oh.' My heart skipped a beat. It unsettled me. Wilson was a very convincing liar.

By the time I got home both Ellen and Beatrice had their suitcases packed and ready in the living room for their departure the following morning. Mom had come home with the stuff from Beatrice's packing checklist and a set of pencils, charcoal and a sketch pad for Ellen. She said there had been a change of plans. She'd organized for the Gambinos to pick Ellen up on Sunday instead, so that she could do the costume for Peter and go to the parade. I knew this was for me; this was her trying. I could see her watching my face for a response. It must have fallen at first – it meant another day of worrying about Barbie Man. Ellen lit up and immediately started organizing: she needed to come with me that night to babysit so she could measure Peter and resize the vest, she'd get him to try everything on, she'd figure out how to attach the sign to the bike and could she also stay at the Sun Bowl to-morrow night for the fireworks after.

Ellen and I walked to the Bouchers' in silence, both of us watchful as we went up the road to cut through the trail. Coming into the tower lot, we could see the rem-nants of the party a few nights earlier. Under the blinking lights, six large black circles on the gravel where the fires had burned looked like moon craters. Further down, the trail was still blocked by branches, a few rusty bikes and tyres.

Ellen was holding a shopping bag with Peter's costume, needles, thread and extra material. She had streamers and strips of fabric and rolls of coloured crêpe paper and tape to decorate the bike. She should have been talking about the costume, or life with the Gambinos and Gabriel, or the art programme she'd been accepted into. Instead she was guarded and nervous. I hadn't told her that Thomas had seen Barbie Man on the mountain. Just one more day up here and we wouldn't have to think about it for two straight weeks. Tomorrow at the parade we'd be surrounded by people all day.

I was worried about seeing Mrs Boucher, worried she would read her own secret in my nervous fluster – talking too much, being jumpy. I found it hard to act normal.

Mrs Boucher had left Peter's Big Wheel in the living room and he kept trying to ride it. He was showing off in front of Ellen, who was taking the streamers and fabrics from the bag.

Peter got off the bike and stood at the table, watching. 'Are they for my bike?'

'Yep,' said Ellen. 'And you can help me, but first let's try your costume.'

Ellen fitted the hat, which was nearly as tall as him. The sign was laid out on the table and Mrs Boucher stood and watched.

'Ah, that's clever, Ellen. Dr Seuss. You see the world like an artist.'

Ellen blushed with pleasure.

I didn't know what Mrs Boucher's life had been like with Mr Boucher. Having seen him with his new fiancée and talked to him a few times, I couldn't imagine it had been good. He seemed superficial and interested in himself. Maybe it was hard for her up here, a house deep in the woods, alone with the kids. Now that I thought about it, my mother and Mrs Boucher weren't that different. Sage's words came back to me: *Don't you want her to be happy?* Mrs Boucher was young, probably still in her twenties. She had a job that was a profession. But that didn't make *her* entitled to an affair and not my mother. Mrs Boucher said she was a feminist, which Mom definitely wasn't. But that confused me too. If Mrs Boucher believed in the best for women, why would she hurt another one so deeply?

Mrs Boucher hugged Bruce, who was lying on the sofa watching Ellen work. 'Goodnight, my littlest chick.' She turned to Peter. 'And you – you behave for Ellen and stop running around like a wild man.' She stood and watched Ellen for a moment. She seemed tired or sad about something and I already regretted spying on her. She smoothed her dress with her hands. 'Okay, then. I'm off. Goodnight, girls.'

I took Bruce to bed while Ellen and Peter worked on the floor, weaving strips of red, white and blue crêpe paper around the Big Wheel. Peter was wearing his Dr Seuss hat with red, white and blue streamers coming out of the top. Ellen had used pipe cleaners to get the streamers to stick up a bit.

I picked up Mrs Boucher's *New York Times*. Some mornings we listened to the radio, but it was on Friday nights at Mrs Boucher's that I connected to the world. She had newspapers and magazines and television. Reagan was on almost every page. We hadn't voted for him. My mother had voted for Jimmy Carter. Reagan wanted to spend more money on nuclear arms, and he was against workers and the environment. My dad died before Reagan got the nomination but he had told me about him because Reagan was one of the actors who had testified against others during the McCarthy trials. My father had hated him for this. He said Reagan lacked honour.

One afternoon the summer before the election, we were driving down Lancaster Avenue and Marie noticed that the car in the lane next to us had a bumper sticker that read *Wyman Was Right*. It took me a minute to comprehend what this meant, that Reagan's first wife, an actress named Jane Wyman, was right to divorce him. Whoever it was didn't like Reagan either. At the next traffic light, we pulled alongside them in the next lane, Mom beeping and all of us waving and giving thumbs ups. The other driver just stared straight ahead. We must have looked like lunatics.

Everything in the paper was depressing: how Reagan was rolling back the reforms made by the civil rights movement in the 1960s and the environmental movements of the 1970s. Workers were in trouble. Air traffic controllers were getting ready to strike, while garbage haulers in New Jersey were already on strike and mountains of trash were piling up on the streets.

Little patriots on bikes, Abbey had said the other night, and I thought that more and more I was becoming like Dad, that things happening to America upset me. This was us in the newspaper, this was what the United States was becoming. Everything we cared about was being destroyed, the forests and our water systems, and here we were making decorations and celebrating this idea of us. I knew this was exactly what had separated my father from other Irish immigrants that we knew, who'd embraced it all and said America was the greatest country on earth. For them it was. They became part of it, took citizenship tests, got good jobs and mortgages. But we'd got stuck. My dad hadn't been able to talk like that and even though he was smart and worked harder than anyone I knew, he'd always seemed to struggle.

Soon Wilson would drive along Horseshoe because I had asked him. I wished I never had. It was like what my dad said about those who investigated others, that they were the ones who were most un-American. I wanted to call Wilson and say *No, don't.* But I didn't know his number and it was unlisted. I couldn't ask Sage.

By the time I'd got Peter to bed, Ellen had fallen asleep on the couch. I watched the TV with no sound, and looked at the clock. At twelve thirty the headlights hit the windows and for a few seconds stayed there. And for a moment I thought, *Oh, thank God, she's not stopping.* But then they cut. I'd made a terrible mistake. I tried to calm myself. Wilson hadn't liked the idea, and he'd never said he'd actually do it.

At one fifteen, the headlights came on and drew closer, making the tree trunks look as if they were moving across the room. Now Mrs Boucher was going to give me money, and I had spied on her. And I had to come back in the morning with Ellen to get Peter ready for the parade. I shook Ellen awake and was glad she was with me right then. I didn't feel like I could face Mrs Boucher alone.

On the ride home Mrs Boucher smoked and Ellen was still half-asleep. I couldn't think of anything to say, but sat upright and alert, half expecting Wilson to overtake us or Barbie Man to step out of the trees and flag down the car. Mrs Boucher dropped us at the top of our street. She rolled down her window as we got out.

'See you in the morning. Thank you, Ellen, for doing this with Peter. I wouldn't have known where to start.'

Ellen mumbled that she was happy to do it. We'd only walked a few yards down the road when I saw that someone was sitting on the quartz rock at the end of our driveway.

'Ellen, Wilson's on our driveway.' I was afraid she'd scream if I didn't warn her. But naming him seemed to wake her up and she waved at him in the dark. We got closer and Wilson stood. Before I could say *Please don't tell me, I've changed my mind*, he spoke.

'Outside the Nike Site. Mercedes W123. From twelve twenty-five until one fifteen.' I knew already, but it still sucked the breath out of me. Why had I asked him to do this? Why had I looked for proof?

'What, Wilson?' Ellen asked.

'Oh, nothing. Was just passing and thought I'd say hello to Stunt Girl, aka Wonder Woman, aka Ellen.'

'In the middle of the night? You're very strange.' Ellen was looking at him like his strangeness was the best thing ever.

22

We stood in the driveway with Beatrice's packed suitcase, waiting for my mom to reverse the car out of the garage. It was six a.m. Ellen and Thomas had said goodbye to Beatrice from their beds, but I'd come down. The sky at the eastern treeline behind the Walkers' turned pink as the sun started to climb. The air was cold, the uncut stalks of grass and leaves still wet with dew; it was the time of the morning we'd once have been heading out to cut lawns in Dad's truck, loading machines, getting ready for a day's work. A chickadee was singing its heart out in the dogwood at the side of the house. We'd had a lawn job where the woman in the house would come out and feed chickadees from her hand, they were that friendly with humans. She'd told us that the chickadee sometimes warns humans. It could be about danger or to foretell luck. I pointed the bird on the dogwood out to Beatrice, his grey sides and tail, black cap and bib, white cheeks and open mouth.

Beatrice had never left home before. I wanted to hold her and not let go. North Carolina seemed so far away. She wouldn't know anyone. Maybe all the other campers would be there with friends from school, from other Southern places, and she'd be all by herself.

'Remember that sometimes you have to talk first and ask girls questions to try to get to know them.' Beatrice looked like she was giving this serious consideration. 'And remember Southerners are always polite.'

'So am I.'

'Yeah, but they're, like, ridiculously polite. Think Sage a thousand times over. So be enthusiastic like . . . all the time. That's what they're like down there.'

'Okay. I'll try.' She looked unsure. It did sound exhausting. Her hair was pulled into low ponytails either side of her head. She was so serious and young.

My mom was wearing a short denim skirt with a suede belt, a white peasant top and her Dr Scholl's wood sandals. She looked like a teenager. The clothes were new, bought, I guessed, for her time away. I put the suitcase in the trunk, and the three of us stood there for a minute on the driveway looking at each other.

'Libby, don't forget: Ellen needs to be ready for the Gambinos by nine because they want to go to ten o'clock mass. The trash goes out Thursdays. Under no circumstances is anyone allowed in this house while I'm gone. I want you home at night by nine o'clock and Thomas by ten. I could be calling around those times.'

'The fireworks are on tonight at the Sun Bowl. They won't finish until after nine.'

'Well, just tonight, then,' and she stepped toward me with her arms out and held me, and I tried to hug her back. This was awkward for us. We weren't practised at it. I wished I could tell her to have a good time where she was staying, that she did deserve it, but the words wouldn't come out of my mouth. I remembered once when she'd tried to go to the beach for one day by herself, just to get some peace, and fell asleep in the dunes. She'd come home with terrible sunburn that blistered and was sick for days.

'We'll be good. Promise.' We moved apart, and I nodded at Beatrice, who was wearing a matching green Danskin outfit of shorts and top. 'People in the South are probably all dressed in flag today. Maybe Bea should arrive in some red, white or blue.'

'Oh God. The Fourth of July. We'll stop somewhere on the road.'

I hugged Beatrice then, her little frame smack against me, and I squeezed her until I knew she couldn't breathe, and she laughed. 'Stamp to scare rattlesnakes and only swim when there's a lifeguard. And have fun.'

'Bye, Libby.' She sat in the back of the car and waved out the window until they reached the end of the driveway.

The blare of the fire engine's siren startled me. The red light started to spin and all those that had gathered broke into a cheer. The parade was starting and ending at the Sun Bowl, and while the loop was only a mile and a bit, it would take about an hour and a half to do the circuit with kids on Big Wheels and tricycles and getting pulled in wagons. We were there from the start. Ellen had end-ed up decorating one of our bikes as well with Meredith Hunter, back from her vacation, and was cycling along. My job was to stay close to Peter and push him on the Big Wheel when he needed it. Of the twenty or so cyclists that had arrived at the Sun Bowl, Peter's bike was by far the best. Ellen had done both sides of the poster board so you could read *I Am Sam, Sam I Am* from behind and in front. The streamers fluttered red, white and blue from the top hat and handlebars. Ellen had put white face paint very lightly across Peter's face and drawn the flag hearts on each cheek. He wore a white T-shirt and the vest Ellen had sewn. Around his neck was a giant red bow made from crêpe paper, with matching bows on his sneakers. The rest of the bikes were just covered in streamers, crêpe paper and glittery pinwheels but Peter and Ellen stood out. She had traced matching hearts on her own cheeks and was also wearing a white T-shirt and a tiny vest made from the leftover fabric.

'That's just so adorable,' I heard one of the mothers say as the fire truck led us down Horseshoe Trail Road toward Forge Mountain Drive. Kids rang their bike bells, and I held on to the back of Peter's seat as we headed down the hill, to keep him from hurtling forward. At the corner of Forge Mountain Drive another group was waiting, more bikes and streamers and two toddlers in strollers being pushed by their dads, who carried giant milk bottles and a big sign with the American flag. Kids cycled into the growing parade as we passed their houses. There was a procession of cars behind us, beeping, and the fire engine blared. Marie would say this was her idea of hell on earth, but large groups of people coming together always got me and I felt emotional. At Paul Lemen we met our first real competitor. He had a bike designed as a fighter jet and the sign read *We Salute Our Brave Military*. His dad was probably an engineer or something, it was so well done. Peter was pedalling furiously, adrenalin-pumped from all the noise and excitement and older kids on their Flyers. We went past our street and when we came up to Hamilton another boy joined us on a Big Wheel, dressed in red, white and blue. Like Peter, he had white face paint, except his face was painted to look sad. Big black teardrops fell from his child eyes. Behind him he hauled a six-foot papier-mâché flag and a sign that read *Please Don't Burn My Flag*.

'Do you think the flag one will win?' Ellen asked, pushing her bike beside me.

'Probably. But they should disqualify parents who do everything. It's not fair.'

'Yeah, well, it's not like we let Peter do very much either.'

Back at the Sun Bowl, the kids circled the basketball court in front of the judges for a few laps. Ellen and I sat on the swings with Bruce while Mrs Boucher did the three-legged race with Peter. I hadn't been able to look at her all day. I didn't know whether I hated her or myself more. Someone announced with a megaphone that they were now going to have the prizegiving, could all the kids bring their bikes; the winners would be asked to do a circuit of the court. Ellen and I stood near the see-saws, watching as they started calling out the prizes. There was Best Effort and Most Original and Most Patriotic and Craziest – the two dads with the giant bottles won that. They jogged around the court like they had just run a marathon, beers in one hand, the giant bottles in the other, and we all clapped.

The man with the megaphone stood up again. 'Now we'll have the first, second and third prizes. In third place, for an original and creative depiction of two great American Sams, is Peter Boucher with *I Am Sam, Sam I Am*.'

There was a small cheer and Mrs Boucher helped Peter put his hat back on and push the Big Wheel on to the court. She gave Ellen a shy thumbs up, and I felt my insides rip. She was always so nice to us.

'In second place,' the megaphone man continued, 'for a patriotic salute to our war heroes, is Scott Jacobs with *We Salute Our Brave Military*.' A huge cheer erupted and a group of men were all slapping each other's backs, one of whom I guessed must be Scott's dad.

'Finally,' the megaphone voice announced, 'in first place, a sentiment that touched the hearts of all of us here, is Duke Costello with *Please Don't Burn My Flag*.' Grown men roared and started chanting 'Duke – Duke – Duke' and there was more back-slapping and hooting while the three boys who'd each won a prize circled the basketball court on their contraptions. I looked at them pedalling, three ideas of America, completing their victory lap to the cheers of mostly grown men.

I thought about Abbey's older brother whooping at the campfire the other night. He had done multiple tours in Vietnam. He and his friends weren't here. I wasn't sure if the flag-burning was a reference to anti-war demonstrations in America or if it was the burning of the American flag in Iran.

'Ellen's should've won.' Thomas was next to me. I was surprised he had come. 'It was the only one that really looked homemade. Those others look like they were made by professional designers.'

Peter was with Ellen and Mrs Boucher, holding a white third-place ribbon and a little bronze trophy.

'Well done, Sam,' said Thomas.

Peter was about to correct him and then broke into a smile. 'Thanks,' he said.

Mrs Boucher was heading home. They wouldn't stay for the picnic. I knew none of this was her kind of thing. She gave Ellen a hug. 'Thank you. I think you've just given him the best day of his life.' I looked at the ground and mumbled goodbye. I felt wretched.

Thomas, Ellen and I wandered around together for a while. Out on the baseball diamond, children sprinted with eggs and spoons and ran wheelbarrow races, and families spread out picnic blankets and lawn chairs. On the hill a group of men had carried up grills and started to fire them up. We'd have hot dogs and hamburgers later and wait for nightfall and fireworks.

By late afternoon, more teenagers had arrived. Ellen wanted to walk around with Meredith. I scanned the crowd. We were surrounded by neighbours and families. There was no one remotely like Barbie Man around. I told her not to leave the Sun Bowl. Thomas disappeared with a kid he knew from swimming. I could smell the hot dogs and hamburgers cooking and saw kids coming down the embankment. The field was getting dark, the sandstone hill lit by the sun dropping behind it. I went up and got two hot dogs, squirting mustard and ketchup across both. Coming down, I met Abbey. I wondered how she'd known about Mrs Boucher and if other people had known it too.

'You're getting just downright social, Libby Gallagher.'

'I know,' I said with my mouth full of hot dog. 'I'm like the mountain's social butterfly.'

'Careful what you wish for,' she said.

I waited while she got her hot dog and we sat up on the hill by the swim club, our backs against the fence, waiting for the sun to fall. On this side of the fence, facing the Sun Bowl, honeysuckle climbed through the shrubbery and wound itself around the links, reaching in some parts all the way to the barbed wire at the top. The air was heavy with its scent. I picked one and inhaled it in my palm. In Ireland, honeysuckle growing around doorways and houses kept away bad spirits. I pinched the bottom of the flower and pulled out the stamen with the nectar. I'd never thought of my father as superstitious but so much of what he'd taught me was how things in nature carried messages between worlds.

Next to me, Abbey started to roll a joint, completely unfazed that there was a field of parents below us. She didn't even try to conceal it, lighting it and holding it between her forefinger and thumb and squinting as she inhaled. She held the smoke in her lungs, clamping her mouth shut, and then offered the joint to me. I shook my head. She held the smoke for a few more seconds, then exhaled and raised the joint high up in the air, gesturing toward someone.

'There's our golden girl.'

Sage was coming across the court, looking up at us. I wanted to get to her before she got to us.

'Abbey, I need to talk to Sage for a few minutes. It's really important. We'll come back.' I ran down the hill.

'Hey,' said Sage. She had on her 1976 Rolling Stones T-shirt with the flag tongue.

'Very patriotic of you,' I said.

'Charlotte begged me not to wear it today.'

Hearing Charlotte's name pained me. I didn't know how to start. I couldn't say what I'd found out. I still wanted to know what she was telling Wilson about Barbie Man, about me, maybe even about Jack. Wilson's *bitter education* remark kept replaying in my head. I didn't know how to put in words this well of feelings.

'What's up with you and Wilson?' My tone was wrong. It sounded like an accusation.

'What do you mean? Nothing. You're the one that left the other night on his Yamaha.'

'You talked to him on the phone about Space Port and Barbie Man. You never told me you did.'

'I have to tell you when I talk to Wilson?' Sage crossed her arms. We were both standing, facing each other at the edge of the field.

'How do you even have his number? It's not listed.'

'Jesus, Libby. I have his number because he gave it to me. Because I buy pot off him. You're so uptight about that shit, I'd never tell you.'

There was that hint that I was childish.

'If it was about Barbie Man you should've said it to me, not him. He's the one that's made it all worse.'

The dark had settled around us, on the hill where the grills billowed smoke, around the swing sets; I felt it sinking into me.

'It's hard to say anything to you,' she said. 'I'm always

walking on eggshells. We can't tell Faye what happened to Ellen. We can't talk about Faye. Or your dad. Especially not your dad. I know you miss him but it's like you're blind to the other stuff and how he was toward your mom. You act like he was perfect and everything is Faye's fault and Faye's a monster.'

I could feel that dread that she would say something we didn't say. I needed to hurt her back first.

'You know, your father isn't so perfect. You should ask him about Mrs Boucher.'

For a second it hung in the air between us and I wanted to press rewind, spin it back into me, because it could never be unsaid or undone.

Instead of lashing out at me she just said, 'What are you even talking about? Ask him what about her?'

Shame seeped through me. I felt smaller than I ever had. Sage was still sort of shaking her head like I had asked her a difficult math equation, and then she started to laugh, seeing something beyond me.

'Oh shit.' I turned around. Tony was walking over with a big grin on his face, carrying two lawn chairs, a blanket and a cooler. 'Oh my God, he's treating it like a date. I said I'd watch the fireworks with him.'

Like that, it was as if she had forgotten what I had just said and all that had just passed between us, oblivious to its significance for her. Tony looked like he had dressed for the date. He was wearing a short-sleeved dress shirt tucked into jeans and he'd parted his hair on the side and combed it back. He looked like Richie from *Happy Days*, and it made me smile despite the empty feeling in my stomach.

'Sage Adams, may I have the honour of watching the sky spectacle together with you?' He bent forward as if to bow.

Sage looked at me, wondering if leaving me like this would hurt my feelings, blind to how I had just tried to hurt her to the core.

'It's okay. I'm going to watch with Abbey.'

Tony and Sage set up in the field where all the families were. Abbey and I went over to the merry-go-round. We lay on our backs waiting, slowly circling. I let my hair trail on the ground and looked at the sky. So much had happened. I couldn't get any thoughts straight in my head. I asked Abbey if she knew where the North Star was. I'd read that you would know where you were if you could find it, like sailors. She didn't. She didn't feel like talking. There were millions to choose from. A rocket shot across from the far hill and white stars exploded above us. Then the whole sky started to crackle. Flames launched across the night, plunged and extinguished above us.

Afterward, when it was all over, I stayed lying on the merry-go-round, looking up, still spinning. I could hear people milling around, folding up lawn chairs, gathering children and bikes. Families leaving together. I suddenly felt cold. Tears burned my eyes. Nothing beautiful lasted.

Abbey said she was heading, and I said goodbye to her still lying on the merry-go-round. I wanted to go home.

Ellen. I had forgotten Ellen. I sat up and looked around. I hadn't seen her in hours. I stood up and started running, first toward the field and then back to the playground. I couldn't see her. Her bike had been left on its side by the see-saws, but she was nowhere to be seen. I had told her to stay in the Sun Bowl. Crowds of people were moving through the dark and funnelling out through the gate. There were packs of teenagers on the road and along the fence and I pushed past them, looking for her. The gate was too crowded, so I crawled through the fence on to the road to see whether Ellen or Thomas were there. How had I let myself forget?

I was shoulder-to-shoulder with the crowd when I saw it. About thirty yards from the swim club driveway. It was parked almost at the trail entrance – a black Camaro. I wanted to scream Ellen's name. I looked around. There were people everywhere and cars were pulling out, but no Ellen. My heart thumped against my ribs. I walked toward the Camaro. Its windows were dark. I was afraid to get close. I stared at the back of it from the other side of the street. I read the plate – *Pennsylvania 3F5-727*. Ellen. There was a dent where the fender emblem should be and an image of Wilson with a hammer flashed before me. It was *his* car. It was definitely Barbie Man's. I looked in the windows as we passed. Was it empty? In the dark, I couldn't be sure. I had that sensation again of just wanting to kneel on the ground. Where was Ellen? I ran.

23

More and more people filed up the street, carrying kids, Big Wheels, lawn chairs. I shouted for Ellen in the crowd, calling into the woods and over toward the Sun Bowl. I ran up the driveway of the swim club. Cars were backing out and turning, switching on headlights. I saw the Hunters getting into their station wagon.

'Meredith!' I shouted, and ran toward them, breathless. 'Where's Ellen?'

Meredith shrugged. 'I haven't seen her since the fireworks started.'

'Didn't she watch them with you? Where did you last see her?' I was shaking her shoulders.

'Up here. We were up here but when the fireworks started she said she wanted to watch them with you, and she went back down to the Sun Bowl.'

'Oh my God.' She stepped back from me. I knew I looked deranged, but I couldn't stop myself. 'What way, Meredith? *Think!* What way did she walk?' I was shouting.

'Libby, is everything okay?' Mrs Hunter had come around from the other side of the car and now stood between me and Meredith. 'What's going on?'

'I can't find Ellen. She's missing. I really need to find her.'

'I'm sure she's just somewhere in the crowd.'

'No.' I was shaking my head. 'No, Mrs Hunter, something bad has happened to her. Something terrible.'

I didn't wait for her to ask what, but started running toward the chain-link fence. The fastest way back was down the hill. I couldn't even find the path; I just fell and crashed through the bramble thicket. I could feel thorns scratching my legs and face, catching my hair and pulling it out. I stumbled and burrs stuck to my cut-offs and hair and hands. I could hear Mrs Hunter calling me from the top of the hill. I was shouting Ellen's name. I had started crying. When I came through the thicket into the Sun Bowl, it was almost empty. Only handfuls of people were left, mostly teenagers. I yelled Ellen's name over and over. The licence plate number echoed in my head. *3F5-727*.

Out on the field I could see two lawn chairs – Sage and Tony. I started running. 'Sage!' I called her over and over. They both stood up as I came hurtling toward them. 'Ellen. I can't find her. Barbie Man's here. His Camaro's by the trail. I can't find her. Help me.'

'Libby. Calm down. Maybe she went home.'

'No, the bike's by the see-saw.'

'She's probably up at the swim club and is on her way.'

'Meredith said Ellen went to find me at the start of the fireworks. She must have walked past him on the way down from the swim club.'

'Are you sure he's here? How do you know it's his car? Did you see him?'

'Sage. It's his car. Believe me.'

'Come on,' said Sage. 'We'll look together.' The three of us started across the field toward the playground. All the bikes that had been lined up were gone and just Ellen's bike was left, lying on its side with the streamers covered in dirt. Sage stopped and looked at it. 'Tony, who lives the closest?'

'Bouchers or Millers,' he said. 'The Millers are closer to the road.'

'Go to the Millers' now and get them to call the police.'

'What?'

'I'm not kidding.' Sage had on her take-charge voice. 'It's serious. Tell them a child is missing and that a man who attacked her before is here.'

'Whoa. What the fuck?'

'I'm not kidding,' she said again. 'Go. Run.' Tony took off and Sage started calling for Ellen. She stopped people, saying, 'We need your help – a girl is missing.' She spoke like a concerned adult. 'A child is missing. Her name is Ellen. Please help us.' More and more people started calling her.

We came out on to the street and I yelled for Ellen. I could hear other people talking – 'A little girl is missing' – and I knew they thought she was three or something.

'She's twelve but very small. It's an emergency,' I said to a woman who was calling Ellen's name. As we came up the hill, I could see Mrs Hunter talking to the man with the megaphone from the Mountain Association, who was putting barbecue utensils into the back of his car. I could hear people down in the field calling Ellen's name. There were shouts for her at the swim club.

Sage was beside me as we got to the peak of the hill, where the Camaro had been parked. It was gone.

'Oh my God. It was there. He's taken her.'

'Who? Who's taken her?' It was the man with the megaphone.

Mrs Hunter came with him and put her hand on my shoulder. 'Libby, try to slow down and tell us what's happened.'

'There was a man here in a Camaro. He hurt Ellen before. He's taken her.' I pointed to the space where he had been parked. 'It was there just a few minutes ago.'

Thomas suddenly appeared. 'Libby, what's wrong? Why's everyone calling for Ellen?'

'Thomas. She's gone. She left her bike and the man's taken her.' A crowd of people had started to form around us.

'What man? What are you talking about? Sage, what's wrong with her?'

'Earlier this summer, a man attacked Ellen and tried to hurt her. Libby saw his car and we can't find Ellen.'

'Thomas, it's the man you saw. The horrible weird man you saw when you were walking with the lawnmower. Him.'

'I don't understand.'

'Ellen was in his car and he wouldn't let her out and she jumped while it was moving.' Sage's voice was calm and clear.

'Libby, what's she talking about?'

I told Thomas what had happened that night on the road, Ellen hitchhiking and the man touching her, how she'd jumped. How we didn't tell anyone. All these people were listening, and I couldn't say we were afraid Mom would get in trouble for throwing her out in the dark to begin with.

Thomas turned to the megaphone man. 'We need the police. Can someone please get the police? Please. We need help.'

'Get Marie.' As I said it, I knew I was going to be sick. I stumbled over to the side of the road and threw up in the decorative shrubbery the swim club had planted at the entrance. I could hear Sage talking to Thomas, who was saying it was his fault if anything happened to Ellen; he was supposed to be the one in charge. Their voices seemed both amplified and very far away. In the distance, neighbours and strangers were calling Ellen's name, and I heard sirens. People were talking all around us, murmuring and whispering, and one woman explained to another, 'It's those kids from the other side of the mountain – you know, the Irish ones with no father.'

Two police cars arrived, and the crowd parted a bit. The megaphone man seemed to be giving an overview of what was happening. 'The sister's over here,' someone said. A policeman came over to me, but my body had started to shake so hard I couldn't talk.

'Does anyone have a blanket?' he asked. 'I'm Officer Day. We're going to find your sister. We need you to be calm and we need you to co-operate. Can you try to breathe a little slower?'

I breathed in deep through my nose and tried to let it out slow.

'Good,' he said. 'Nice and slow. Just a few more of those.' I breathed and he put his hand at my back and guided me over to Thomas and Sage. 'Okay,' he said. 'We're going to find her. First I need a description of your sister and a description of the man you think has taken her.'

Someone had brought a picnic blanket and put it around my shoulders.

'Our sister's Ellen Gallagher. She's twelve years old,' said Thomas.

'But very small for her age,' I added. 'Not even seventy pounds. She only comes up to here' – I showed them half-way between my elbow and shoulder – 'just a few inches past four feet.'

'Okay. And the man you think may have hurt her?'

'Tall. Very, very tall. He has long blonde, almost silver-white, hair. All the way down to below his belt. And long fingernails on his right hand.'

'Age?'

'Thirty, maybe?' Officer Day was writing it all down in a notebook. 'I know more,' I said. 'He drives a black Camaro. He lives in Pottstown and his licence plate number is 3F5-727, State of Pennsylvania.'

Thomas was staring at me like I was a freak. 'How do you know all this?'

Officer Day turned to one of the others: 'Can you run that?' From inside the car I could hear the feed of information: 'Suspect . . . black Camaro . . . the plate . . .' The crackling of the transceiver. Officer Day turned back to me. 'Do you know this man?'

'I saw him about a week ago when we were in the King of Prussia mall. We saw him in Friendly's downstairs and then again upstairs in Space Port.'

'And you say the suspect lives in Pottstown. Did he tell your sister this?'

I hesitated. 'I don't think he told her anything like that. I think we heard it. Me and my older sister heard that there was a guy from Pottstown that fit that exact description.'

'So you did report the incident to some people?'

I had told Mrs Boucher, who was a member of the legal profession. She hadn't reported it or even told my mother. Grady Adams was a medical doctor. He knew and he hadn't told. Wilson was over eighteen. Even Marie was now an adult. I was going to get so many people in so much trouble.

'No. Not like that. We didn't tell anyone. Just my older sister knew people and we heard there might be someone like that in Pottstown.'

'Marie knew?' Thomas looked at me like I was Judas Iscariot. 'Libby, stop fucking around. This is serious. Tell them everything.' He knew I was holding back and he was right. I had to say everything.

The radio broke in then: 'Affirmative on the Pennsylvania plate 3F5-727. Camaro. Vehicle registered to Julius Korhonen, Ash Drive, Pottstown, over' – crackle – 'Units dispatched, over.' The second squad car reversed and started down the hill, the light spinning but the siren silent.

Officer Day turned to me again. 'Are your parents home? We're going to need them to file a statement to say Ellen is missing.' I shook my head. 'Can you give us a number of where they are?' I looked at Thomas. Neither of us knew where Mom was staying.

'Our father isn't alive,' Thomas said. 'Our mom took my youngest sister to camp in North Carolina. My eldest sister Marie's an adult. She's in charge. She's in Philadelphia right now.'

'If you don't know the number for your mother, can we have your sister's?'

'It's at the house,' Thomas said. 'I don't know it.'

'Did this man know Ellen's name or where she lived?' Officer Day asked me.

'Not her name but she said she lived on Valley Forge Mountain when she first got into the car before he did anything. And he could have found out her name because she had on our school uniform.'

'What time did you see his car here?'

'Just after the fireworks, like maybe half an hour ago or forty minutes, but then ten minutes or so later it was gone.'

'Why do you think he came looking for her tonight?'

I was about to say that maybe he'd come looking for others when Officer Day stepped aside to let someone push through. It was Grady Adams.

'Sage? What's happened to Ellen?' He'd been running and was out of breath.

I focused on Officer Day's question. Barbie Man had come to kill Wilson. But he must have seen Ellen and . . . maybe he'd taken Ellen to get her to name him. To show him where he lived? But then, what would he do with her?

I started to talk. 'Someone helped us when Ellen got hurt. He is the one who found out who the guy was and he went to Pottstown with some boys from around here and they beat him and messed up his car and cut part of his hair bald. I think he's looking for them.'

Thomas kicked the ground. 'Are you all fucking crazy? What's wrong with you, Libby?'

'Who was this person who helped you?' Officer Day had the pencil poised in his hand.

'It was Wilson,' said Thomas. 'Right?'

The two policemen exchanged glances. 'Wilson McVay?' asked Officer Day.

'Yes,' I said.

'We are going to need to take statements from both of you at the station in Phoenixville. We'll have to call your older sister to come there.'

Grady Adams stepped forward. 'I know these children. I am happy to come with them.'

Officer Day shook his head. 'I'm sorry but it has to be someone who is a legal guardian or related.'

Thomas backed away from me, and Sage came closer, putting her arm around my shoulder. Tony was there, trying to be helpful.

'People,' said Officer Day to the crowd still standing around, 'unless you have information relating to this incident, can I ask that you find your vehicles and leave.'

The crowd backed off a little. I saw Abbey watching with the others even though she'd left ages ago. She'd probably heard the sirens.

Officer Day turned to me. 'Can you show me where the Camaro was parked?' It was just a few yards away and everyone moved as I showed the policeman the exact place where I'd seen it. Officer Day turned to the other cop and asked for the light. It was the kind of floodlight they'd used the night we pool-hopped. It lit the ground and Officer Day and his partner walked around. I stood back while they combed over the area. Someone tugged on my blanket. It was Abbey.

'Your brother took off,' she whispered. 'He's gone down the trail.'

I looked at Sage. She'd heard it too. I felt weak then and just sat down on the ground. Where would he go? To see if Ellen was at home? No. He knew she wouldn't have left the bike.

Sage sat down next to me. And I loved her all over again, infinitely, because she just understood it all without me having to say, and she loved me. Grady came over too. He sat on his haunches and took my wrist and felt my pulse. He squeezed my arm.

'They'll find her, Libby. She'll be okay. I just wish I had said something from the start. To your mother or someone. It just didn't sit right with me not to say anything.'

Sage looked at me and shook her head to try to tell me again that it wasn't her. I already knew it wasn't. For the second time that night I could see her trying to grasp something, like a picture that comes into focus and then recedes.

'Sage,' I said, 'tell Wilson? That Ellen's gone and Barbie Man could be looking for him?'

The two officers helped me into the back of the patrol car. 'Where's her brother?' people had started asking. I could hear the murmur of his name: 'Thomas Gallagher . . . was here a few minutes ago . . .'

'Did you see where your brother went?' Officer Day asked me.

'No. He was next to me. Maybe he went home to see if she's there?'

Officer Day told the other cop to call it in and I listened: Thomas's name, Ellen's name repeated by a voice muffled by static and interference as we made the three-point turn and headed down Horseshoe. Families were still standing on the side of the road, looking in at me sitting in the back of the car as we drove past. I looked back at them, desperate. Tears fell but it wasn't like regular crying. I wanted my mom. *Please help me.* What would he do to Ellen? She should have been at the Gambinos' tonight, making custard and cakes with Gabriel, wearing aprons. This was all my fault. What would he do to her? I couldn't think of that, her slight frame and his giant one, him hurting her. I dry-heaved in the back and Officer Day said, 'Pull in, she's going to be sick.'

I stood out on the side of the road and threw up in the grass, and Officer Day said, 'Just take a second there in the fresh air.' Cars coming down from the fireworks passed me as I bent over, hands on knees. It was right near the spot where only a week earlier I had stood with Grady Adams and Mrs Boucher and the dead doe. I thought about how Ellen had jumped that night. And what was Thomas doing now? How I had done nothing that time at Jessie Warren's house. Wherever Ellen was right now, she would fight. Maybe she'd seen Barbie Man and had run for her life and hidden. Even Thomas, who barely left his room, was out there, somewhere in the dark, trying to save her. I had to get a grip on myself, so that I could act.

263

Everything was moving in slow motion, the sway of trees, cricket sounds, drivers slowing down to gape through the dark glass, me looking back, searching for Ellen's pale face. The Walkers passed, the whole family looking straight ahead, as if they didn't know me. I breathed in, like my PE teacher had said, to be ready to encounter the other warrior, to be brave.

'I'm okay,' I said to Officer Day, who had stood a few feet away, trying to give me privacy. He handed me a Kleenex. I blew my nose and we got back into the squad car. 'Can we go to my house first?' I asked. 'I need to get my sister's number in Philadelphia.'

The house was in total darkness and I felt better going in with Officer Day and his partner. I shook the handle of the garage doors until they unlocked and then rolled them up.

'You should get that fixed,' Officer Day said. We went up to the hallway outside the living room.

'Ellen?' I called. 'Thomas?' No response. 'I'll be right down,' I said.

I ran up the five steps to the next hallway and went into our room. Marie's number was on a slip of paper on the bookshelf. I stuffed it in my pocket, then took off my red-and-white-striped shirt and opened the drawer that held the clothes Marie had left behind. I needed something dark. I grabbed a black T-shirt and opened the closet. I took down the B. Altman box with the Marksman airgun. We had only used it a couple times out in the woods. Marie thought Thomas would be annoyed that she'd gotten one and not him, so we'd never let him know. Mom would have killed us, and then killed Dad. I put the pistol into my back pocket and a handful of darts in the other and pulled the T-shirt over them. I went back into the hallway.

'There in a minute,' I called. 'Just going to the bathroom.'

Inside, I locked the door, turned on the sink to make noise, went over and pressed the toilet handle down, lifting the window as it flushed. I stepped out on to the thin ledge and jumped across to the lower roof above the dining room. I landed on my hands and knees, feeling the scraped burn on my right knee. I prayed they hadn't heard the thump. I moved down the roof, to where its lowest point met the ground, and jumped again. I landed on my feet and sprinted straight up through the woods. The trail was ahead.

24

At Forge Mountain Drive, I crossed the road and slipped into the woods instead of going up the road. This section of the trail was less defined than the one behind our house. When it rained a small stream ran through it, and in heavy downpours it could wash out, its shape shifting, boulders carried several yards, loose shingle dumped in sheets and the water redirected, gouging even deeper into the earth.

I walked close to thickets and trees, avoiding the gully that had swallowed the path. In front of me were sycamores. I could feel the strips of fallen bark underfoot. The American sycamore sloughs off its bark like a snake. Ghosts of the Forest, they're called, for their spooky white-grey branches. There had been a lawn we took care of in Penn Valley with sycamores all across the front, and as the lawnmower chopped up the fallen strips of bark the dust would catch in my throat and stay there for days.

The waxy leaves of rhododendron brushed against my bare legs. I thought about copperheads nesting under the rocks below me, feeling the vibration of my footfall, coiled like springs, waiting to strike. There was movement in the underbrush beside me and I jumped. Whatever it was, I could hear it moving away in the thicket, a deer or fox that I'd startled. Could it be a coyote? Once, Thomas and I had heard a high wailing sound in the woods. Not one animal, but like a chorus of howls and cries. 'Are they dogs?' I'd asked. Thomas thought coyotes. He said there were increasing numbers of them throughout Pennsylvania, but not to worry because they didn't bother humans.

I walked until the trail neared the road, and cut through a property in order to come out on High Point. I would have to go the rest of the way by road. I ran down the short hill to Forge Mountain Drive, turned left and sprinted toward Paul Lemen. There were headlights in the distance, coming up the hill, and I turned into the woods behind the houses and waited for the car to pass. Pushing through thick understorey, I moved toward a light in a window. A woman was standing in its frame, like she was a painting, drinking a glass of water. I waited. When she turned and walked away, I ran across her backyard to the side of the house. The blue glow of a television flickered through the curtains. I crouched low, my head beneath her window, and pressed along the side wall. The air conditioning unit was running, one of those that stands apart from the house and spins and makes your voice go funny if you talk into it.

I squatted there against the wall, beside the humming unit, and took the Marksman and one dart out of my back pockets. I released the slide latch, pointed the barrel up and pulled the slide out until I heard a click. Then I pressed it all the way in, feeling for the second click. The gun was cocked. I pushed on the safety and then the loading button at the front, tipping up the barrel. There are two slots on a Marksman. I felt them with my finger, holding the bottom one where the darts go. I searched for the dart in the fold of my T-shirt and forced it forward into the barrel. My hands were shaking, clammy and unsteady. I put the gun in my lap and wiped my palms on Marie's shirt, then I unlocked the safety. It was ready to fire. Gripping the gun, I tried not to hit the trigger. I didn't even know for sure if the dart would hurt someone. In the woods, darts fired from a long distance bounced off trees, but even from five yards they pierced through bark and into the heartwood all the way down to the dart's shaft. (I'd told Marie that of all the things we could shoot, I didn't want it to be trees.) If I had to shoot tonight, I would need to be up close.

I stayed up against the wall and when I got to the front corner of the house, I looked across the road to the McVays'. There were no lights on at the road, and I couldn't see any through the trees. I hadn't seen Wilson at the fireworks. Maybe they were already asleep. I sprinted as fast as I could across the road to the end of their drive-way, then went into the woods between their house and the neighbour's. I knew there was a shed with a carport on that side; I'd seen Wilson working in it. If his motorcycle was there, it meant he was too, and I would ring the bell. As I got closer, I could see a single utility light on at the side of the house.

I nearly walked right into the shed before I saw it in the darkness. I leaned against the back of it, still holding the Marksman. I thought I smelled cigarette smoke and wondered if Wilson was in the shed, but there was a window next to me and it was black inside. The driveway was empty. Wilson's dad's Buick wasn't there either.

I heard an engine in the distance. A motorcycle decelerating, taking the turn from Forge Mountain Drive, coming down the hill. There was a rustle somewhere close, maybe a cat or something under the shed or on the other side. I stayed still, listening. I thought I heard a cough, like someone clearing their throat before spitting. Then the light was coming up the driveway through the trees. Wilson. I put the gun in my back pocket. The motorcycle passed where I was crouching and turned at the top of the driveway. I walked toward it along the side of the shed, slowly, my hand trailing against the wood cladding. Wilson's headlight blinded me, and I stopped. There were two people on the bike. The second person was too big to be Ellen. My eyes adjusted to the glare, and I saw that it was Thomas. I was about to shout to them, but they were both looking at something else. Their stillness stopped me. Against the headlight a dark shadow fell like a tree across the lawn and me. Someone was moving toward them, his shadow enormous in the headlights: Barbie Man. He must have been on the other side of the shed waiting. He stepped out in front of them, and I wanted to scream *Drive away, Wilson! Run, Thomas!* Why weren't they doing anything? He walked toward them. His left hand was still in the sling, but in his right hand he had a gun.

'Kill the bike!' he shouted.

The engine cut. The headlight spluttered out and all of them were just dark shapes outlined by the dim light attached to the house.

'Off. Fucking kneel.'

Thomas eased off the back of the bike and knelt on the ground, his arms at his sides. Wilson leaned down over the Yamaha like he was trying to get something from his boot.

'Get off the bike. Hands where I can see them.' Barbie Man stepped closer, waving the gun. The bike toppled on its side as Wilson swung his leg over it. In a single movement he lunged toward Barbie Man, tackling him. They fell together, Barbie Man landing on his slinged arm, screaming. Thomas tried to stand up and at the same time there was a popping sound, a flash, and then a blast reverberating around us, like aftershocks. He'd shot the gun. He'd shot Wilson.

Wilson was on the ground, scrambling on his side to get away from Barbie Man. He looked bewildered, checking his shirt. Barbie Man was sitting on the ground, pointing the gun at him. Wilson wasn't hit. Barbie Man had missed.

'Kneel on the fucking ground. Over by him.' Wilson stood and took slow cautious steps backward to where Thomas was kneeling.

Barbie Man tried to stand. Even in the dark, I could see clots of black blood spouting from his nose. He tucked the white sling close to his body and stumbled, still pointing the gun at Thomas and Wilson. He was in pain. He walked in a circle twice, his body bent, then stopped and turned. Then, suddenly, he moved fast toward them, almost running, long strides, and kicked Wilson in the face with his heavy black boot. I heard the crunch, the sound of bone splintering. Barbie Man stepped back again and took another walking kick at him, this time in the ribs, and Wilson fell toward Thomas. I wanted to scream to Thomas *Get out of the way, get away from both of them.* Wilson was slumped across Thomas's knees. Barbie Man seemed demented. 'Fuck you!' he shouted, kicking the Yamaha on the ground, shattering the headlight.

Wilson's neighbours in the blue-glow room with the curtains drawn must have heard the shot and his shouting. *Call the police, please*, I willed them. Thomas was leaning over Wilson, whispering something to him, trying to help him sit up. I took a few steps toward them.

'Get the fuck off him,' Barbie Man shouted at Thomas. He pointed and waved the gun wildly. 'Move away from him.'

We're all dead, I thought.

He paced toward them again, kicking Wilson in the ribs a second time. Wilson's body didn't make a sound.

'Fucking cunt, thinks he can come into my town and fuck me up?'

I was holding the Marksman now.

Barbie Man took the bandana off his head. 'You do this to me, motherfucker?' he shouted. 'You come and cut me up?'

He walked over to the fallen Yamaha, gun still on Wilson and Thomas. He took the cap off the gas tank, dipped the bandana in with one hand and sloshed the fuel all around. Then he angled the gun into his bad arm and took out a lighter from his pocket. He lit the gas-soaked bandana and jumped back. Thomas moved toward Wilson again as if to protect both of them from what was coming. Even I took a step back. There was a burst of white light and then an explosion like a rocket as a fireball blasted into the air. Patches of fire floated to the earth and sizzled out on the grass. The gas tank on the Yamaha looked like a can that had been torn open and lingering flames kept burning. Barbie Man was now just a few feet in front of me, still shouting. What had he done to Ellen when he was like this?

'Move back!' he shouted at Thomas. 'Get away from him.' Thomas moved backward on his knees, his arms raised, and Barbie Man dragged Wilson's limp body by his suede jacket and then knelt down beside him. Was he going to kill him?

I moved forward. I was in the yard now, out of the trees. I took quick quiet steps toward them and just a foot from Barbie Man, I raised the Marksman. Thomas saw me at that moment; his eyes locked on mine for the briefest second, and then he looked away. Barbie Man was bent over Wilson and I could feel the adrenalin surge through me. If I hit the skull it could bounce off; I had to go for the neck, the vulnerable flesh and tender veins. He suddenly reached back, put his gun into the back of his jeans, and pulled a knife from a sheath on the side of his boot. I could see the strip of white flesh on his back below his shirt. What was he going to do to Wilson with the knife? My hands were shaking. Now I had to do two things at the same time: shoot him and get his gun. Pull hard and keep aim. Breathe in. With two fingers, I pulled the trigger. As I felt the air pressure release, I grabbed the gun from his trousers and stumbled backward. Barbie Man fell over Wilson, and Thomas catapulted on to him.

I was holding two guns. Barbie Man was screaming.

Thomas rolled away and sat up. Barbie Man was lying on the ground, his left hand impaled through the palm and stuck into the earth. He looked like a pinned insect with just one wing, something in a grotesque natural history museum. He was trying to sit up but couldn't. He twisted on to his side and reached toward the knife, but Thomas got there first and pulled it out, throwing it across the lawn toward the woods. Blood spurted from Barbie Man's palm and dripped from his hair where the dart had hit his neck. Had Thomas stabbed him? I handed Thomas the gun.

Barbie Man's nose was still streaming and he tried to use his right hand to support himself but he collapsed back on to the elbow.

'Where is she?' Thomas asked. 'Where?'

Wilson mumbled something on the ground.

'Car,' Thomas said. 'Libby, check his car. By the shed.'

The Camaro was backed into the carport at the side of the McVays' shed. When I opened the door on the driver's side, an interior light came on. The car smelled of cigarette smoke and patchouli. A yellow rabbit's foot hung from the rear-view mirror. On the passenger seat was a black comb, white hair and lint caught in its teeth, and a pink plastic mirror like a child would use, with a small plastic bag of powder sitting on it.

I kneeled on the driver's seat and looked into the back and on the floor. I thought of Ellen sitting inside here with him that night, how terrified she must have been. Where was she?

'She's not here,' I shouted.

'Check the trunk.'

I went to the back of the car, pushing pine branches out

of the way. I paused a second, terrified of what I might find. I lifted the trunk lid. It was empty, just some leaves in the bottom.

'She's not here, I shouted again.'

I wanted to go kill Barbie Man and stamp on the hand where he was bleeding. I walked back toward them. Wilson was lying still. He was breathing but it didn't sound right. His eyes were open, and he looked back at me. Barbie Man was propped up on his elbow a few feet away; his hand on the ground still pumping blood.

'Where is she?' Thomas asked again.

'Fuck you.'

'Libby, shoot him again.'

'You'll be fucking dead if you do.' Barbie Man tried to sit up further.

Thomas stepped back. 'Don't move,' he said. He motioned me to come over. 'Be in front of him in case I have to shoot. Get him in the eye or the front of the neck.'

I pulled another dart from my back pocket and cocked the airgun again. It took several attempts, my hand was shaking so hard.

'Where is she?' I asked. 'What did you do to her?' I walked closer, trying to aim.

'What the fuck are you talking about?'

There were sirens in the distance. Barbie Man heard them too. He made a half-hearted swing for me and at that exact moment a firework sounded.

Barbie Man looked down at himself. There was blood on his shirt.

'Oh my God, Thomas. You shot him.'

Barbie Man sank back down, bent over himself. Had Thomas killed him?

'I thought I shot into the trees,' Thomas said.

Then Barbie Man pulled a dart out of his T-shirt with his right hand. It was me: I had shot him again with the Marksman without even knowing it.

'Tell us where she is,' I said.

'Don't know . . . what the fuck you're talking . . .' He was groggy; his voice dragged and he tried to lie down. His face was pasty white.

'No, don't go to sleep,' I shouted. I went toward him and for an awful sickening moment I held his hair in my hands, trying to pull him up.

The sirens came closer and a police car turned up the McVays' driveway, the red and blue flashing through the trees, the headlights bringing us all into view: Thomas holding a gun, Wilson foetal on the ground, Barbie Man half-conscious on his side, me above him still holding the Marksman.

A voice shouted, 'Put the gun down.' Officer Day.

'We can't find her. He won't tell us where he took Ellen.' I could hear the panic in my own voice. I started moving toward the police car.

'Hold on. Let's drop the guns.' I looked at the Marksman in my hand.

'It's just a dart gun. It's not real,' I shouted, and dropped it. I put my hands in the air. 'She's not in his car. He won't tell us where she is.'

'Something's wrong with his breathing.' Thomas was leaning over Wilson.

I could hear them calling in the ambulances. Other cars arrived. A searchlight on top of one of them flooded us all in an unreal wash of white. We looked like ghosts. One of the cops wrapped Barbie Man's hand and was pressing on it, and I could see his fingers with the long nails cupped with his own blood. There were officers looking inside the Camaro and in the trunk, maybe for traces that Ellen had been there. Thomas was still beside Wilson, and I sat down on the grass next to them. There was a police officer talking to Wilson and speaking into a radio. 'Possible traumatic pneumothorax. Don't let him move until the paramedics arrive,' said the voice on the radio. Wilson was pale and his breathing was fast. I wanted them to make Barbie Man tell us what he had done with Ellen – make him talk, not fix him.

'Libby . . .' Wilson's voice was lower than a whisper.

'Yeah?' I leaned in toward him.

'Where. Would she. Go.' His words sounded like they were being swallowed. Caught in the light, his face shocked me. It was so swollen that his eyes had disappeared, like lines drawn in marker on a misshapen balloon. 'Where. Think.'

I shook my head. Not the Bouchers'. I wasn't there. She wouldn't go to a neighbour's house. And then I remembered that there was one place I hadn't thought of.

'I know,' I said. 'I think I know.' I turned to Thomas. 'If she ran, I know where she would go.'

25

It was my dad who told me that horses and pack animals weren't native to North America. They were brought by European settlers. These types of details about America interested him most. No horses or mules meant that the natives had travelled mostly by foot, and while they sometimes used their bark or dugout canoes and had dogs to carry packs, for thousands of years they walked. Making paths. He loved this – how they'd felt and listened to the woods, how they must have watched the deer and foxes and shadowed their tracks through the undergrowth, how they'd always found the driest and most direct routes. He said that their footfall still marked the landscape and that those traces spoke something about man's potential relationship with the surface of the earth – quiet, instinctive, respectful.

I thought about how, all of our lives, the paths we followed had been started by the first people here; almost every road had first been a trail. Dad would say that being *on the warpath* wasn't just a figure of speech – it referred to an actual trail, a real place. Maybe it was a path that gave warriors an advantage when confronting an enemy, and they had learned this from their elders, how to travel to fight.

I led Officer Day and another cop, who said he was Officer Schuster, down the trail toward the Kingdom –

probably a Lenape path before it was a horse and hiking trail. He pointed a flashlight at the ground and his partner angled a high-powered beam straight ahead, casting the trees and path in phantom white, like in a horror film. Thomas and I walked ahead, out of their beams, several times, and they asked us to slow down.

The crooked tree was ahead of us, visible even before the policemen's lights hit it. Looking at its bend, its pointing arm, it felt as if something living in this place was directing us toward Ellen, and I prayed to whatever it was that she would be here.

'This way,' I said, leading them off the Horseshoe Trail to circle into the Kingdom from behind. We ducked under branches and pushed through mountain laurel into the canopied clearing.

'What is this place?' asked Thomas.

'The Kingdom. It's mine and Sage's. Ellen knows about it. She's been here before.'

'Ellen.' Thomas called her name softly, like a question.

Officer Day directed the beam of light around the circumference of the clearing. Nothing. We all stood silent and listened. He swung the light back again slowly, shining it up and down tree trunks, as if, somehow, we would see her perched up in the branches or down inside the tangle of rhododendron roots.

'She's not here,' said Thomas. 'Jesus Christ, Libby, she's not here.'

'We need to get the two of you back to the station,' said Officer Day.

'No. This is where she would've come. I'm certain.

When Sage and I buried stuff we told her that in an emergency this was the best place to hide.' I knelt at the foot of the red oak and pushed the earth off the board and lifted it. 'Can you shine the light here?' I asked. There were cans of beans and Campbell's cream of chicken soup, a tube of Crest toothpaste and two rolled-up sleeping bags. There was one missing. Definitely.

'This is your apocalypse survival plan?' Thomas asked.

'She's been here. I'm positive. The *Lone Ranger* and *Garfield* sleeping bags are here but the *Star Wars* one is missing. There should be three. No one else knows about this except Sage, and she doesn't even come here any more.' The sleeping bags had belonged to Sage's brothers and we'd retrieved them from Goodwill bags Charlotte had put in the trunk of the car.

'Are you sure?' asked Thomas.

'Positive. She must've gone home. She waited here for us to find her and when we didn't come, she went home.'

'There were definitely three?' Thomas was afraid to hope. Marie called him 'Doubting Thomas', saying it would make him a good scientist, able to question things, to see the possible pitfalls.

'Please,' I said to Officers Day and Schuster, 'we have to go back to the house.'

'We left a squad car at the house. They'd call it in if she went there.'

'She's waiting for us, then. For me and Thomas. She got home and saw the police car in the driveway, and she's afraid. Please. Can we go there first?'

We would have to cut off the trail to get to our house,

but it was only a few hundred yards down from the main trail. If Ellen had gone back home, we were already so close to her. Thomas and I nearly ran all the way, the two policemen following. We turned right off the trail, on to the path that led to our house, and both started sprinting, shouting her name. I could see the bathroom light still on, where I had crawled out hours earlier. There was a light on in the kitchen. A police car was in the driveway, its parking lights on.

'ELLEN . . . ELLEN!' I shouted, and Thomas did too. We stopped where the path ended at the steps leading down to our drive. 'ELLEN!' I glanced at Thomas, the expectant look on his face. Where was she?

'Here.'

A voice from under the low dogwood on the little hill where we'd buried our cat and goldfish and toad and dead things we found like birds or chipmunks. I could see her trying to stand up inside the *Star Wars* sleeping bag under the low sweeping branches.

Thomas reached her first. He lifted her in the sack and sidestepped down the embankment, holding her co-cooned shape. He sat on the ground with her, hugging her swaddled body, and I sat with them and we waited there for the policemen to catch up.

As Thomas, Ellen and I traipsed up the sidewalk of Phoenixville police station, Marie pushed through the double glass doors and came running out to us.

'How did you get here?' I asked, feeling for her number in my pocket. 'I never gave them your number.'

'Sage called and she and Grady came and got me. They're still here.'

I looked at Marie and wondered what the police made of her, and if they believed she was even an adult. She had on Doc Martens, a black miniskirt and a cropped T-shirt with rips. Ellen was still wearing her Fourth of July outfit; the heart flags she had painted on her face to match Peter's were smeared across her cheeks like bruises. Her thin blonde hair was tangled and her white shirt was streaked with dirt. But it wasn't Ellen that Marie was looking at with shock, it was me.

'Jesus, your hair.'

I lifted my hands either side of my head and felt the immense tangle. I looked down. My arms were covered in dried blood. There was dried blood in the cuticles of my fingernails. 'Oh God. Marie, it's not my blood. Please, get it off me.' I felt panic, like I might start clawing at my own skin. 'I have to get it off.'

'I need to take her to the restroom,' Marie said to Officer Day. Sage and Grady Adams were sitting in plastic chairs in the waiting room, but they weren't looking over at us. It was more than just giving us space; I had done some irreversible damage. I could see it in the way Sage sat and the way Grady didn't do his polite-Southern-father routine. They were sitting in their own devastation, and I was the cause.

In the mirror of the police station bathroom, I looked even more horrifying. There was his blood on my face, or maybe some of it was mine. My hair was caught in clumps of burrs and sticks.

'You're going to have to cut it,' Marie said. She turned on the hot faucet and handed me a bar of soap. 'Wash your face and your hands really well, and when you get home you can have a bath.' She took a toothbrush out of her backpack. 'Use this like you would a nail brush and we'll throw it away. But get it all off you.'

It took several hours for our statements to be taken. We sat in a room together, Marie with us. Grady and Sage were still in the waiting room. The police gave us cans of Coke and bags of potato chips from the vending machine. Later, around four in the morning, Ellen and I went to the bathroom together. She finished first and went back out. When I stepped into the hallway, Sage was hugging her, but she didn't look at me. I knew the message was to stay away. I didn't blame her.

We told our stories. Ellen had to begin with that night in the car when Julius Korhonen picked her up. Officer Day asked why she was on the road, to explain how she ended up getting out of our car and standing on the road in the dark.

'It was almost dark. But not quite. That time that's more like twilight,' Ellen said. 'And I was being horrible, losing my temper, and my mom couldn't control me . . .' I glanced at Marie. We knew Officer Day was thinking about what kind of mother would leave a girl this size on the side of the road.

Marie said she really didn't know anything about who went up to Pottstown with Wilson or exactly what they did.

I found myself defending Wilson again. 'He was trying to help us,' I said.

Ellen told her story from the fireworks, how she had turned out of the swim club parking lot to come find me. Meredith Hunter just wanted to follow a group of boys from her middle school around and she was getting on Ellen's nerves. It wasn't Barbie Man's car she'd seen – she saw him, standing in the middle of the road, looking around, taller than everyone else. She thought he was looking for her, so she ran straight across to the trail, past the tower, and kept going. She waited in the Kingdom and when she thought for definite that she'd waited long enough, that Thomas and I would be home, she walked back, only to see the police car in the driveway. She didn't know what to do so she decided to hide under the dogwood until she saw one of us.

Thomas had gone straight to get Wilson, convinced that Barbie Man would make Ellen take him to Wilson. They'd gone out on the Yamaha to see if they could find Ellen or the black Camaro, then back to Wilson's in case he came for them there, not expecting him to already be waiting. He definitely hadn't expected to see me coming out of the woods holding a gun.

'A gun?' asked Marie.

'The Marksman.'

'You're serious? You armed yourself with a toy?'

'It's not a toy and it looks real in the dark.'

We had to describe repeatedly what had happened to cause Barbie Man to get stabbed in the hand. I didn't know. The knife was his. Thomas had thought he was going to stab Wilson or slit his throat he was so out of control.

Officer Day asked Marie for our mother's contact phone number in North Carolina.

'I'm sorry,' Marie said. 'We left my apartment in such a rush I didn't bring my bag with the information sheet my mother gave me. It had all her contact details and the emergency numbers. I'd call my roommate but she's away right now.'

I knew Marie was lying to protect Mom, but I worried we had still told the police too much and that maybe she'd be in trouble already. Would they take us away? From each other? What would happen to Beatrice?

The police spoke to the hospital. Wilson had a broken jaw and a punctured lung from a broken rib, which was why his breathing had sounded so difficult. He was having surgery to wire his jaw shut. He'd be in hospital at least a few days but should be okay. 'What about . . . the other one?' Thomas asked.

Officer Day said, 'Don't worry. You didn't kill anybody, son.'

At the end of the interview, we stood in the hallway for a few minutes.

'That's my T-shirt,' Marie said. I looked down. It was the black one I had put on before I left the house.

'Oh, yeah. I borrowed it.'

'It's one of my favourites,' Marie said. I looked at it. It was the Ramones' 'Blitzkrieg Bop' shirt, *Hey Ho Let's Go!* written across the front around the American seal.

We stepped out of the police station into early-morning light. The Schuylkill River was flushed in pink and gold, a chorus of birds sang from unseen trees or ledges somewhere, and the earth felt clean. We were safe and together.

Grady and Sage walked ahead of us. Despite everything I had done, they were still here, waiting to take us home. Grady told Thomas to sit in the front. I got into the back of the Mercedes and slid all the way over to the far door. Marie sat next to me, then Ellen. Sage sat on the other side.

We drove along the river and I pressed my face against the glass and watched it pass. In the distance, the cooling towers of the Limerick nuclear power plant were visible. In a few months clouds of steam would billow out of them. Sage and I had signed petitions and written to our representatives to try to stop construction. Outside Phoenixville we passed farmland, and I kept my face against the window so I didn't have to look at Sage.

During the journey, Ellen fell asleep on Sage's shoulder. When we turned on to our street, Marie nudged her. 'Wake up, Ellen, we're almost home.'

There was a car parked in our driveway and someone was crouching in front of the failed marigold patch I had tried to plant. A very small woman outside the front door looked up at the house.

'Who's that?' asked Thomas. I sat forward, leaning over to peer through the windshield.

'Oh God, the Gambinos. I forgot. Ellen was supposed to be going with them this morning to start art camp. Whatever you do, don't anyone tell them anything.' I didn't think Mrs Gambino could comprehend it all.

'How are we going to get out of this?' said Marie.

'No. Please. I want to go.' Ellen was awake, sitting up. 'I have everything packed. Tell them I was at a sleepover and I'll need to sleep today.'

287

We stumbled out of the car and said thank you. Ellen ran to the garage to go in and get her stuff. Marie went to the front to talk to Mrs Gambino while Thomas and I stood awkwardly by Gabriel.

'Hi, Gabriel,' I said. I saw him take in my hair and clothes. He was wearing a pressed white shirt with shoulder pads, and his hair was parted and slicked back like the boy from *The Munsters*. I actually thought he looked a bit new wave but that was most likely by accident. He was a strange kid.

'These are dying,' he said, pointing at our marigolds. I looked at the overgrown grass which was still yellow, at the sludge at the bottom of the garden where the septic tank was overflowing, at the weeds growing between the steps up to the woods, so high you couldn't even tell there were steps.

'Yeah, they are,' I said. I could hear Mr Walker across the road turn the ignition on his sit-down mower. I could see all the signs of our chaos, of how we were not coping.

'What happened to your hair?' Gabriel asked.

26

We tried conditioner and mayonnaise and gently taking hair off the burrs strand by strand, even cutting them out, but it only got worse and the tangles were moving closer to my scalp. When we used to cut the grass at one of the houses on a cul-de-sac in Penn Valley, Dad would always say to 'mind the burdock', a crowd of purple flowers that grew down the side of the embankment leading to the Schuylkill Expressway. We'd see their burrs, green in the summer, turned brown by the fall clean-ups. Sometimes they got caught in my socks or my sweater, but until yesterday I had never run head first through a whole hill of them. Marie put a towel around my shoulders and let me hold a mirror in my lap while she cut chunks of hair.

We were all exhausted, but Marie warned that if I went to sleep on my hair, she'd have to cut it as close as Annie Lennox's. I said, 'Please make it more Belinda Carlisle.' With Marie there, home felt safe again, like there was an answer for everything. I sat very still as she cut and watched the nests of hair drop to our bedroom floor. In the end it was like a short bob that fell just above my chin and had a few layers. Marie said this framed my face more and that she liked it on me. I was so tired it didn't seem to matter. We left the fallen hair on the floor without sweeping it up and went to bed in the bright morning.

*

I woke to the smell of pancakes. The afternoon sun was streaming through the leaves and throwing patterns across the wall next to my bed. For just a moment I didn't remember, still between sleep and waking. I lifted my hand to my neck and its nakedness was like a jolt, summoning the night before.

Thomas and Marie were in the kitchen. Marie put two pancakes in front of me and a bottle of Aunt Jemima maple syrup.

'Where did you get the ingredients?' We lived on a diet of peanut butter and jelly, Campbell's soup and canned SpaghettiOs with meatballs; we didn't actually ever cook.

'Well, we had milk and butter. I went over to the Walkers' and knocked on the door and said, "Hi, Mr Walker. I didn't get a chance to do the grocery shopping. Could I trouble you for three cups of flour, two eggs, and would you have any syrup?" And he said, "Oh yes, no problem, of course", and then he asked me, "How's your sister?" And I asked which one and he said, "Ellen." I said, "Oh, she's fine." And he waited, as if I might say more. Then I said, "She's headed off to a prestigious art camp today."'

Thomas was eating through a pile of stacked pancakes. His mouth full, he said, 'They taste better for having come from the Walkers.'

Marie spoke to the camp director, saying she had misplaced the name of the hotel where our mother was staying. He gave her the forwarding number and Marie called it and left a message with reception saying it was an emergency and could they ask her to call home. We waited and talked about the night before and all that had happened and might happen and what exactly we would tell Mom. When the phone rang, the three of us went silent.

Marie picked up and I instantly knew it wasn't Mom because of the way Marie spoke, polite and friendly. Both Thomas and I were watching and Marie looked over at me. 'Yes, okay, Mrs Boucher. Oh, we're all fine. I'll tell her. Thank you for letting us know.'

When she'd hung up, I waited for her to say it.

'Mrs Boucher says she doesn't need you to babysit next Friday. She sounded a little weird.'

I could feel the heat seeping into my face. Both Marie and Thomas were looking at me.

'What's going on, Libby? What's wrong?' Marie knew something was up. 'Is it because we're involved in this that she doesn't want you near her kids or something?' She sounded angry.

I shook my head. 'It's not that. It's something I did.' I told them the story of the car headlights cutting out all those nights, how I'd known for a while that she was seeing someone and that she wanted it kept secret. I told them all the reasons I suspected it was Grady Adams, him knowing about Ellen, the night he hit the deer.

'How does that mean they're having an affair?' asked Thomas. 'Your story makes no sense. You have no evidence or proof.'

'That's the worst part. I went and got proof.'

Marie stared at me. 'You what?'

'I know.' I could feel the shame all over me. 'On Friday night I asked Wilson to drive up and see if there was any car parked along Horseshoe Trail Road. I feel so shit.'

Marie looked disgusted with me. 'If Mrs Boucher and Grady Adams are having an affair, that's none of your business. Seriously.'

'I know. I know.'

'What did Wilson say?' Thomas asked.

'It was a Mercedes. Just like Grady Adams's, parked by the Nike Site.'

'I'm still confused,' said Thomas. 'Why would Mrs Boucher ask you not to babysit? Did you say something to her?'

'No. I told Sage.'

'Oh shit, Libby.' Marie put her head in her hands.

'I'm sorry.'

'Is that why she wasn't talking to you at the police station?'

'Yeah. I think so. He must have admitted it to her on the way to get you in the city because I could tell she'd been crying. She never looked at me.'

'You shouldn't have done it,' said Marie. 'That was their business, not yours – or Sage's. And now Charlotte will know.' The thought of hurting Charlotte tightened my insides. She had always been kind to me, and I loved her ferociously for liking my father.

I couldn't even bring myself to tell Thomas and Marie that I had only told Sage in order to crush her own idea of her father when I thought she'd questioned mine.

We waited for Mom to call. When it was almost dark, I dialled Information and asked for the number of Phoenixville Hospital, then called and asked if I could speak to

Wilson McVay. I got connected to the nurses' station, and a woman told me he couldn't receive calls. Marie called her boss to say she wouldn't be in for the next few days, that her younger siblings had been victims in a criminal incident and we still hadn't been able to contact our mother.

Mom called at nine. Marie spoke to her and outlined everything: what happened to Ellen when Mom kicked her out of the car, Barbie Man showing up at the fireworks, Thomas and me being vigilantes, stabbing and shooting the man with a dart gun but not doing a good enough job of it to kill him. Marie was trying to give the facts but be funny. It was like she was the mother, trying to reassure Mom that it wasn't such a big deal and we were all fine. Our mother stayed quiet on the phone. She listened and then said she was on her way. She was leaving North Carolina and driving all night. It would be nine hours before she got back to the mountain.

Wilson was sitting up when we went in to see him, me, Marie, Thomas and my mom. Every speck of skin on his face was bruised, even his eyelids. The swelling had distorted its shape. He'd had surgery to wire his broken jaw shut and they'd inserted a chest tube through his ribs to drain the air around the lung, where a broken rib had punctured it. He would recover but it would take the rest of the summer.

'Libby,' he wheezed when we came into the room. 'My gallant knight. Did they cut your hair as ritual punishment?' His voice was hoarse from surgery and it was hard to understand him talking through closed teeth.

'You look dreadful.' Marie said what we were all thinking.

'Thank you very much,' he said.

'Hi, Wilson.' Thomas was hanging back in the room, uncertain how to act.

'Hey, Thomas. Thanks, man. You and Libby.'

Thomas gave a nod of his head to acknowledge this, shy and proud. I thought about what he had done, what I had done, both of us that night. While I felt like shit about some of the choices I'd made, I now knew I could fight when I needed to.

Mom was quiet. She stood near Thomas at the foot of Wilson's bed, holding the rail with both hands. I know the sight of Wilson shocked her; he made visible the violence we'd been through. Wilson's broken bones and swollen body made it real.

Wilson looked directly at her. 'Faye, I'm sorry,' he said.

'No. I'm sorry. We're so sorry. It's my fault you got pulled into this.' She started to say something else and stopped, then started again. 'I would do things differently if I could. I wish I could change what I did.' She hadn't said it to us, but she could to Wilson, and we were here too. Later, I would tell Ellen: 'Mom will never get over it, leaving you on the road, even though she can't say it.'

Marie chatted to Wilson about some bands. A nurse came in to check his blood pressure and we shuffled toward the door. Wilson said something garbled.

'What?'

'Libby's hair. Very new wave. It's good.'

I touched my bare neck. 'I think I'm still really a hippy.'

'I'm working on her,' said Marie.

294

When we left the hospital, it was Mom who suggested we go to the Guernsey Cow for ice cream cones. We bought double scoops and walked through the barn, which smelled like soured milk. We sat in the car then, and my mom left on the radio while we finished our ice creams. 'She's a Rainbow' came on and even Thomas sang. The sun was setting and everything and all of us – Mom, Marie, Thomas and me – were washed in a golden-orange light. The farmland, cows, picket fences and silos were pink, catching the sun before the coming dark. Everything was beautiful and for a moment we were held together by our longing to be what we had once been. I could see my mother as she sang. I could see her face, see how like a child she was in some ways. She hadn't slept and had spent the whole day at the police station, and I wondered how much they had questioned her about why she'd kicked Ellen out of the car and why she'd left her children home alone. She must have felt accused. But here she was, eating ice cream. And she had driven through the night, straight back to us. I knew she loved us in the way that she could. And when I'd been most afraid, I had wanted her. There in the car she sang with us and every time the part about combing hair repeated we burst into laughter because of mine.

On Wednesday morning Mom drove back to North Carolina. None of us said anything to her about going back. I didn't feel angry or resentful. I knew she felt outside of what had happened, that she didn't know how to be in charge, that being here made her feel guilty. She needed to go back to what she had left so suddenly. She would be close to Beatrice, and somehow it was okay. Marie was already taking care of things. Before she left, Mom had gone to the Gambinos'. She and Ellen had had to be questioned together a second time, and afterward she had taken Ellen out to Gullifty's in Rosemont, just the two of them, and they'd talked. Ellen told us that Mom had said she was sorry, that Ellen had been so brave, braver than she could imagine anyone in that situation being. Ellen said it was all going really well until Mom told her she needed to work on her bad temper.

When Mom left to go back to North Carolina, I stood with her in the driveway.

'I did look for her that night, Libby,' she said. 'I took the car and went and looked for her.'

'I know. Marie heard you leaving. We figured you were trying to find her.'

'I wish you felt you could tell me things.'

I looked at the ground.

'I'm proud of all you did, Libby. Your father would be too.'

She left us $40 this time, and Marie and I took the bus to King of Prussia to go food shopping at the Acme. It was there that we saw Sage and Charlotte Adams.

We had gotten a shopping cart even though we had to pack light to carry the groceries up the mountain in backpacks. Marie said she was going to cook properly for us and we picked up fillets of steak and green beans and potatoes. We chose three ears of corn. Our dad used to buy paper bags full of corn from stalls on the back roads in New Jersey and bring them home and tell us to start shucking. We'd done it outside to avoid mess. Marie and I got flour, eggs and maple syrup to take to the Walkers because, as Marie said, she didn't want them to have one up on us. Ever. We were in the baking stuff aisle. Marie was reading a recipe for brownies on the back of a Hershey's block of chocolate. I was looking at the boxes of brownie mix where you just add eggs and water, when I turned and saw Charlotte and Sage coming toward us with their shopping cart. Sage was in her J. C. Penney's waitressing uniform. Charlotte had sunglasses on even though she was inside and wore a madras golf skirt and pink tennis shirt, but when she got closer I could see she looked dishevelled, and I knew she knew. They had stopped but hadn't seen me yet. Sage was speaking to her, leaning over, intense and serious. Charlotte turned and saw me just as I was going to look away.

'Libby,' she said, and it came out like a sob. I took a step toward her. 'Libby, your hair. I didn't recognize you. Can you believe he's done this to us?' And Charlotte Adams put her arms around me and held me, and she was crying in the baking section of the Acme supermarket. I put my arms around her thin frame and tried to hug her back, feeling awkward and tall. I'd only ever seen Charlotte as elegant and distant. She was always kind but reserved and this was unfiltered raw emotion; she was showing us how hurt she was. Her hair was flattened at the top and back as if she had just got out of bed, and she seemed suddenly small and diminished.

'Charlotte, stop it,' said Sage. 'Please. Come on. Leave the cart. We're going back out to the car.'

'I'm so sorry, Mrs Adams. I am so, so sorry.'

'I know you are, Libby.' Her shoulders were shaking she was crying so much. 'I've always thought you and you father . . . had empathy.'

'Charlotte. Mom.' Sage took her by the hand and pulled her away from me, and they left, Sage with her arm around her mother as if she had tucked her under her wing.

Marie and I stood in the aisle and looked at their abandoned shopping cart and our half-full one. Whenever someone mentioned my father, it went through me. I had hurt all these people who had treated me like their own and brought me into their homes. I started to shake. I had failed her idea of me and my father's.

Outside, I sat on a bench and watched the traffic flash up and down Route 202 and cried. There were cars everywhere, across the parking lot, on the highway, and construction and noise. Dump trucks trailed clouds of dust to and from the asphalt plant and building sites. Jackhammers clanged against rock and bulldozer blades screeched metal on pavement. The sun was blinding and hot. I couldn't stop crying. The Rolling Stones' 'Paint It Black' kept going through my head. Even in the blazing sun, everything was overcast and tainted. Me most of all. Nothing could ever be put right. Marie was inside, paying for the groceries, and when she came out pushing the cart, we gathered the bags into our backpacks and walked over to the bus stop. Every few feet I had to wipe the fluid running from my nose, and Marie walked beside me and knew it was better to say nothing at all.

27

Thomas had practically become a celebrity on the mountain. Stories circulated about how he and Wilson took on the giant with the gun and Thomas struggled for the knife and stabbed him. Meredith Hunter had come up to see how Ellen was and, even though Ellen was away, she stayed and recounted to us all the variations of the stories they'd heard. She said that one of the Walkers had told them that Thomas had stabbed the man over and over.

'No wonder they practically threw the pancake ingredients at me,' said Marie.

I barely played a role in these stories. It was all about how Wilson and Thomas had saved me and Ellen and pinned the guy down with a knife.

'Don't worry,' Marie said. 'They always make it about men heroes. The world makes better sense to them that way.'

I didn't care. I wasn't proud of any of it and I didn't want people to even know I'd been there. But in a weird way it was helping Thomas and bringing him back out into the world. One night he came home, and he'd been pool-hopping at the swim club. And he was spending time with Jack again.

'Was Sage there?' I asked. But he said he hadn't seen her since the night at the police station.

*

A week or so after he came out of hospital, Wilson pulled up our driveway on a new motorcycle, which he said was a loaner from the dealer.

'Aren't you supposed to be resting in bed? I thought they said no driving.'

'I'm fine. I'm just going for a little spin. I thought you might like to come.' His voice was muffled from the wires. He took off his helmet and I could see his face again, the shape of it, even though it was still bruised yellow and orange in places.

'How do I know you're not swilling down your pain-killers recreationally and stuff?'

Wilson laughed. 'I haven't taken them, not even medicinally. They're shit. There's much better stuff in our medicine cabinet at home.'

I looked at him and tried to raise my eyebrows.

'I swear, I haven't taken anything at all. Not for days. It's safe.'

'Where are we going?' I asked.

'To a place with no trees.'

'I don't think I'd like that.'

'I want you to see it.'

I looked up through the light and leaves at the blue sky and remembered that night on the motorcycle coming back from the tower, how I'd felt.

'Okay,' I said, and picked up the helmet on the back of the bike.

'No, you have to change. Long jeans. And boots if you have them.'

'I only have wellies.'

'What?'

'You know, like rubber boots they wear in Ireland. My dad always brought them back for us.'

'Okay, those and jeans and bring a light jacket.'

I wore a white T-shirt, a green corduroy jacket, jeans and black wellies. I had started wearing earrings after my haircut, and I had big silver hoops in, a bit Belinda Carlisle, even though I wasn't a GoGo's fan. I'd put on mascara and eyeliner too. Marie said it was a new look, edgier than my ethereal long straight Crystal Gayle hair, and that it suited me. I hadn't gone anywhere with it yet, just around the house. But standing back outside by Wilson's bike, I felt more grown-up, comfortable with my ridiculous boots and short hair, someone with my own world inside me.

I forgot when I got on the back of the bike that Wilson was injured and I held on to his sides. I felt the jolt of pain go through him, how he buckled.

'No,' he said, 'lower', so I held his hips instead and by the time we were out on Route 23 I had my fingers hooked through the loops of his jeans and trusted myself not to fall.

We headed west, through Phoenixville and out beyond it on Route 724, past clapboard houses with American flags stabbed into their front lawns and through towns where the Fourth of July bunting still criss-crossed the road. We saw fields of corn and cows, yard sales and flea markets and heaps of rusted junk and more cornfields. I could feel the heat of the sun on the back of my bare neck, and the cooler shadows of trees passing on the road beneath me. I was so lost in the landscape that I almost missed it: a sign for Pottstown. Was Wilson taking me there? I tapped him on the shoulder, and he pulled to the side of the road.

'I don't want to go to Pottstown.'

'We're not. It's just a town on our way. Anyway, he's not there. He's in prison.'

'Are you sure?'

'Yeah. He was arrested in the hospital and the cops took my statement there and they had yours. They had a search warrant for his house and found stuff. He was arraigned last week. No bail. We don't have to worry about him.' Wilson put his hand to his jaw.

'How do you know?' I asked.

'My lawyer.'

'Are you in trouble because of all this?' Had my mom gone to a lawyer those few days she was here? Did she need one?

'No. Well, maybe for beating him up in the first instance, but I had a lawyer long before that because of other stuff.'

'Yeah,' I said, as if I really knew what he was talking about. Maybe it was for robbery or for that night they said he punched out all the windows or possibly for dealing drugs, which he still did.

I got back on the bike and we continued west.

After Reading we passed Minersville. I knew already we were in mining country. Everything looked like it had slumped slightly, even the sky sagged, as we passed coal trucks and anthracite signs and lots of American flags. A few miles beyond Buck Run, Wilson turned off the main road. We went down two small roads and on to a dirt path that sent up white dust all around us, like ash. The path ended at a chain-link gate and a sign that read *No Trespassing* and another that read *Blasting Area*. Other vehicles had driven right over the fence; just to the left of the gate, a whole section lay flattened on the ground. Wilson drove over it. We had come through a tunnel of trees but in front and all around us now was nothing – no vegetation, no trees, no colour. Wilson kept on driving forward but the landscape was completely bare.

We climbed a hill but the further up we went, the more the traction under the wheels seemed to give, and it started to feel as if we were sinking. Wilson stopped and we both stepped off the bike. The earth beneath my feet moved as if there was nothing substantial below us, and I sank several inches in my wellies.

'What's wrong with the ground? What is this?' I thought maybe it was a quarry.

'It's a strip mine.'

'What is that?'

'They blast away the earth to get to the coal instead of digging for it. It's like tearing off the skin, the fat and the muscle of the earth to get to the bone. Sometimes they take off whole mountain tops, explode them off, so they can get directly to the coal seam. Six hundred feet of mountain or more, and then they dump it all.'

There must have been thousands of acres here, all stripped bare, like a scar. Nothing would ever grow here again. It would be dead forever. Far away, I could see forests, a blue-green mirage moving like a sea of water, but here the earth was all the same pale brown. There was no sound. No birds. No movement of water. Nothing.

We walked up to the highest point on the empty hill and sat on the strange surface. I felt as if it might swallow me into its nothingness. This is what earth without trees would feel like: no texture, no substructure, no roots or connections to give it composition, no history, just a sense of collapsing. I had never been to a place so bleak.

'How is this allowed?'

'I don't know,' he said. 'All those beautiful trees. It makes me sick.'

I looked over at him sitting in this vast empty world. 'Did you kill our cat?'

'What?'

'Did you kill our cat, Mr Franklin?'

'That's a bit of a non sequitur.'

'I don't know what that is.'

'It means it had nothing to do with what came before it. I didn't kill your cat or anybody's, ever. I've never hurt animals.'

'What have you done that everybody is scared of you, the police know you, you have a record and you're only nineteen and have your own lawyer?'

'That's what you're thinking about?'

I waited, lifting the strange earth and letting it fall through my fingers.

'It wasn't just one thing. It's a long list of things. Do you want like a rap sheet?'

'Tell me the worst thing.'

'I can't even say. Most people would say armed robbery

or maybe one of the drug charges. I've done plenty of stupid things. But it's some of the things I did when I was mad, so mad I couldn't even think, wrecking things and people, that I feel worst about.'

'Why were you so mad?'

'I don't know. My dad, maybe? Myself. I just wanted to destroy things and, I don't know, get put away.'

I wished I hadn't asked. I remembered Marie saying about his dad beating him senseless, and I didn't want to know the side of him that raged.

'It's messed up,' I said.

'Yeah. I've been to plenty of shrinks. They think so too.'

'Do they think you can get better?'

'Maybe. They say I would do better away from here, away from my dad – and I did when I was at military school. I don't know . . . I can't leave my mom.'

I wanted to ask if it was because he was protecting her from his dad, but another part of me didn't want to know more.

I made a pillow of my jacket and lay back on the hillside of dirt. Wilson did the same, having to lie back first on his elbows, and then ease himself down. We lay there like washed-up living creatures on a strange planet.

'Wilson?'

'What?'

'Have you seen Sage?'

'Yeah. A few days ago she and Tony De Martino came to my house.'

'Oh.' Sage was still hanging around with Tony. I wanted to ask how she was but didn't.

The sun was warm, and I could tell by Wilson's breathing that he had fallen asleep. I lay on my side, facing him. It was true what Sage had said, he was handsome. Strong-featured, tan, and when he laughed a series of lines appeared either side of his mouth. His dark hair was tipped with blonde from the sun. His face was slack with sleep but you could see the fullness of his lips and, even though it was swollen, the line of his jaw. A man, not a boy, as Sage would say. He was good-looking, but because he was crazy girls steered away from him. I wondered if he'd ever had a girlfriend. I was still cautious about him. I knew something wasn't right, but at the same time I trusted him with my life. I wondered who he'd be if he'd had a different father.

I dozed too, and woke to a rumbling that I could feel all around me. I sat up. Wilson was down by the bike, and I felt and heard it a second time. Almost like thunder, and waves of vibrations beneath me, except the sun was shining. Was it an earthquake? I grabbed my jacket and ran down the hill to Wilson. It was like running down a snow bank.

'What is that?'

'Explosives.'

'Are they near? The sign said we shouldn't be here.'

'No. It's like a mile away. But we should head anyway.'

We stopped at a gas station in Reading, and I got a hot dog with mustard and a bag of potato chips. Wilson drank chocolate milk through a straw. By the time we hit 23 it was almost dark. We pulled into the driveway. There was a Datsun parked in it.

'Jack Griffith's here. Will you come in with me? And let me carry the helmet? Just for effect. And try to act normal.'

'Yeah, with your rubber boots from Ireland, your corduroy and all the dust, you look really biker-chic.'

We went in through the rec room door, and Thomas and Jack were sitting there. Even though they'd never talked about what had happened, Thomas and Wilson had some understanding since that night, and I could see Thomas's face brighten when he saw him. Jack mumbled a 'hello' to both of us, and we said 'hey' back.

'Wilson!' Thomas said. 'You feeling any better? Is the chest tube out?' He looked at me then. 'Where've you guys been? What's with the wellies in July?'

Wilson acted right at home. He sat down on the couch opposite Jack's chair, and I plopped down next to him and heard him suck in his breath. I kept forgetting the broken ribs. We were both holding our helmets.

'We went up toward Buck Run and Centralia,' Wilson said, 'out beyond Reading, looking at some of the strip mines – you know, for Libby's tree research.' He made it sound like I was a graduate student. I told them about the strip mining, the strange earth like a moonscape, how despairing it felt there.

'What happened to your hair?' Jack asked me. We all looked at him.

'That's a bit of a non sequitur,' I said.

I could feel Wilson smile.

I looked directly at Jack and it wasn't hard and I didn't feel embarrassed about anything that had happened.

307

Thomas interrupted and asked more questions about the strip mine, the kinds of explosives, the risk of floods and landslides if there were miles of no vegetation. He asked Wilson if he would take him up.

'Yeah, I will. Maybe next week,' said Wilson. His voice was getting even harder to understand through his closed lips, and I looked at him and could see how exhausted he was.

'You should go home to bed and stop talking,' I said.

'I will.' He stood up, and I said I would walk out with him. On the driveway, I strapped the helmet to the seat back.

'Thanks,' I said.

'Glad to be of service. Again.'

I laughed. He was pale and tired, and I knew he was in pain. I held his shoulders for a quick moment. 'No, really – thanks. Like, for everything.'

I went back though the rec room and said, 'Goodnight, you losers' to Thomas and Jack, like it was old times when they were building nerd labyrinths for their marbles, before death, and adultery, and secrets and betrayal and heroism and strip mines had come into our lives, and I climbed up the stairs, not giving a shit about my wellies, or my hair or my dirt.

28

That summer when I so desperately tried to reel us all in, I didn't understand the forces spinning us apart. I didn't know it was my last summer on the mountain, that I wouldn't live with my mother or my siblings again, that Thomas and I would board with other families for the remainder of high school and that Ellen and Beatrice would start the next school year in a different state. I didn't know that my mother would move with them, that we would all leave the mountain, and maybe for her it was to be closer to Bill and maybe it wasn't. We still didn't know.

Even without knowing all that was to come, I already wanted to go back to before, to hold us all together in the car driving through Pennsylvania Dutch, so squished and inseparable I couldn't tell where my skin ended and my sisters' began; I wanted to be in the back of Dad's pickup truck, us and the machines, after a day cutting lawns, driving home and the air cooling us as we drove, grass blades and leaves in a swirl around us, or lying on the living room floor in our separate spaces, listening to old reel-to-reel tapes of a time when we were looking forward to who we would be in the future. I wanted to hold us there. Together. Summer evenings in the driveway playing kick-the-can against the dark, calling from azaleas and dogwoods, running the trails. I wanted to be on the moss hill in the Kingdom smoking Charlotte's Kents with Sage or looking up through the canopy of a maple in October, wearing a sweater against the cold, wading through leaf fall. I wanted Beatrice in my bed curling my hair, needing something from me, Ellen coiled beside us, wound against the world; I wanted Marie back, across the room from me, making sense of it all, and Thomas in his room looking up at the spinning universe. Even now sometimes I want to be driving west down 252 and Ellen's tired head falls on my shoulder, and I don't shrug it off, and she stays there with us in the car; to drive, again, all of us together, through the covered bridge, to feel the wooden planks beneath our wheels, to climb the mountain, knowing the turns by heart by the feel of them, to be going home.

Beatrice came back from camp with braids all over her head and wristbands made for her by new friends. She had a bag of embroidery thread and was busy designing us all anklets and bracelets. She'd canoed, been white-water rafting, had camp-outs with ghost stories, hiked a mountain, seen rattlesnakes and water moccasins and had started to say 'y'all'. She was taller and tan. She said it was the best time she'd ever had.

'I was practically the only Yankee there,' she said.

'Did they actually call you that?' asked Thomas. 'Yankee?'

'Yeah. There was just me and a girl from New York City.'

'I hope you did us proud,' said Thomas.

'They got me to say the word *water* over and over. And they'd all repeat it "Wudder, wudder".'

'Yep, you definitely showed them what we're made of,' said Thomas.

'That's totally a Philadelphia thing, the way we say it,' I said. Sage had told me a thousand times it was a word we'd destroyed.

Ellen came back from the Gambinos' and art camp saying that if she never saw ravioli, cannoli, panna cotta or prosciutto again, it would be too soon.

'Stop bragging,' said Thomas. We salivated at her descriptions of what they ate. Gabriel had taught her how to make tiramisu, soaking the ladyfingers in coffee and amaretto, making the mascarpone mixture, finishing it with chocolate shavings using a potato peeler. She and Gabriel had made us potpourri. We each got a sachet. Ellen said he used rose petals, lavender, orange peel, mint, sweet woodruff and rose oil.

Ellen had gotten attention at art camp. One of the teachers there taught in a private school in Maryland that had one of the best art departments on the East Coast. The teacher had spoken to the school, and a week or two after Ellen came home they called my mother offering Ellen a full scholarship. It never occurred to me that she would actually go.

In the mornings the rest of that summer, after Mom had gone to the hospital, Thomas and I listened to the radio in the kitchen before Beatrice or Ellen woke up. The royal wedding was at the end of July, and it seemed every station had nothing else to talk about. In the days after the wedding, three hunger strikers died in Northern Ireland. I listened to the radio and thought how much it would have

311

upset Dad that there was more talk about Princess Diana's wedding dress than there was about the three young men who died.

I walked the mountain that August. I looped Forge Mountain Drive, paced the trails and sat in the Kingdom. I went down the north-west trail to the bottling factory and over the ridge behind it. I discovered an old quarry in the middle of nowhere. At night I pulled ticks from my scalp over the sink and then crushed them against the beige porcelain with my thumbnail. I walked south and came through the woods to Valley Creek, near the covered bridge. I walked and walked the mountain, memorizing its surfaces, as if my feet knew before I did that I wouldn't ever be going back. I broke into the bunker on the Nike Site, through a rotted window frame. I didn't find nuclear secrets, just cobwebs, spiders, a broken office chair and a dead mouse that had turned almost to dust in a trap on the linoleum floor, only the long tail intact. Sometimes I sat up there looking at the bindweed choking the fence, the dead dandelion and chicory. I counted how long it had been since I had pulled weeds with my dad – one year and eleven months. I rewrote days working with him where I could name nutsedge and pokeweed and could haul the tarpaulin of leaves myself, and could tell him then, in the past, all the tree facts I knew now.

Charlotte Adams was the first to leave the mountain. It was Wilson who heard. She had rented a house in a new development near Gateway Shopping Center.

'But why didn't Grady leave?' I asked him. 'Why Charlotte?'

'I don't know,' said Wilson. 'He has his doctor's practice up here. Maybe that's too hard to move. Maybe Charlotte just wants to get away from all this.'

'How about Sage and the boys? Who will they live with?'

'Don't know. Maybe both.'

We had driven through the development when it first opened one night on the way home from school. All the houses looked the same. I had resented it before it ever existed because it had once been beautiful meadow that was steadily destroyed by cement trucks and bulldozers.

Every time I thought of Charlotte Adams, it was as if my insides were being scooped out. That night, after the Acme, I'd told Marie how it scared me to see Charlotte like that, so uncomposed, so unlike herself. She had always had this elegant detachment that I thought was her, being Southern and refined and all that. But Marie said she liked Charlotte Adams even more after the Acme.

'It would be far scarier to have met her and instead of seeing her messy and upset, she looked blank and perfect. Like a Stepford wife. She's been fucking betrayed, she's upset, and she showed it. She's real.'

One afternoon, I got a ride with Thomas and Jack as far as Paoli. I went into a Hallmark store and bought a card for Charlotte Adams. I'd looked at the whole selection. *Good Luck in Your New Home* seemed tactless. *Thank You* kind of strange. I bought a blank message card, one with Monet-like flowers. I didn't know what I would write to her.

I walked the five miles back to the mountain, up North Valley Road to Diamond Rock, and started to climb, past the octagonal schoolhouse and up Horseshoe Trail Road. Locals along here had tried to make the road private-access and sometimes they harassed drivers who dared to come through. I wondered if anyone would give me trouble. I walked and walked. The road was gravel and full of potholes. I looked down at my Converse, now grey with wear and washing. I'd nearly reached the point where the trail met the top of the mountain, below the Nike Site, when I heard the crunch of gravel under wheels. There was a car behind me, going very slow. I stepped on to the grass verge so it could pass but didn't look back in case it was one of the crazy locals trying to keep it private. But the car didn't pass. I stopped walking, and the car stopped. The ignition cut out; I could hear the fan still whirring. A door opened.

'Libby?'

I turned. Mrs Boucher was standing at the open door of her Volvo.

'I thought it was you. I wasn't sure because of your hair.'

I had developed an involuntary response when people mentioned my lost hair: I touched my neck.

I tried to smile at her, but my mouth wouldn't work, and I could feel my lips twitching.

'Is everything okay with you and Ellen and all that happened? I heard about it. I should have checked to see.' I could tell Mrs Boucher was nervous.

'Yes,' I said. We were all fine. Just Wilson was still recovering. The wires had been cut the week before and he was coming back on to solid food. 'How are Peter and Bruce?'

'Fine. In Florida on vacation right now with their dad and his new wife.'

'Oh. The wedding.' I had forgotten.

'Yeah. A few weeks ago. The same day as Charles and Diana. It was actually on purpose.' She laughed her wry laugh. And I rolled my eyes as if to say *I know, how tacky*. She shut the car door and walked around toward me. 'Can we sit for a minute?' she asked.

I shrugged. I didn't know what we had to talk about. Was she going to ask me why I'd told Sage? We sat on a log on the side of the road. Mrs Boucher took her pack of Marlboro Lights out of her bag and lit a cigarette. Her hand had a tremor. I suddenly felt very tired. I'd been walking for miles, it was hot, and I had a card for Charlotte in my bag. I wanted to go home and write it.

'I'm very sorry, Libby. I let you and Ellen down. I should have reported what you told me right away. I had other stuff going on in my life this summer. It's all very messy, and I felt I couldn't face all of you and your mother. I just avoided it. I've felt so guilty.'

'Oh, it's okay,' I said. This wasn't what I'd been expecting. 'Does someone else babysit for you now?'

'What? No. Oh – no, Libby. I haven't been out and the boys had the wedding coming up and then the Florida trip and there's been so much going on.'

'I thought you were angry with me.'

'No. Why on earth would I be angry with you?'

I breathed in and just said it. 'Because I told Sage about you and her dad.'

Mrs Boucher held her cigarette in mid-air.

'You knew?'

'Yeah.' I felt miserable and put my head between my knees. 'I feel like I've ruined their lives.'

'Well, that makes two of us.'

I thought about that, how Charlotte Adams had left. 'Yeah. I guess you probably feel even worse.'

Mrs Boucher gave a half-laugh. 'Believe me, I do.' I did believe her. She seemed unhappy, different. I wondered if my mom felt unhappy about her situation. I felt an ache in my chest when I thought about how she was willing to take such small slivers of love from someone, how I knew she deserved more than that.

Mrs Boucher kept smoking and then she said, 'I didn't know you told Sage. I doubt Grady knows that. He was going to tell them all anyway. So you have to understand that you didn't do anything. I'm sure Sage knows this.'

'Sage and I aren't really friends any more.'

'That's really sad. I'm sorry to hear that. She's probably needed you.'

Had Sage needed me? When my father died, Sage came straight to the house. Had I called her, or did she just come? I couldn't remember. She was just there, every day for a long time. She and Charlotte brought black clothes for us to wear, and Sage did Beatrice's hair for the funeral. The one time Thomas choked out a sob, it was Sage who moved across the room to him. Charlotte sat with my aunt in the kitchen and talked and listened to stories about Dad because Mom wasn't able to. When everyone moved away from us in those few days, kept their respectful distance, Sage came toward us. My Irish aunt was confused by our empty house. Where were all the neighbours and friends? No one made tea for us, visited, brought us food. She couldn't understand America. Everything felt wrong to her about our world – except Sage and Charlotte, who came every day. They were the only ones who made any sense to her at all.

I had always waited for Sage to come to me. In my room, I took out the card I bought for Charlotte and wrote it to Sage instead, just one line: '*I miss you.*' On the envelope I wrote *Sage* and, underneath, *Kingdom before dark?* I cut through the trail to Hamilton Drive and walked as far as her house. There were no kids gathered at the nets playing basketball, no scattered bikes on the driveway. The Mercedes was parked over by the clinic. I knocked on the kitchen door and no one answered. I wedged the envelope between the glass and the metal frame of the storm door. I didn't know if Sage had moved with Charlotte or was working but if she didn't get it today, she'd get it another day, and she would know that I finally came and looked for her.

I walked to the Kingdom then. It was nearly a year and a half since the phone call had come from Dad's cousin in New York. I see that day in slow motion. I was outside with Ellen on the street, and Thomas called to us and we came running up the azalea path. There was the moment before the path, us on the street playing four-square with the Hunters, an in-between moment, running up through afternoon light to the pine at the top of the hill where

Thomas was standing, and then Thomas's face telling us something terrible, forever terrible, had happened. We had run up the path, and we were one thing at the start, and we were something else at the other end, in just a few hundred yards. Walking into the house, Marie on the living room floor, my mother upstairs on her bed, crying.

The crooked tree was ahead of me. When my dad had first pointed it out, he'd called it a wayfinder and said the Indians had bent the tree at a time in its sapling life when it was flexible and could withstand the strain. I wondered if, in tree age, I was past my sapling time. I waited for Sage in her brother's *Lone Ranger* sleeping bag and must have fallen asleep because I woke in the dark. She hadn't come.

I walked back home. The crickets were out, and the lights of my house blinked through the trees as I came off the trail. Ellen or Thomas had turned on the outdoor lamp post, and I could see that the grass was nearly knee-high again. I thought about what we had been since that day on the azalea path, how we had each tried to measure the world, order it in our own way, naming or drawing it, making lists, trying to stave off its disorder by mapping its galaxies, plotting its paths. I wanted to order my section of that world, to keep it and look after it.

Inside, Ellen was sitting at the kitchen table. I went to the drawer under the stovetop and took out the kitchen scissors.

'Sage called,' she said. 'She's at her mom's. She said to tell you her brother read the card over the phone. She said to write this down for you. It's weird.' Ellen handed me a piece of folded paper.

I sat on the bottom step in the hallway and opened it.

'Wild Horses'
Not today or tomorrow but soon.

I went back outside to the end of the driveway with the scissors and in the circle of light from the lamp post, I knelt on the ground and started to cut the grass.

Acknowledgements

I am deeply grateful to so many, but my first debt is always to my seven sisters and brothers – my wolf pack and my country. Grainne, Maeve, Brian, Kieran, Deirdre, Aideen and Siobhan, thank you.

To my mother, courageous and always unconventional, I am grateful that you always blazed your own way. You left gifts in the wake. To my band of nieces and nephews, you are the coolest people I know. All of you. To my cousin Mary Devins Felton for showing me that the glass is full, I am grateful.

It was in The Sandy Field Writers Group in Sligo that some of the scenes in this book were first put to paper and shared with the most generous group of readers and writers, especially Nora McGillen, Rose Jordan, Niamh MacCabe, Julianna Holland, Mairead McCann and Bernie Meehan.

To Mike McCormack who encouraged me to start a novel, to Sinéad Gleeson whose generosity set me on this journey, and to Mia Gallagher who read an early section, I am so thankful.

I am grateful for my colleagues and friends at IT Sligo, especially Tommy Weir, Rhona Trench and Jo and Frank Conway, without whom I would be lost. Thank you Eoin McNamee and Alice Lyons, not only for your friend-ship but your words. To all the students and staff on the

Writing + Literature and Performing Arts courses, thank you for inspiring me every day.

For their absolute friendship, even when I've been truant, and for reeling me back into the world I am forever thankful for Lisa Johnson Viveros, Thérèse O'Loughlin, Julie Ellwood and Molly McCloskey. For her daily unflinching support through all my states of panic and writing despair, thank you Louise Kennedy who is a total touchstone in my life. Thank you also Cecilia Mace Hardy, Isabel Grayson, Catherine McGlinchey, Mary Quill Eglinton and Siobhan and all the Hennessys in Sooey.

The River Mill in County Down provided sustenance and space to write. Thank you, Paul.

To my agent Peter Straus for his belief and invaluable guidance and to all at Rogers Coleridge & White who have been so generous and supportive, including Eliza Plowden, Stephen Edwards and Tristan Kendrick. I feel so fortunate to have you on side.

Louisa Joyner, my editor at Faber: you rewrote my reality when you chose *A Crooked Tree*. Thank you for your perceptive edits, your guidance and exuberance. You and Libby Marshall are heroes. Thank you also to Lizzie Bishop and Josephine Salverda at Faber. Thank you Noah Eaker, my editor at HarperCollins, for your thoughtful insights and editorial care. I am so grateful to you, Mary Gaule and all at HarperCollins. The book is better for your input.

I now have first-hand experience of the refined art of copy-editing and thank you forever Silvia Crompton and Miranda Ottewell for your scrupulous care and expertise.

To my oldest friends Crissy Cline Ortlieb and Jeannie McGovern Fogal: I was blessed to have spent my youth in the woods with you. You made me better.

To the family I have made, my children Dúaltagh, Brónagh and Aoibhín – everything is good because you are in the world. Michael, for all, thank you.

Finally, I am infinitely grateful to those who are gone – my grandparents and my father.

Sign up
for free

Become a Faber Member and discover the best *in the arts and literature*

Sign up to the Faber Members programme and enjoy specially curated events, tailored discounts and exclusive previews of our forthcoming publications from the best novelists, poets, playwrights, thinkers, musicians and artists.

Join Faber Members for free at faber.co.uk

faber
members